BAITED

BAITED

Colleen O'Brien

UNBRIDLED BOOKS
2025

This is a work of fiction. Names, characters,
places and incidents are either the product of the author's
imagination or are used fictitiously. Any resemblance to
actual persons, living or dead, business establishments,
events, or locales is entirely coincidental.

Unbridled Books

Copyright © by Colleen O'Brien

All rights reserved. This book, or parts thereof,
may not be reproduced in any form without permission.

NO AI TRAINING: Without in any way limiting
the author's or publisher's exclusive rights under copyright,
any use of this publication to "train" generative artificial intelligence
(AI) technologies to generate text is expressly prohibited. The author
reserves all rights to license uses of this work for generative AI
training and development of machine learning language modes.

First paperback edition, 2025

ISBN: 978-1-60953-155-3

E-book ISBN: 978-1-60953-156-0

*Map by Amelia Hagen-Dillon from
Cairn Cartographics, with permission (work for hire)*

1 3 5 7 9 10 8 6 4 2

First Printing

For Mark, Dalton, Merritt and Jack

*And for all those who love Glacier Park
and treat it with reverence*

CAST OF CHARACTERS

Dyer Family
Clancy
Sean (deceased)
Truman

Law Enforcement Rangers
Mack Savage
Jed Turner
Layne West

East Glacier
Patrick Hughes
Rosie Boswell (brother Shane)

DNA Study
Liz Ralston
Penelope Keller

Trail Crew
Ezra Riverton
Marion Roberts
Nate
Clancy Dyer

Additional Park Service
Vera Fisher (adoptive parents Tori and Oliver)
Marty
Sandy

Meeks Family
Grady
Josie
John
Patty

Ranch Owners/Meeks Family Employers
Maureen Thomas
Fred Thomas

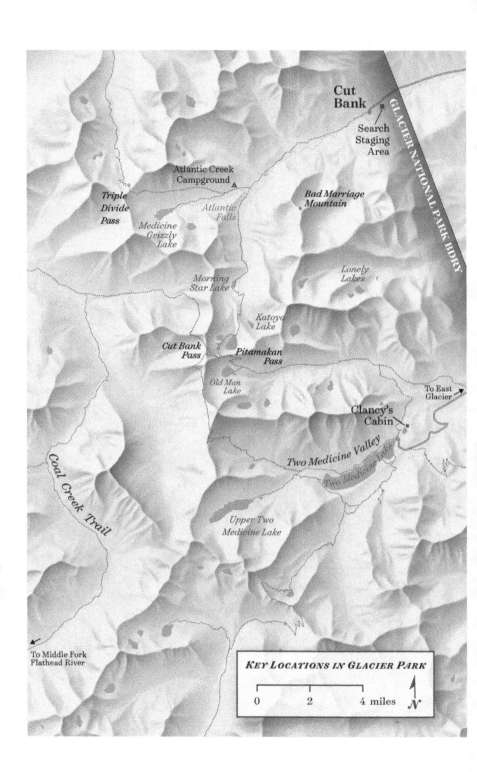

PROLOGUE

FAKER

◆

March 2004

Maureen Thomas knew pretending to have cancer was wrong, but she never could have predicted the repercussions, the events that her faux illness would set into motion. Maureen, a mom, a devout Catholic, a woman who until now had been honest to a fault, drove to a state park and arrived on time for the imaginary appointment she'd penciled on the calendar.

Walking helped. Not much else did. She strode through empty campsites and up hillsides desperate for a sign of spring. She studied bare patches of ground for shoots of buttercups, watched the skies and fence posts hoping to glimpse a mountain blue bird, lurid and alive. She tried to pray, but her thoughts shot-gunned.

The night of the Russell Art Auction, it had been a relief to pee. She'd needed to go for ages, but Fred, locked in a bidding war over a Scriver sculpture depicting cowboys branding a calf, occasionally reached for her hand. She did not want to leave him. From the privacy of a bathroom stall Maureen heard, "You get to sleep with him, *and* you never have to look at that hideous depiction of animal cruelty."

A second voice laughed. "His poor wife."

Maureen was too late to see who had spoken. She told herself it did not matter. She despised how women treated one another with vitriol, especially when it came to men, blaming each other while absolving the philanderer. She stood at Fred's side in silent shock as his fellow board members, work colleagues, and art enthusiasts approached to congratulate him, glasses raised. She surveyed the crowd, but no one's appearance screamed, *I'm Fred's mistress, your worst nightmare, younger and smarter and hotter, funnier and more deserving of his love.*

Once home, she took to her daughter's empty room and, still wearing her dress, climbed beneath the covers. Fred came to the door. She told him she wasn't well, which felt true enough.

Surely, Maureen Thomas thought as she stared up at glow-in-the-dark stars, there were options, a million ways to respond when one's husband has an affair, but she could think of only two: to stay or to go.

Maureen did not want to leave. She did not want her life to change. Fred laughed at her jokes. He was her best friend. She loved him, his easy confidence, his wit and capableness. And she especially loved their children, the family they'd created together. No one else on the planet remembered their kids when they were little the way she and Fred did, their favorite board books and inability to say their s's, their ridiculous demands and amusing misspeaks. When unboxing something new, they still read one another the "constructions." With the kids now in their twenties and the possibility of grandchildren on the horizon, the real fun was about to begin.

But Maureen could not turn a blind eye to a betrayal so devastating it had dried her mouth, sent her blood to rushing audibly and trapped her in an emotional firestorm. Add to that Fred's acumen as a divorce lawyer, she knew him to be ruthless. More than once over the years she'd thought that she would not want him as an adversary. He could see to it that she walked with nothing. Maureen had not held a paying job for almost thirty years. That night, she stayed because she was too afraid to leave. She did not sleep.

When Maureen emerged from her daughter's room two days later, she thought of Kafka's story and believed it would have been only slightly more disorienting to have awoken as an insect. Maureen, who loved to cook and to eat, stopped. She nibbled an occasional cracker, called the secretary at the Catholic grade school and begged off volunteering for the rest of the year. She bowed out of book club, Catholic Daughters, and decorating the church for Holy Week. Pounds melted from her frame. Her clothes hung loose.

The rumor originated at church. An acquaintance cornered her. "What kind of cancer is it?" Maureen could not bring herself to correct the woman, to verbalize the true source of her suffering. She attempted a smile, then turned and left. The rumor proliferated like knapweed, spread fast and took over. Maureen received phone messages and cards. She existed outside herself. Often, her mind flew to the afternoon she believed she'd set their home on fire.

Seventeen years ago, with the kids all at school, she'd slid a roast from their cattle ranch into a 450-degree oven to sear. After twenty minutes, she would reduce the heat and add the vegetables. They had just finished renovating their kitchen and Maureen delighted in her aloneness. With the workers finally gone, she could relax. Fred had wanted to add on to their ranch house outside Babb but Maureen, for once, asserted herself. They spent six weeks or so up there in the summer, and she and the kids often went hiking or camping in Glacier. She loved it but they barely used the ranch house. This was where they lived, here in Great Falls in their old Victorian with its pitched roof, original wavy glass windows, and antiquated kitchen. Maureen wanted a dishwasher, a microwave that didn't consume half the counter, and a garbage disposal. After insisting and insisting and finally withholding sex, she'd gotten it all plus a double oven, gas range, and farmhouse sink.

She chopped the carrots and onion and ran upstairs to fold laundry. Fred called. He told her Patty Meeks had her baby, a girl. The infant needed surgery for a cleft lip and palate. John Meeks had called him to find out what the ranch insurance would cover. The news weighed on Maureen. The Meeks Family, how hard they worked running cattle and caretaking and all the rest on her family's behalf, made her uncomfortable. Fred saw it differently. "They love it," he claimed. "They're outside. They're together. They live life on their own terms." He told Maureen he compensated John better than most hired men, "It's fair," he assured her. But Maureen had grown up poor and she knew the world was rarely fair when it came to what owners paid workers.

"What can I do?" she asked, wanting to help. Fred told her she should send a gift "like normal." John would forward them the bills. They would cover whatever insurance and Patty's benefits did not. He said they'd named the baby Josephine. Maureen's heart softened. That was the name of the lake where she and Patty took the kids for picnics.

Maureen did not bother to put away the laundry she folded that afternoon. The kids could do that. She set out on a walk. The grass was greening. Tulips muscled up out of the cold ground. It could have been one of hers, one of her babies born with a lifelong malady. Patty was Blackfeet with thick dark hair, strong cheekbones, and almond-shaped eyes, who even in muck boots and a chore coat wore mascara and eyeliner and looked like she'd stepped out of a magazine. It would be harder for her, Maureen thought, to raise a daughter with a facial scar than it would have been for Maureen, who, while not a complete slouch in the looks department, did not put nearly the stock in her appearance that Patty did. Maureen knew it to be yet another privilege of wealth, to wear cheap sweatpants and not bother to comb her hair or wash her face before she walked the kids to school.

She realized it was time to get them. Maureen loved seeing her children after they'd been away all day. As she stood on the playground waiting for her daughter and sons to race through the door, she remembered the roast, the oven set to sear.

She ran. As she passed the dour playground attendant, she hollered that she would be back. Maureen's tongue felt thick. She tasted iron. Her feet pounded the sidewalk. She could not get enough air, but she could not stop. Her new kitchen, ruined. Their home. She'd fought so hard for what she wanted, gotten distracted by the news about Patty's baby and destroyed it all. If only she could go back, back to before.

As she turned down the alley, she heard the *bleat* of the smoke detector, insistent, steady. She ran harder. She burst through the door and up the back steps into the kitchen. Her beautiful new kitchen with its tile floor and granite counters. Smoke billowed from the edges of the oven. She flipped it off and grabbed potholders, yanked open the door. Heat hit her like a wall.

There was no fire. Only smoke. Her chest heaved. She emitted a single shuddering sob as she whisked the roaster out the back door, dropped it on the sidewalk, and turned on the hose. Steam billowed like the smoke. A charred husk of meat crusted the metal. Maureen drew air deep into her lungs. She'd ruined supper, not their lives.

Her children waited in a cluster by the swings. She told them she was sorry she was late and announced the birth of Grady's sister, Josephine Meeks. Her kids loved Grady, followed him around the ranch, and deferred to him even though he was younger. Her daughter, always attuned to the emotions of others, knew something had upset her. Maureen explained that she'd been frightened. "Fear," she told her, "is the enemy of joy."

Now, as Maureen strode through the desolate campground, she remembered running home that spring afternoon, her belief that she'd destroyed their home, their lives. It was how she felt now, all the time, desperate to discover the extent of the damage, wishing she could return to before. Cattails waved in the marsh. Maureen longed to see a red-winged blackbird, spot the return of something beautiful. The temperature dropped below freezing. She walked and walked and her thoughts darted to Josie. Adolescence wasn't easy for anyone, let alone a girl with such a scar. Clouds filled the sky, the wind picked up. Sleet stung her cheeks. She knew signs of spring must exist, but she had not found them. She drove home carefully though she wasn't sure exactly why. Maybe a quick car wreck was the answer to how all this would end. As she turned onto their block, she saw Fred's fancy car in front of the house. He rarely came home in the middle of the day. She wondered if the rumor had reached him.

Fred met her at the door. "You have the cancer." He said it with the article, trying to be funny. Folks around Babb called it that, "the cancer." Her kids would say it to each other and crack up. And now Fred said it and his arms wrapped around her. His body pressed hers, lifted and dropped, rose and fell.

They sat close on the couch, and Fred told her he would have a trail built through the aspen above the ranch house. She could hike without ever encountering Glacier's crowds, all the people whose germs might tax her immune system. "From the ridge," Fred told her, "you'll be able to see Chief."

The weight across her shoulders eased at the thought of Chief Mountain, a monolith that rose above the plains like a guardian. She realized she wanted to return to the ranch, the thick trees, the wild country. Once spring had a foothold up there, say early June, she'd go. Alone. Safe in the place she loved, she believed she would be able to decide. She would know whether to stay or to go. Fred's hand wrapped around hers. Maureen grasped it, held on.

PART I

GONE

Monday, June 21, 2004

CHAPTER 1

MISSING

The morning she discovered Ezra missing, Clancy Dyer hadn't once thought about her brother, Sean. She and Ezra were late. Clancy dashed through the aspen, hollering, "'The day is a woman who loves you.'" Ezra had taken to quoting some Montana poet. Clancy had no idea if *Hugo* was the guy's first or last name, but if ever there were a day deserving of that line, this was it. Sun careened off leaves laden with moisture. The sky stretched a cloudless blue. The mountains, ribboned with falling water, appeared scoured and fresh. She and Ezra planned to climb Bad Marriage after work to celebrate his imminent divorce. The clear air held a chill. Clancy drew her hands up into the sleeves of her fleece. A woodpecker beat a steady rattle. They'd burned daylight, and Roberts, their boss, pissed about his lost resin wad and riddled with aches borne of decades working trails, was gunning for any reason to make their lives hell.

She called in a singsong, "Ez-ra, time to wake uh-up. Roberts got a burr up his knick-ers. We need to ro-oll. Oh, Ez-ra, we get to scrape Triple Div-i-ide. And climb Bad Mar-r-iage." Roberts had taken Nate and his six feet of brawn and hit the trail. They were headed toward Morning Star Lake.

The aspen thinned. Clancy stepped out of the trees and into the sunlight. The smell stopped her cold. She buried her nose in the crook of her arm. The air stank of iron and rot, excrement and decay. Just beyond her feet spread a rectangle of crushed green where Ezra's tent must have been. A metal stake secured a length of webbing to the earth. Clancy's limbs twitched with the need to go, get away. She made herself stand still and scan the tall grass, the brush. She spied it. Along a thicket of willow lay Ezra's tent, collapsed and shredded.

"Ezra?" Nausea rose in her throat. "Ezra!" Waxwings sprang from a bush. A sharp bark made her jump. She swung toward the sound, expecting a coyote or fox, maybe a deer. But there was nothing but trees, brush, deadfall. She turned. Tatters of orange nylon lifted on the breeze, fluttered, and sank.

She ran back the way she had come, back through the aspen, across the meadow and up a rise toward the main trail. She needed to find her crew, get ahold of Roberts's park radio, call the Com Center and summon help. She needed rangers, people like her dad and Mack Savage who ran search and rescues, found the missing, saved them.

She wished Roberts and Nate were still around, wished they had never left. The day before, they'd all worked extra. Roberts made them clear a logjam from the outlet at Morning Star Lake. When they finally returned to camp, they could feel the storm building. The guys were out of pot. Usually when this happened, Roberts sent one of them to East Glacier on a bogus errand like bar oil or chain saw gas. But they were gypsied up the Cut Bank Valley, with no town close by in any direction. The time it would have taken Ezra or Nate to hike out and drive the miles of rutted dirt road to the highway and then to East Glacier meant they simply had to suffer. All of them.

Roberts started supper and cleaned his pipe. Unbeknownst to Clancy he perched the resulting resin wad atop an upturned basin they used for rinsing dishes. The sky darkened. Thunder rumbled in the distance. They wolfed down their stir-fry. The wind kicked up. It was Clancy's turn to dry. She wanted to be inside her tent when the storm hit. She mistook Roberts's clump of resin for a rodent turd and flicked it into the cow parsnip.

Roberts went ballistic. He let loose a barrage of cuss words and called Clancy, among other things, a "trails hobbyist idiot." Ezra sent them to their tents, hollering that there was no reason for all of them to get wet. "I've got it," he insisted.

Roberts was still pissed about the resin this morning. Scorn rolled off him like an odor. Tardiness rankled the man, and this was the first time any of them had risked his wrath by being late. "Don't dawdle," he told Clancy. "I expect you at that pass before noon. Way before. You mess up, I'll know." He and Nate left with the chain saw, shovels, and their Pulaskis.

Clancy dawdled. She brewed herself a bonus mug of jasmine green tea, which she enjoyed while she read about the route up Bad Marriage in the climber's guide. "From there, the route is obvious."

She rolled her eyes at J. Gordon Edwards's ubiquitous line. Clancy had learned the hard way that whatever *obvious* elk or goat trail Edwards had found might well have grown over or been relocated at the whim of the wildlife by the time she schlepped toward a mountaintop. She sipped and studied her topo, glancing up at Bad Marriage still covered in white. Snow and ice might turn them back before the summit, but it would be fun to try.

She expected Ezra to saunter into their kitchen area all bedhead and half-open eyes, his reddish beard a tangle. No one could have slept through those crashes of thunder, bursts of lightning, and ripping winds bowing the sides of their tent. Clancy figured Ezra had finally fallen asleep when the storm passed, and eventually the sun was bound to roust him.

It hadn't happened. She'd waited as long as she could. Twenty minutes? A half hour? Longer than she should have. She knew that now. Clancy hit the main trail and ran faster. She ran toward her crew, toward help and contact with the rest of the world. She ran so she wouldn't feel alone, ran because it was coming for her. She could feel it pressing closer, not a predator or violence but the darkness, the consuming hole of loss. Clancy ran because she couldn't save her brother, but maybe if she ran hard enough, got help soon enough, she could find Ezra.

For the rest of that summer and for always, Clancy would wonder if instead of fleeing for her tent the night of the storm, she had stayed and helped Ezra stash their dishes amid the wind and rain, how her life might have gone differently. She would have convinced Ezra to hunker down for the evening, persuaded him to leave the hard conversation with his pert-nosed, high-maintenance wife for another day. In this fantasy, she convinces Ezra to play cribbage while the storm buffets her tent. He leaves, discovers his shelter destroyed, and returns. They sleep without a hint of romance or attraction, dry and safe. When she tells herself this story, it leads to another, one heavy with nostalgia for an impossible future.

CHAPTER 2

BOUNDARIES

◆

Glacier's Hudson Bay District Ranger Mack Savage drove the winding road below Divide Mountain without braking. He cheated the center line. Morning sun blinded him. A Black Angus stood in the middle of the road. Mack swerved. Missed it by a breath. Open range meant if you hit it, you bought it, and Mack already had a full freezer.

As district ranger, he was in charge of the entirety of Glacier National Park east of the Continental Divide from the Canadian border south to Marias Pass. His area included half a million acres of the most spectacular wild scenery in the country. Trailheads originated at Belly River, Many Glacier, St. Mary and on up the Sun Road to Logan Pass, more at Cut Bank, Two Medicine, Autumn Creek and Marias Pass. Hundreds of miles of trail and almost a hundred of road snaked through his district, and every inch was under his authority. He led law enforcement and delegated backcountry and campground management to his area rangers. He felt personally responsible for the place, its wildlife, his coworkers, and the millions of visitors who traveled to the park every summer. He wanted every person, every animal to remain safe. There was no job he'd rather do, no place he'd rather live, no life he'd rather lead.

Earlier that morning, Sandy in the Com Center had relayed a message from Layne West, a law enforcement officer so green his fellow rangers had nicknamed him Shrek. Mack had stuck him in the Cut Bank Ranger Station. With miles of bad dirt road for access, a primitive campground with fourteen sites, and spotty park radio coverage, not much happened there. At least not until this morning, when Layne had patrolled the campground and discovered "a massive grizzly behaving strangely."

It wasn't so much that Mack didn't believe the report. It was that just about everyone described their first grizzly bear that same way. Whatever the situation, Mack appreciated the excuse to leave his office on this, the most beautiful day of the year.

He negotiated the hairpin curve at the top of the rise and reviewed the morning's oddities. His girlfriend's dog, Muffy, was missing from outside his house, lead and all. Liz was going to go nuts if he couldn't find the Karelian. She had planned to come home for the night but had not shown. She had left a voicemail on his office phone. He'd gotten it first thing this morning. She said she was canceling the meeting with east-side law enforcement rangers. This surprised Mack because she'd insisted upon getting every law enforcement ranger in the same room to address the sabotage of her DNA study and gone to great lengths to make it happen. She ended the message with "I love you." Hearing the words on his machine perplexed Mack. She'd never said it in person. Why would she tell him on an office voicemail? Given that the dog was gone, he'd probably never hear those words again. Could be a predator had gotten the pooch, but there was no sign of a tussle. Liz might have grabbed the animal, but dogs were forbidden on Glacier's trails, and she devoted every waking moment to her DNA study. Why would she saddle herself with Muffy?

Mack's truck rumbled down the washboard gravel toward the Cut Bank Campground. Liz had gone over his head about the meeting with law enforcement, all the way to the superintendent, who was a spineless opportunist afraid to ruffle feathers, especially Liz's. Why would she cancel? Mack had tossed a pregnancy test into his pack. He'd driven to Browning to purchase it the day she told him she was late. Last he knew, Liz and her staff were working the Cut Bank Valley. He hoped to find her, slip her the test, and finally know.

The truck bounced over the useless cattle guard marking the boundary with the Blackfeet Reservation. Cowboys simply cut the fence and ran their cattle into the park's lush meadows. Layne was waiting in the gravel parking area in front of his cabin, blond curls rimmed by his flat hat. He had the leather strap fastened underneath his chin. The rookie climbed inside the truck and talked nonstop as Mack drove to the campground. "I got your message about the meeting. My cell phone works in the northeast corner of the kitchen. Canceled. It's too bad. I'd been looking forward to it. Not much company here most days. Guess it worked out. If I'd left for St. Mary like I'd planned, I wouldn't have seen the bear. Could've led to an unfortunate visitor encounter."

Mack half listened. Bad Marriage poked behind snow-topped twin triangular shapes, the sort schoolchildren would draw if you asked them to depict mountains. The peaks lifted toward a flawless blue sky. When they arrived at the campground and climbed from the truck, the bear didn't so much as glance their way. Mack switched off the handheld he carried on his duty belt. What he saw confused him, and he didn't want the grizzly spooked by the squawking of his radio. He told Layne, "Swing the gate and post it 'Closed Due to Bear Activity.'" He raised his binoculars. "Call the status into the Com Center." Layne dashed off. Mack hollered for him to take the truck. The park boundary was almost a full mile down the road from the campground where the agitated bear dug. The project would keep Layne busy and give Mack time to think. The rookie had nailed his report.

The grizzly's muscled hump rippled as it excavated site 7. The bear rolled onto its back and wriggled as if it suffered an angry itch. Something had drawn the bruin to this spot, something compelling enough that the usually wide-ranging creature had shown no sign of leaving for over an hour without a food source in sight. Mack suspected Liz's bait—fish guts combined with rotting cow blood.

She had devised a study using DNA technology to determine the number of grizzly bears in Glacier. In order to lure the creatures to stations surrounded by barbed wire, she developed a fish-gut-and-cow-blood combination that bears found irresistible. Liz also identified rub trees scarred by claw marks and riddled with bear hair and affixed barbed wire to them as well. She distinguished each tree by nailing a numbered, metal medallion into its trunk. Liz hired wildlife biology majors and anyone she could to collect the snagged hair from the rub stations and trees and then she sent it to the lab. The hair contained enough DNA to distinguish individual bears.

Had Liz or one of her minions spilled the lure in a public campground? If a bait mishap led to a bear harming someone, sabotage would be the least of Liz's problems. Luckily, eager-beaver Layne had prevented that scenario. Mack couldn't shake the persistent thought that the bear in site 7 had something to do with Liz's canceled meeting, her missing dog, and her recorded proclamation of love. He just didn't know what.

Half an hour later, Mack and Layne climbed a hillside. Mack handed the young man a shotgun and a supply of miniature beanbag ammunition. He lifted his binoculars and studied the bear. It dug, upending earth, tossing rocks. Mack looked over to see Layne's hands shaking as he loaded the gun. "I've never shot at a grizzly." He forced a tight smile. "Heck, I've never shot at much of anything."

"I know," Mack said. "I'm the one who qualified you."

A month ago, Layne with his curls and the chiseled looks of a Rodin statue couldn't stand still and wouldn't shut up when the law enforcement rangers gathered at the rifle range. Each had to pass an accuracy test before they qualified to carry firearms inside the park. Bits of sleet pinged their jackets. Layne, a last-minute hire, bounced around in a sky-blue Patagucci windbreaker. His uniform had not yet arrived. He fired off a spate of questions: "Is it always this cold in May?" "Have you ever shot anyone?" And "Does my cabin have internet?" That was when Layne's colleagues started calling him Shrek. One of them broke it to the guy that not only would he not have access to the World Wide Web or email, but park radio coverage was spotty in the Cut Bank Valley. And if he owned a cell phone, he might want to use it as a paperweight. Phones probably worked even worse than the radios. Mack couldn't help but think the kid was too dapper, too soft for the job. He scheduled him to shoot last, not to be mean or induce hypothermia but because he hoped the fellow would calm down without an audience. As the temperature dropped and the wind rose, the rangers who had already qualified sought indoor projects. Nothing like a little inclement weather to get the paperwork moving.

Mack didn't know if Layne shook from the cold or nerves, but the blue jacket trembled. The poor guy was lucky to send the bullet in the vicinity of the target. After several minutes of errant shooting, Mack set a gloved hand on the young man's shoulder. "Let's call it for now."

Layne's face fell. He couldn't have looked more bereft if Mack had taken away his birthday. "I have to qualify to do the job."

Mack nodded. "I'll qualify you provisionally. Spend some time here at the range. Practice. We'll come back in a week or two and see what you can do." Mack found no reason to be a hard-ass about the guy he'd banished to the dead end of a dirt road. Sure, the very remoteness of Cut Bank demanded a law enforcement presence to prevent local cowboys from wantonly grazing their stock in the pristine meadows and meth dealers from setting up production trailers, but Layne would be lucky to have cause to issue a food storage citation, let alone shoot at something.

That was what Mack had thought, but now here they were, getting ready to fire a beanbag at a bear's butt—tricky for anyone, let alone Layne. The aim was to haze the animal out of the campground, make the grizzly associate the spot with pain and stay away.

As he lowered the binoculars, it dawned on Mack what he should've asked when he first arrived. "Who stayed at that site last night?"

Delighted to have a different project, Layne handed Mack the shotgun. "I'll check. I've got the payment envelopes on my desk." He scrambled down the hill. "Back as fast as I can." Layne's housing in the Cut Bank Ranger Station sat about three-quarters of a mile from the campground and a quarter mile inside the park boundary. The trailhead that led up the Cut Bank Valley and into Glacier's backcountry began a couple hundred yards west of where the bear was digging. Numerous vehicles sat in the parking area including a Park Service stock truck. He should look for Liz's truck and get a count so he had an idea how many hikers were up the valley. But that could wait. He focused his binoculars back on site 7. He loved watching bears, even those that perplexed him. Confounding behavior seemed the order of the day. As his mind worked to make sense of it all, he recalled the afternoon Liz demanded her meeting with law enforcement.

A little over a week ago, she had stormed into his office, slapped a file on his desk, and growled, "Make it stop." Liz's dark hair rebelled against its hairband. Loose strands poked every which way. Anger flushed her apple-round cheeks. Blue pockets bulged below her eyes. "This ends now."

He eased his chair back from the desk. "Have you slept at all, Liz?"

"Do you know what those assholes did?"

"It's nice to see you, too." Mack had missed her. She'd been consumed by her study and hadn't been home in days. It'd been more than two weeks since they'd slept together.

"Pubic hair, Mack. They stuck pubic hair on my barbed wire. Along with grizzlies, I'm tracking smart-assed human males."

He almost stifled his grin.

"Not funny, Mack. Not one bit." During intense moments, a vein at Liz's left temple bulged. Mack watched it pulse. "They are also ripping down my wire, stealing my tree ID tags, and destroying my hair-snag stations." Liz paced.

"Suspects?"

She stopped in front of him, her green eyes hard. "I had the idea for this as an undergrad. The technology finally caught up, and I pried funding from Washington, D.C., the fiscal flipping conservatives." Her jaw went rigid. "These men—the park biologist, the tribal biologist, the Fish and Wildlife Service guy, the state techs—they're pissed. I don't know if it's because I'm a woman, because they didn't think of it themselves, or if they just want to keep right on darting and collaring. But every one of them would give his left nut for a reason to dismiss my study and me." She took a breath. "I am not paying the salary of a lab tech so she can analyze pubic hair."

"Maybe we should talk about this at home. Over supper. And a beer or two."

"I will not allow these people to derail my entire project." Mack noticed her favorite hat jammed in her back pocket. It was purple and made of some high-tech fabric, lightweight and warm. He had once spent an unplanned night in the backcountry with his cheek against the softness of that hat. She collapsed into a chair.

Liz suspected everyone from a charismatic East Glacier climber she claimed had a cultlike following of backcountry enthusiasts to a Blackfeet Indian elder who gave campfire talks through an interpreter even though he spoke perfectly good English. And she wasn't done there. She swore the Park Service's own visitor use assistants, permit writers, and especially trail crew had to be part of the sabotage. "It's happening all up and down the east side. These reservation people have no respect for anything." Her nostrils flared. "I am just trying to do my job."

"Why don't I cook you dinner?" Mack had learned long ago that his relationship with Liz worked only when he maintained solid, nonnegotiable boundaries. He knew he could not fully support her study and remain true to himself. He had a job to do, too, and it did not require him to bow to Liz's every whim. She shook her head. Mack tried again. "I need a statute. They're ripping down wire and destroying man-made structures inside a proposed wilderness area."

"Bull." She punched a nail-bitten finger in his direction. "Don't tell me it's not illegal. You pick and choose which regs you enforce. Bust them for destroying federal property, marijuana, public nuisance, whatever. These are not upstanding citizens. Threaten them with anything you want. Just make the sabotage stop."

Ever since Liz had traveled to D.C. last fall and secured funding for her study, Mack had been dogged by the sense that her project would destroy their relationship. She'd been working around the park on one wildlife project or another for years. They'd gotten together eighteen months ago, a relationship record for him.

"I've got maybe another seventy days before weather shuts me down and a senator who wants my data calculated and my population findings published by early next year. What I don't have is statistical wiggle room, the time or personnel to redo work we have already done, or the energy to convince people like you to do their flipping jobs." She chewed her bottom lip for a moment. "I would hate for Senator Donaldson to hear about a lack of cooperation from Glacier's Law Enforcement Division."

Mack swallowed. "Liz, you've got a public relations problem. Siccing Donaldson's office on me won't change that. In fact, he is your problem." Mack had not wanted to tell her. He'd thought she would figure it out. Her study and its methods had drawn ire. Everyone from Park Service naturalists to backcountry rangers to local bear enthusiasts took issue with it. He'd fielded complaints for weeks. The elderly Blackfeet woman who cleaned bathrooms at Two Medicine had said, "Tell that lady friend of yours, you tell her. Don't go messing with them." She narrowed her eyes. "Their power, it comes back on you."

"The senator who sits on Appropriations and got my study funded is my problem?" She raised an indignant eyebrow. "Why are you fighting me on this? I need you in my corner. I can't do it all."

Mack kept his voice even. "Why would a staunchly conservative senator who has trouble conceiving of an animal that isn't livestock convince his Republican cronies to fund a grizzly DNA study?"

"Donaldson's a nice man, Mack. He holds the elevator for Senate pages. He probably wants to know how many bears exist."

"Montgomery Donaldson does not give a crap about the well-being of grizzly bears or any other wild animal."

"Maybe we can delist them. Wouldn't that be an incredible success story? Wouldn't the proven recovery of the creature at the top of the food chain speak volumes for the effectiveness of the Endangered Species Act? We need to know how many there are. My study is going to provide the most accurate population estimate we've ever had."

"Your number might well pave the way for Donaldson and his rancher buddies to shoot grizzlies on sight with no repercussions." Mack leaned toward her and spoke slowly. "Montana will open a hunting season. Can you imagine the gold mine that will be? Hunters won't have to travel to Alaska to harvest a rug. Struggling ranchers can diversify into hosting and guiding grizzly hunters. It'll be a boon for everyone except the bears."

"I'm a scientist. My job is to collect data, analyze it, and publish."

"It's irresponsible to ignore the repercussions of your study, Liz. Most likely your census will lead to grizzly hunts in Montana and dead bears. That's the only conceivable reason Donaldson wants your numbers."

She stared out the window. The pines rustled in the wind. The tension drained from her face. Her anger seemed to dissipate. Mack figured it was because she'd decided she'd won and her threat about the senator would get her what she wanted. "My project does not kill bears, Mack. It is the least invasive method of studying wildlife ever devised." Liz stood. Mack kept his gaze locked on the moss green of her eyes. "What's better for bears, Mack, some remote possibility of a hunt or the reality of human handling?"

"You need to know that a lot of folks believe your study will result in a death sentence for grizzlies." He exhaled. "That's why they wrench it."

"If you support me, do something. Because if you don't, I will." Liz headed for the door. Mack watched her go. Instead of leaving, she locked it.

Afterward, Mack nuzzled the crook of her neck. They curled together on the floor behind his desk. "I can't believe we did that."

Liz ran her fingers through his hair. "Office sex. Quite unlike you, Mack. Wickedly unorthodox. What would Truman Dyer say?"

Mack's boss, Truman Dyer, wore his uniform shirt ironed and his park-issue hiking boots polished. The previous summer Mack had led the search that recovered the body of Truman's son after a climbing accident. Mack had walked with the man up the trail to an overlook at the edge of St. Mary Lake. Cloud shadows darkened the mountains and the wind whipped fierce. Mack hoped it could whisk away the pain. Dyer's son Sean had fallen and sustained a head injury. "It was quick." Mack had little else to offer. There was nothing he could do, so he did nothing. He sat on a cool rock and allowed the man his grief. He stayed with him for a long time and watched the wind rush the water the way it ripples a field of wheat. Mack attempted to make peace with his helplessness while Truman collected himself to tell his wife and daughter.

Not a soul on the planet meant as much to Mack as that boy had to Truman. That was when he'd resolved to make it work with Liz. After months of dating, he knew she had her moods, her sharp edges, and a temper. She could be impulsive and was often her own worst enemy, but he admired her dedication, her passion, her bullheaded ability to make things happen. Not many women survived in the world of bear biologists. Mack craved a relationship that mattered.

He kissed her softly and smiled. "I think Truman would understand." Mack stood and pulled her to her feet.

"I'm late."

Mack glanced at his watch.

She shook her head in annoyance as she tugged on her work pants. "I haven't had time to get a test. Too much sabotage."

"The pill?" Mack stared at her.

"They only work if you remember to take them." Liz double-knotted her boots. "Or if, when you remember, you have them with you in the backcountry." She sighed. "I don't even know what day of the week it is."

Mack's mind whirled. He'd tracked her cycle for nearly a year, found it helpful when she turned sour and meaner to realize she would bleed in a couple days. "April." He studied her, felt he should be able to tell by looking if his baby grew inside. "You didn't get your period last month."

The phone on Mack's desk beeped. "Dyer. Line one." His admin assistant's voice came over the intercom as well as through the flimsy door. Vera sounded pissed.

"You'll help?" Liz snatched her hat from the floor and returned it to her pocket. "Get your gung-ho law enforcers to catch me some bad guys and pick up a test?"

Mack still wasn't certain who the bad guys were. "I love you, Liz."

She gestured to the blinking light on his phone. "You'd better answer that."

Now, on this stellar Monday morning in the Cut Bank Valley, he watched the bear dig, focused his binoculars on its claws ripping open the earth, desperate for some reward just out of reach. The pregnancy test was in his pack. Either way, he tried to tell himself, it would be good news.

CHAPTER 3

HELP

◆

Farther up the same valley that same morning in the Atlantic Creek Campground food prep area, Penelope Keller slapped a biting fly. The vicious insects made it impossible for her to journal. This, Penelope reminded herself, was the first day of the rest of her life. Last night's storm had done it. Ezra had not shown. He had broken his last promise. Bursts of thunder jolted her inside her sleeping bag. Wind strained the sides of her tent so severely she believed the poles would snap. It came to her with a crash of thunder on top of a bolt of lightning, like a message from a higher power: Be done with him.

Half an hour ago she had climbed from her tent wearing makeup, journal in hand, ready to begin her Ezra-free life amid downed trees littering the campground like scattered toothpicks. But beyond mud and a bit of water pooled in low spots, the place was the same. The patch of blue sky straight above her indicated a bluebird day. She twirled her blond hair around a finger and picked at her oatmeal. She had no appetite. But if she didn't eat it, she'd have to pack it with her. The idea of schlepping oatmeal along with two Nalgene bottles of bear attractant while alone in Glacier's backcountry caused her hands to tremble. Penelope set her cook pot on the ground and waved away flies.

Yesterday her boss, Liz Ralston, had accompanied her on the hike to this wide spot in the trees, but as soon as they arrived, Liz announced that she had a meeting she needed to attend in the morning and headed back out the way they had come. Penelope was elated. Her husband, whose trail crew had been spiked out just a mile away for a week, was going to stop by so they could discuss Penelope's favorite topic: the future of their relationship. She waited, watched dark clouds build, felt the wind gather steam. Penelope loved Ezra. It sounded so simple, but it had gone so horribly wrong.

She had taken the DNA study job so she could work the same valleys as Ezra. She knew he'd met someone, was seeing her, probably sleeping with her. The guy could be insatiable. But Penelope needed him. He'd promised they would have a baby.

When she didn't have a visual on her husband, Penelope thought about him. She thought about him while hiking, while attempting to affix barbed wire to trees, and while curled in her sleeping bag listening to the wind. She recalled the flash of his grin and his hazel eyes, how one of his front teeth slightly overlapped the other, the scratch of his auburn beard when he kissed her. She planned to cut him a deal. He could continue to live in their house just as long as he ditched the girlfriend and gave her—them, really—one more chance.

All of that was in the past. Penelope promised herself she would obsess no more. What would she do with her time? She needed to feel her feelings. As she reached for her journal, Penelope heard the crash of vegetation, the flurry of footfalls. Something was coming toward her. Fast. Despite herself, she thought of Ezra. It could be him. Penelope stood and turned to greet her visitor. An animal burst from the brush. Penelope screamed. She had not screamed with such intensity since she'd left home.

The creature pounced on her oatmeal pot. It attacked her breakfast as if it hadn't eaten for days. Penelope, shaking, realized the animal was a dog. Black-and-white, neither big nor small—she would not have been more shocked if it had been a penguin. The Park Service strictly enforced Glacier's dog ban. Domestic canines put the park's coyote and wolf populations at risk for parvo, not to mention that bears and dogs infuriated one another and dogs had been known to chase wildlife to exhaustion.

Behind the dog strode her boss, wearing a pack that towered above her head. Liz's round face, haloed by hair more unruly than usual, was flushed with exertion. Penelope stomped her foot. Mud and flies flew. "You could've called out."

Liz's eyes were huge and green. She looked joyful, happier than Penelope had ever seen her. "Shouldn't you be packed and ready to hit the trail?" Liz asked. "You know, working, like I pay you to do."

Penelope raised a brow plucked to perfection. "You had a meeting. What happened to marshaling the law enforcement rangers to protect your project?"

"No longer necessary. Instead, we're building a new hair-snag station. I have the perfect spot off trail and impossible for saboteurs to locate unless someone tells them." She nudged Penelope with her elbow, and the young woman caught a faint whiff of gasoline. Had

Liz discovered that she had been mapping their station locations for Ezra?

"No two-handed hammering today," Liz chirped. "We're going to meet Grady."

"Why do you smell like gas?" Penelope demanded.

"You've got eyeliner problems. Why bother with makeup? Is that lipstick on your teeth, or are your gums bleeding?" Liz told her she'd hired a packer. "He starts today."

"Did you say Grady?" Penelope ran the tip of her ring finger beneath each eye.

"He's the answer to my woes, dear. Possibly yours as well." Liz pulled free of her enormous backpack. "Grew up on a ranch outside Babb and is ferrying supplies in via mule." She rummaged in the top pouch and retrieved a protein bar. Liz explained that thanks to having canceled the meeting, she and Penelope would be able to help Grady construct his first hair-snag station. She'd left a note on the seat of the stock truck, told him he wouldn't have to do it alone. "We need to get going."

"Why would some guy I've never met be . . ." Penelope carved quotation marks in the air, "'the answer to my woes'?"

Liz bit into her breakfast. A squirrel offended by their presence chittered from a pine tree. "Unlike the fiasco you married, Grady has common sense."

Penelope wished she were a different sort of person, above such obvious ploys, but her interest was piqued. A boyfriend? She could take up with another guy, and Ezra, riddled with jealousy, would want her back. Humans desired what they couldn't have. Ezra was no different. This could work. In the meantime, her boss was a far cry from the company Penelope had hoped for, but anything was better than pouring bear bait by herself. She picked up her cook pot coated in slobber and shuddered. "I can't imagine who you'd have to sleep with to get permission to bring your dog."

Liz crouched and cupped the pooch's face in her hands, rubbed its head. "We're no longer asking. We're doing."

"Won't your boyfriend have a problem with that?" Penelope admired Mack Savage. He was kind, capable, and handsome, with neat brown hair, light blue eyes, and a strong jaw. She could not help but wonder why he was with Liz. When Penelope had first heard Park Service women call Mack "Softy Savage," she'd thought they were referring to his leniency as a law enforcement officer, his tendency to only warn pot smokers and food storage violators, but then she'd caught on. Those women were not talking about arrests or citations. Penelope figured Liz scared him hard. Their relationship fascinated her almost as much as her own.

"Once I publish this study, everyone who is anyone in wildlife biology will know who I am. I will forever alter wildlife research." Liz stood and stretched. "Mack and the rest of these yokels, their opinions do not matter."

Clancy ran up the trail that bisected the Cut Bank Valley, past meadows and through stands of lodgepole. She ran toward Roberts and Nate, the radio, and help. Clancy knew Ezra had planned to sever his relationship with Penelope the night before. His batshit crazy wife had hired on with the DNA study he abhorred so she could stalk him on Glacier's east side. She was overnighting at Atlantic Creek, less than a mile away from their spike camp. Earlier

Clancy could not wait to hear how it had gone. Now she just wanted to find him. Had the storm waylaid him? Had he gotten to Penelope and decided to spend the night? While contrary to his purposes, it wouldn't have surprised Clancy if Ezra had given in to pity sex. It would not have been the first time. If he was at Atlantic Creek with Penelope while she feared for his life, Clancy was going to chew the guy a new one.

The trail tunneled through a stand of lodgepole that melded into a verdant smear. Worry weighed her chest the same way it had last summer when night fell and her brother Sean had not returned from climbing Going-to-the-Sun Mountain. Her throat throbbed. She broke out of the trees. The mountains squeezed closer. The trail turned to talus. Clancy ran faster, desperate to find Roberts and Nate.

Her toe caught a root, and she sailed. *It's not the fall that kills you*, she thought as she set her teeth and hit hard. *It's the landing*. Pain stabbed her right knee. Her palms stung. Nothing felt broken. Muck soaked her work pants. As surely as she knew she was okay, she knew Ezra was not. An animal snorted.

Clancy's eyes flew open. *Bear*. Velcro gave with a *rip* as she freed her pepper spray. Still on her knees, she scrambled to turn and face what was coming. She flicked the safety free with her thumb and locked her arms. A dun-colored mare rounded the curve and tossed its head. The creature's rider wore a chore coat, jeans, and a light-gray Stetson. Mules loaded with tools and boxes moseyed along behind. There she was, all distressed, and who should appear but a guy on a horse wearing a whitish hat. The rider hopped from his mount in one fluid motion and raised his hands. "We come in peace. Put down the weapon." His grin lifted lopsided. Chewing tobacco bulged beneath his lip. Clancy still held the canister at the ready. Flustered and wired with adrenaline, she worked to holster her bear spray. The fellow reached out a gloved hand large enough to cradle a watermelon. Clancy grasped it, and he hauled her to her feet. Emotion caught in her throat. Her chin quivered.

"No shame in falling, just in not getting back up." He maintained the endearing grin. His eyes were the warm brown of creamed coffee. "I'm Grady, and this here's Ruth, Barb, and Sandy." Clancy shook her head. He thought she was upset because she'd fallen. She wasn't that soft. The names of the animals were familiar, but her brain seized. Mired in fear for Ezra, her memory wouldn't function. Her mind did that to her, shut down under stress, froze when she needed it most. She could not place the names and gave up trying.

"My . . ." Clancy struggled with how to refer to Ezra. How could she describe the guy she'd hiked with for hundreds of miles, the guy she teased relentlessly about his messy love life and his Casanova attitude, the guy whose rugged looks and crass charm landed him in a heap of trouble, the guy who gently woke her when it was time to get back to work after she'd consumed her peanut butter and jelly and dozed against her pack, the guy who'd found her brother, the guy for whom, with the exception of sleeping with him, she would do just about anything.

The night before, the wind had gusted and snapped the tarp covering their kitchen area. The last thing Clancy had seen before she'd ducked inside her tent was Ezra, his hood cinched tight, his hands red with cold as he stowed their cookstove inside a metal bear-proof box.

"My friend, my coworker," she explained to the packer, the inside of her bottom lip secure between her teeth, "he's gone." The story tumbled out—the tent ripped from its stakes and shredded, the smell, the sickening knowledge that Ezra suffered out here somewhere, cold and wet and alone.

With the same grace in reverse, Grady climbed atop the mare and reached down. "Let's get you to your crew."

"Can you run mules?"

Grady laughed and shook his head. "From up here, you're less prone to trip." Clancy accepted his hand, stuck her boot through the stirrup, and swung her sore knee over the horse. Grady scooted, made room. "Hold tight." He clucked his tongue and Ruth started moving. Jostled, Clancy hugged his middle. The slope of the saddle angled her toward him. Her chest pressed against his back. He urged the animal up the trail with a pump of the reins and a squeeze of his legs. The mules plodded along behind, keeping pace without protest. He smelled of woodsmoke and wintergreen tobacco, and despite his thick work coat, Clancy swore she could feel his warmth. When it came time to pull away, she knew the front of her would feel colder than if she'd never pressed against him at all.

The horse meandered through thickets of sweet pine heavy with their damp spring smell. Anxiety stung beneath her ribs. Ezra needed help and she needed to be moving. "I'm worried. I should get down, run."

"Hang tight." His voice was kind. "They can't be far."

Clancy's mind raced as if to make up for the fact that her body couldn't. What had happened to Ezra? Who or what had shredded his tent? What accounted for that smell? Why hadn't she found Roberts and Nate yet? Had something happened to them, too? Had Ezra gone out in the storm to visit Penelope as he'd planned? Was he with her now at the Atlantic Creek Campground?

Clancy had her arms around a guy she'd never seen before who packed mules. It had been months upon months since she'd been physically close to an attractive man. The tight fist of regret clamped her chest at the memory of her heavy drinking and the one-night stands in the wake of Sean's death. She'd had to stop. The sex had meant that for a while she could feel something beyond the maw of sorrow. That had been the upside. The downside came with morning and the avalanche of shame.

Clancy's first summer on trails, they'd been building the two-stringer bridge over Atlantic Creek when Roberts had yelled, "What's the golden rule?"

She responded, "Don't sleep with anyone on the crew."

He shook his head. "I was going for 'Measure twice, cut once.'"

None of the guys she worked with tempted Clancy. No way did she want to become one of the women they made up nicknames for, joked about. Never would she risk inviting morning-after awkwardness to her workdays or on their ten-day hitches.

She shifted in the saddle. What was it with the animals' names? It plagued her like an unreachable itch. Clancy studied the meadow that stretched to the creek. Purple patches of shooting stars lifted amid the green. With a rush of relief, she said, "You named the stock after the women who work in the head shed?"

Grady chuckled. "Someone in the barn was thinking." After a moment he added, "Don't tell your dad."

"You know who my dad is?" Clancy's father was the park's chief law enforcement ranger. From West Glacier, he oversaw every district in the park.

Grady turned to meet her eye. There was that grin, lopsided and beaming. "Marty filled me in. He says you can't keep a secret."

"You work for Marty?" Clancy harbored a soft spot for the man. The guys didn't like him because he refused to pack ridiculous quantities of alcohol into their spike camps. Roberts always designated her to stay behind and lead Marty and the string to their spot. He was older and quiet, gentle with the animals, and one of a handful of Blackfeet working in Glacier despite the reservation's 85 percent unemployment. Never mind that the park was the Blackfeet's ancestral homeland and the government had connived over the centuries to destroy them by many means—everything from military massacres to disease to destruction of the buffalo and ripping children away from their families, absconding with them to boarding schools. Those schools, where priests and nuns beat them for speaking their language, cut their hair, crushed their spirits, and worse, had traumatized generations of Blackfeet families. How every Native American wasn't permanently walking around mad enough to spit astounded Clancy. She couldn't imagine the rub of knowing the mountains sacred to your people for thousands of years had been taken from your tribe and turned into a park where people recreated. Now, where their ancestors had once sought visions, people climbed for fun and scarfed their peanut-butter-and-jelly sandwiches on sacred summits. It seemed the least the park could do was hire Blackfeet for the good-paying government jobs.

Marty had asked one morning as he loaded the mules, "Can you keep a secret?"

"Nope." Clancy grinned at him and shook her head. "Not in my skill set." She spent the whole hitch wondering what it was he would have told her if she'd answered differently.

The horse slowed, stretching to nibble grass along the trail. Grady nudged her onward with his heels. "I'm sorry about your brother."

"You and Marty must've had quite the chat."

Grady shrugged. "Marty's a family friend. He mentioned it."

Even after almost a year, Clancy still wasn't sure how to respond to expressions of sympathy. "I miss him."

Grady looked over his shoulder. "I have a sister, Josie. I worry, can't imagine the world without her." His face was solemn. "It has to be awful."

They rode in silence. The horse was not in a hurry. Clancy tried to quell the antsiness that twitched her legs. "When did Marty hire you?"

Grady shook his head. "Ms. Ralston, the bear lady, I work for her."

"You don't look like the DNA study type." Grady lacked a few layers of expensive polypropylene and the noses-up, our shit-doesn't-smell-as-bad-as-yours, our-work-is-actually-important attitude of Liz and her DNA people.

Massive Douglas firs dictated the trail's curves. Hooves clomped against chunks of scree. Clancy relaxed her arms. Her hand knocked against something solid and heavy in the pocket of Grady's work coat.

Before she could ask if he knew that unless you worked as a law enforcement ranger, firearms were illegal inside the park, Clancy spotted her crew. Nate, six feet of brawn, had his black-framed glasses perched atop his ball cap, the one Clancy knew read *Virginity Rocks*. Ezra had given it to him as a birthday gift, promising it would help get him laid. Her crew, what was left of it, sprawled in a meadow, their jackets bright red and yellow. Both men reclined against their packs, with the canvas bags for hauling dirt, shovels, and the chain saw scattered around them. They'd driven the axe ends of their Pulaskis into the ground so the adze ends and long wooden handles lifted like some primitive turnstile. Even at this distance, she could hear Roberts complaining about "the uniforms." It was a favorite topic of his. The brass with the fat salaries and all the power who never stepped out from behind their desks, never so much as got a scuff on their park-issue Danners. It had bothered her during her first season. She felt defensive about her dad. But last summer during the search for Sean, Roberts had treated her entire family with kindness. Now Clancy dismissed his rants, figured they had nothing to do with her father, just Roberts blowing off steam. Better that he unleash on higher-ups than on her, Ezra, and Nate.

She rose up in the saddle. Roberts's radio and her connection to help was within sight. Nothing against the good-natured stoners she worked with, but she wanted Mack, his search-and-rescue experience and EMT training, and the multitude of personnel and resources he and her dad could marshal. Clancy needed them all in this valley searching for Ezra, and she wanted it an hour ago. "Roberts!" she shouted. As soon as his name escaped her mouth, she knew she'd made a mistake. Clancy felt a sharp tug.

Grady leaned back hard, pulling the reins taut. The mules kicked. Their loads shifted. Clancy eyed the rocky bank, the ten-foot drop from the trail to the meadow. If one of the string went over, they'd all follow, a horrendous tangle of animals, tools, and boxes. One of the mules snorted. Nostrils flared. They kicked. Clancy slammed her eyes shut and felt the horse shift, crow-hop. Grady said softly, "Settle in, girls. Settle in." He clucked his tongue and lifted loose from the saddle, swaying with the pull of the ponies, the lengths of rope that tied the pack string together. Clancy clenched her work coat, squeezed her legs against the horse. When he sat down, she opened her eyes. Grady had them angling down the bank. The guys were on their feet.

"Quite the entrance." Roberts raised his eyebrows. With a look he told her she'd done something stupid, had best explain why she was on the back of a horse when she was supposed to be scraping scree from the Triple Divide Pass trail, and it had better be good.

Nate's face lit up with his insouciant grin. "Nice rodeo."

Clancy wanted off the horse so badly she almost jumped. Grady pulled his boot free from the stirrup. She kicked her toe in. Before she had it secure, Clancy swung her other leg across the animal's back. The weight of her pack shifted, dragged at her. She tried to grip the saddle. Too late. With her toe still in the stirrup, the rest of her slammed to the ground. For the second time that morning Grady smiled down at her in the wake of a spill. Clancy didn't have it in her to care. "Ezra." She desperately tried to right herself by pushing up on her hands and one foot. "He's gone." Nate hoisted her to standing, reached out and held the stirrup. She leaned against him and pulled her boot free. Clancy turned to Roberts. "Call it in."

"Bastard owes me money," he huffed. "Lots of money this time."

"Help, dammit," Clancy yelled. "Could you just help?" She heard the mules' breathing, felt their heat.

"You should know," Grady said, "something's burning back there."

Clancy swung to face him. "A fire? Why didn't you say?"

"Just this side of the ford a ways. Right about where Ms. Ralston told me you have your spike camp. Smells nasty." The wind rushed high in the trees. Grady met her eye. "I didn't want to add to your trouble."

Roberts frowned. "Ezra's missing. There's a fire near, or possibly in, our camp." He shook his head. "Maybe our boy don't want to be found."

Grady dipped his chin. "Got people waiting." He flicked the reins, turned his horse toward the trail. She watched him go, kept her eyes trained on his back. The mules followed. Her chest where she had pressed against him felt chilled, just as she'd known it would. Clancy swallowed, fought the familiar sting of being left behind.

CHAPTER 4

HARASSED

◆

That same morning in the hamlet of East Glacier, Patrick Hughes tucked his gangly legs beneath the counter, took his usual seat next to the window, and signaled his buddy the cook. His order acknowledged with the lift of a chin, Patrick grinned. Today he was hiking with the woman he loved. He refused to allow the fact that she was dating someone else, a married someone at that, to dampen his enthusiasm. Patrick sought the deep satisfaction borne of adversity, and this situation was no different than scaling St. Nick without rope. Just as in his successful solo of Glacier's most technical climb, the reward would be well worth the effort.

Rosie's honey-colored hair caught the light even on cloudy days. She had a great body, toned and strong, smooth skin, and light blue eyes. Whenever Rosie smiled at him, she looked like she knew a secret—a good one. He never regretted time he spent with her.

Tourists and locals packed every seat in the small diner. The new server filled a glass with Squirt. "Pop," she grumbled, "breakfast of champions for toddlers."

Patrick spotted a table crowded with high chairs, parents, and grandparents and shrugged. "The youngsters aren't old enough for coffee." The server shot him a grin, and he asked if she knew where Rosie might be.

"Probably sleeping. Didn't get out of here till after midnight." The diner closed at nine, so it had to have been crazy busy. Hopefully she was still up for a hike.

He studied the mountains. Snow drenched the peaks, but they could tackle one of the passes. Across the road, Two Medicine Area Ranger Jed Turner stepped from his patrol car and made for the door. Patrick ducked into a section of the *Great Falls Tribune*. Before he could read more than the first paragraph about Great Falls' urban chicken controversy, he felt a sharp tap on his shoulder. Patrick forced a smile and swiveled.

"We need to talk." Turner's nostrils flared below his tidy mustache. His jaw jutted with aggression.

"Shouldn't you be checking a campground for food storage violations or arresting people for selling fish to their aunties or whatever it is our tax dollars pay you to do besides drive around Two Med aimlessly?"

For years Patrick and his buddies had referred to Ranger Turner as "gay" in a general derogatory sense. Then six months ago, the man had walked out on his wife and two kids and begun dating guys from Calgary he met online.

"Don't pretend you pay taxes." Turner leaned close. "I had an interesting call this morning." He waved at the server. "Coffee, miss." He faked a smile. "Senator Donaldson's office phoned. They're concerned about sabotage of the DNA study." His mouth twitched. "If I was to happen to glance in the back of your Subaru at some trailhead and notice a pile of barbed wire, we'd need to bring you in for a conversation." The server swung the coffee mug onto the counter with enough force to slosh it beyond the rim.

"You're threatening to set me up?" Patrick raised an eyebrow. The server slid him a plate of veggie browns bookended with a double side of thick-cut, applewood-smoked bacon. "Did you hear that?" Patrick asked her. "This officer of the law, sworn to preserve the park for the American public, for folks like me who actually get to enjoy it instead of trolling for petty offenders the way he does, just said he plans to plant incriminating materials inside my vehicle."

Turner reached over and snatched a piece of bacon. "Sooner or later, we'll arrest you. We'll take you in because you're camping without a permit or packing a blade longer than four inches or violating some other regulation you don't even know about. And when we do, we'll find a reason to keep you." He took a bite, his fingers raised delicately. "We've got your number, Hughes, and Senator Donaldson is getting your name." Turner sipped his coffee and set the mug on the counter with forced gentleness. "We'll see what happens when you're on my turf." He tossed a dollar in the coffee spill and took a step toward the door. "Please," his eyes narrowed, "come visit the Two Medicine Valley."

Patrick had a theory about the town of East Glacier and why every fall people like Ranger Turner retreated west of the mountains to what Patrick considered "the dark side"—the Flathead Valley with its gray skies, espresso stands, tattooed Christians, and big-box stores. Patrick believed East Glacier culled those it deemed unfit —skiers and snowboarders who required a ride to the top of a run, folks who couldn't handle hurricane-force winds as a matter of course or drive icy roads during whiteouts or look beyond the reservation poverty to see the beauty. He felt fortunate to be among the chosen and tore into his breakfast.

"What'd you do to him?" The guy on the stool next to Patrick looked to be around thirty and had used some sort of product to spike his hair. He wore a wrinkle-free, button-down shirt, khakis, and dress shoes. A silver cuff clamped his wrist. "You must be local."

Patrick wondered what gave him away—his hair months overdue for a cut, his tan from spring skiing, his face lined by weather? Or the fact that a cranky park ranger knew his name? "How can I help?"

"I have a friend, a high school buddy, who lives around here in the summer. Name's Ezra, Ezra Riverton." The guy held his mug with both hands, like he was cold. "You know his place?"

This kind of thing rankled Patrick. People landed in this remote gem on the Blackfeet Reservation for all kinds of private reasons, and to Patrick's mind they should stay that way. "Who should I tell him is asking?"

"I'd like to surprise him." Light glanced off the metal adorning his wrist. "He works trail crew."

"I'll pass along the message. What was your name?"

"Tell him Skip's in town. And we need to get together."

"Anything else?" Patrick just wanted to find Rosie and go hiking.

Skip pulled out his wallet. "Take me to his place. I'll make it worth your time."

Patrick stood to his full height and tucked a few bills beneath his plate. "You don't have that kind of money." He smiled. "No one does."

An hour later, Patrick drove a rutted gravel road until they came to a chain that spanned the cattle guard and blocked their entrance to the Cut Bank Valley. "What the hell?" Rosie asked. She was the youngest sister of Patrick's college roommate. He'd harbored a crush on her for years. Shane had called Patrick and said Rosie seemed depressed. She was drinking too much and had lost her spark. She wanted to live in the mountains. Patrick landed her a job in the diner and Shane bought her a train ticket. Except for her objectionable choice of boyfriend, she seemed to be doing well.

"Bears. This valley runs thick with them. Probably have one in the campground." Patrick threw the car in reverse and gunned the vehicle into the timothy. "Doesn't mean we can't walk around it." He backed down a small rise until he could no longer see the road and no one on the road could see them. "We just shouldn't get caught."

While Patrick donned his gaiters, Rosie leaned against the vehicle and gazed up at the mountains. She asked what the one in the middle was called. "Bad Marriage," Patrick said.

"You are so full of it." Rosie laughed. "Ezra would have mentioned that."

"Say what you will about your boyfriend's unfortunate union." Patrick shrugged. "I'm not making it up." He tightened the last bit of webbing around his calf, struggled into the harness for his binoculars, fastened the powerful magnifiers into place across his chest, and pulled on his pack.

Rosie pointed. "Do you have any idea how dorky you look?"

"Function before fashion, my dear. This isn't New York. No one cares how you dress or what you look like. You just get to be you." He led her along the boundary fence until they could hear the rush of the creek swollen with spring runoff. He placed a boot in the middle of the bottom strand of barbed wire and yanked the next highest upward. Rosie shrugged out of her pack, tossed it over, and slipped easily between the two wires. He grabbed the top of the fence post, planted his boot, and hopped to the other side.

"Ezra's crew is back here somewhere." Rosie sounded gleeful. Tight pigtails that would've looked ridiculous on anyone else over the age of seven sprang from the sides of her head.

Patrick moved swiftly through a stretch of thick brush. "You're still chasing that nightmare?"

"He's a good guy."

"He's married. He's often stoned, of questionable morals, and he's not good enough for you." He glanced over his shoulder. Sunlight tangled in her hair. Color rose on her cheeks. The color of her eyes matched the sky. "But other than that . . ."

"His wife is nuts, insanely jealous with an emphasis on the insane. You won't believe what she's putting him through." Rosie struggled to keep up.

"You shouldn't believe anything he's telling you about Penelope. Isn't that the first rule of mistresshood? Don't believe what he says about the wife."

Rosie laughed. "You watch too much Lifetime television for women. Ezra married her for a half-price lift ticket at the ski hill. How could she have believed it would work? They're barely married. I'm not really a mistress."

"You. Are a walking other-woman cliché." Patrick doubted that anything he said would change how Rosie felt or whom she dated, but he still needed to say it.

"She's threatening to take everything. The house, the goldfish, the equity, half his camper. Ezra doesn't have the money to fight it." They meandered into a meadow crammed with wildflowers—

lupine, sticky geranium, and biscuitroot, a riot of purple, fuchsia, and yellow. "I wish you could know him like I do. He's passionate about grizzly bears, a defender of wilderness, and the victim of a crazy woman."

"Know him biblically. No thanks."

Rosie laughed. "You have the maturity of a twelve-year-old."

"I'm wise enough to pursue only one woman at a time."

They made their way along Cut Bank Creek. Dew blanketed the grass and sedges. Patrick asked after Shane, and Rosie told him her brother made so much money managing investments that he'd offered to purchase a place in Montana and let her live in it. "I suggested he buy Ezra's house."

"Because that wouldn't be complicated." Patrick stopped and turned toward her. "You know Penelope's got a tenuous grasp on her mental health. How do you think she'd feel about the woman shacked up with her husband in her house? Are you trying to get yourself killed?"

"You're jealous. That's what you are."

They reached the water and walked along the bank. "Your infatuation with that stoner impairs your decision-making."

"You're just bummed you and I didn't last beyond that one night."

Patrick felt himself blush. He had replayed it over and over. He picked her up at the train station. Her awe and delight in the view, her new boss, her room above the store infected him with joy. She was more attractive than he remembered, a smattering of freckles, long honey-colored hair, and an impish grin that seemed at once to delight in the world and hold some private wisdom separate from it. He helped her schlep her bags and backpack up the stairs to her home for the summer and drove her to his place—a trailer house a couple miles south of town with a woodstove and a view of snow-covered Calf Robe, Ellsworth and Henry to the west, and rolling plains sliced by the Two Medicine River to the east. Potatoes baked in the oven, a salad chilled in the fridge, elk steaks marinated on the counter, and a huckleberry pie cooled on the table. He grilled the meat and she caught him up on the lives of people he'd once known. After they ate, he spread a blanket across the deck, and they watched the stars appear. She tensed with cold, and he offered her more of the comforter. She curled close. He kissed her and asked her to stay. She did.

In the morning, during the drive to town, she told him she wasn't looking for a relationship. Next thing he knew, she'd attended a trails barbecue at Park Service housing and was seeing Ezra. It wasn't that she didn't want a relationship, he realized; she just wasn't interested in one with him. He was too available. He knew that. But he couldn't change who he was, not even for Rosie.

Now, on this bright morning, he fought to find the right words. Cut Bank Creek rolled wide, water lifting and rushing to a froth as the current braided its way downhill. Maybe he should just tell her how he felt? What was the worst that could happen? Instead, he said, "I'm not going anywhere."

"Ezra built a trail for a woman with cancer this spring. Said he met some great people, ranchers, real Montanans who love the land."

Had she heard him? Patrick wondered. Maybe she had and chose to ignore it? Maybe there was nothing for her to say to that. Patrick told her, "He built a trail because he got paid." He angled toward the trailhead. "I don't like you being with him." There, he'd said it. He estimated they were due south of the car campground. "This morning some guy in the diner asked me where Ezra lives, said they went to high school together."

"Ezra didn't go to high school."

"Everyone goes to high school."

"Ezra homeschooled in Idaho. He told me his parents didn't want him subject to 'the indignity of public indoctrination.'" She stopped. Her face twisted with disgust. "What is that smell?"

"Must be getting close to the vault toilet." Patrick lifted his binoculars from his chest harness and glassed the area. He grinned. He saw the back of a ranger, his gray polyester shirt and green trousers unmistakable. Beyond him a grizzly excavated a campsite. Just as Patrick had said, the valley ran thick with them.

CHAPTER 5

TORCHED

◆

Clancy struggled to keep up as Roberts double-timed it down the trail toward their spike camp. She practically had to jog. The man was twice her age and smoked half a pouch of tobacco a day along with oodles of pot. Still, he could leave her in the dust if he so chose. She wanted to get back to camp, find out about the fire Grady had reported. But she couldn't shake the sense that they should be looking for Ezra as they hiked. At this pace, she needed to keep her eyes on the trail.

They had spent a ridiculous amount of time hemming and hawing about calling the Com Center. Roberts had refused to do it until he'd assessed the tent and the fire for himself. He also insisted that they fill in the pit Nate had dug as a source of dirt to raise the tread on the trail. "Doubt we'll be back this way for a while. Best tidy up." Clancy had never shoveled so fast, but the task still felt interminable and wrong. Now they were finally moving, and the knot of anxiety behind her ribs eased. Nate whistled tunelessly behind her.

"I know you think I'm an ass, but I'm right about this," Roberts said and then, more softly, "Your brother died, Clancy." She scrambled to stay at his heels, strained to hear. "Sean went missing and when Ezra found him, the worst had happened." Roberts was trying so hard to be kind. It didn't come naturally. "I'm not calling you paranoid exactly." He paused and glanced over his shoulder. "I'm just saying that what happened last summer might well be clouding your thinking here."

"Maybe he was catholing it," Nate called. "Started a fire when he burned his toilet paper."

"Why," Clancy didn't bother to wring the annoyance from her voice, "would he cathole when we've got a perfectly good low-rider?"

"Bet you were using it." Nate sounded like a second grader telling his potty joke. "Maybe he got tired of being Roberts's whipping boy?" Nate's playfulness made Clancy want to slap him. Something had happened to Ezra. It had nothing to do with Sean's death or her grief. Maybe they'd believe her when they smelled what she had and saw Ezra's shredded tent.

"He'll probably be standing there waiting for us, stoned out of his head on his private stash," Roberts said. "I'd bet you all the money he owes me, he was holding out on us last night."

Had Roberts or Nate gone looking for Ezra's pot after he left to visit Penelope? Did one of them have something to do with all this? Why would Ezra borrow money from Roberts? And an even better question, where on earth had Roberts come by money in the first place? The guy worked trail crew during the summers and drew unemployment while he downhill skied all winter, same as lots of trails folks. Fun but not terribly lucrative.

"One thing I've learned over almost thirty years." Roberts shook his head like even he couldn't believe how long he'd been at this. "Never call the guns into the backcountry, not if you can help it. Exhaust every other option. You get a bunch of those pricks together, they're bound to find someone to cite and someone else to arrest. It's what keeps them buckling into their flak jackets every day. Sure, they serve and protect, but only after they've done so for their own ass."

"I'm sure he didn't mean your dad, Clancy." Nate seemed to be the only guy on the crew who remembered that her dad was the chief ranger. As she scrambled to keep up, Clancy toyed with Roberts's theory. Maybe Sean's death did distort her interpretation of Ezra's upended tent. Since her brother had died, she'd certainly found the world more tenuous. Sean, who'd always been afraid of heights, went climbing alone and never came home. They searched an entire day and found nothing but his signature in the summit register. The next day Ezra, Clancy's steady, funny stoner trails buddy, managed to downclimb the northeast face of Going-to-the-Sun Mountain and locate Sean's body.

Afterward Ezra sat with her in the deep cool of Sunrift Gorge, tossing stones into the rushing creek. He answered the questions that burst in her mind like a shotgun blast. Even now, almost a year later, they'd be hiking along and she'd wonder, "Was he wearing a stocking cap?" Ezra understood how her mind flew back to that time, those two days that had shattered her world, how she worried the details like pearls of grief, trying to string them into a cohesive story. He didn't ask, "Was *who* wearing a stocking cap?" He simply turned toward her and said, "Blue with a darker blue stripe." Clancy knew the one. Their mom had gotten it for Sean at the feed store. It fit his inordinately large head. She tried to smile, and they continued up the switchback.

During her first day on the job two summers ago, Roberts sent Clancy and Ezra off to dig drains. As they hunched beneath a tree seeking refuge from the cold and rain during their morning break, he offered her a toke. When she shook her head, he drew his fingers through his beard and asked, "What kind of environmental studies major are you?" The question struck Clancy as hilarious, and she still hollered it at him as they barreled up some painfully steep stretch, hiked in a downpour, or through a plague of biting flies. After Sean died, Clancy didn't have it in her to return to the university in Missoula. The idea of reading deep ecology essays and arguing about postmodernism inside a stuffy classroom struck her as banal. She could not muster the energy to care. She felt betrayed by a world that chugged merrily along without Sean in it. She told herself she'd go back to college when the coursework didn't smack of privileged people performing mental gymnastics with no relevance in the real world.

Hundreds of miles of cleared trail formed the bedrock of her friendship with Ezra. The guy led a complicated love life, would climb peaks with her after work, and shared his chocolate. Add to that the crazy stretch of crumbly rock he'd downclimbed to find Sean and recover his body and, well, she owed him.

As they left the main trail and veered toward camp, an acrid smell burned in Clancy's nostrils. Nothing had been on fire when she'd left. It had to have started after her departure but before Grady and the mules happened by. It made her shudder, the thought that someone had been watching, waiting to see her leave, and then slunk in and set a fire. Ezra sprang to mind. Could he have been observing her the whole time she was reading the climbers' guide and charting their route up Bad Marriage? She shook her head hard at the thought. That would be low. Roberts's paranoia was rubbing off on her.

The social trail led straight to their kitchen area. The tarp they'd strung high between trees shaded their crude counter and the log rounds that served as seating. "We got contraband."

Clancy assumed Roberts meant pipes and other paraphernalia and she could not have cared less. "Call it in already." She stood with her feet wide, hands on her hips.

"Patience." Roberts trained his gaze on Nate, pointed at the DNA study's tree ID tags and coils of barbed wire hanging from stobs like trophies. "That shit needs to disappear."

"We have to find Ezra," Clancy demanded.

"Gotta know what we're dealing with first."

Nate and Clancy followed Roberts toward Ezra's tent site. "Ezra," Roberts hollered, gruff and commanding. He marched down the path, tramped through the aspen. When Roberts hit the clearing, he stopped and shook his head.

A raven croaked. For a long moment none of them spoke. Nate sucked in air and said, "Shit."

Ezra's tent had melted into a charred black clump. Wisps of smoke lifted from the shriveled mass. Clancy looked over at her boss, feeling indignant and ready to let him have it. But the look on Roberts's face stopped her. He'd gone pale. His eyes narrowed. With a slow shake of his head, he said, "Our boy's long gone."

Roberts dropped to one knee on the flattened patch of ground where Ezra had pitched his tent. He ran his thumb across the webbing staked to the ground. "Looks to have been cut." The air bit with the edge of the earlier stink topped with acrid notes of that which was never meant to burn—nylon, damp grass, wildflowers—having gone up in flames.

"Gasoline," Nate said. "Some sort of starter, anyway."

"Now do you believe me?" Clancy pleaded. "Something's happened to Ezra."

Roberts got to his feet. "Something like he owes me money and probably other people, too, and he's had it with that psycho wife of his." He shook his head. "Something happened, sure. But don't go thinking Ezra didn't have a hand in it. He only looks dumb."

"Why did Ezra borrow money?"

Roberts turned on her, his eyes bright with anger. The man's distress had morphed into aggression. "I didn't ask. I didn't ask for the same reason you shouldn't." He dropped his gaze and muttered, "None of my damn business." Roberts shrugged out of his pack and removed his Pulaski from the ice-axe loop. He swung the tool and drove the adze end deep. Dirt and vegetation flew. A black line sprang up between them and the tent. "No one goes closer." He turned to Clancy. "Check the gas can." He eyed Nate. "Down the shitter with the wire. March the tags to the creek. Make sure no one finds them. Ever."

Instead of heading toward their kitchen, he ducked into the trees with his radio. Twigs popped beneath his boots. Clancy knew talking into the thing, being heard by the whole park from the superintendent to the maintenance folks scrubbing toilets, rattled him as few other things did. It was the only time she'd ever heard him tongue-tied, the only part of the job that pierced his veneer of cool.

Clancy found the gas can where it sat beneath their makeshift kitchen counter—a weathered board they stashed in the brush to use year after year nailed to a platform constructed of arm-thick branches. She lifted it. Empty.

Nate was off ditching the DNA materials. Clancy couldn't see Roberts. The man could dig whatever lines he chose. He'd be pissed, but Clancy was used to that. She dashed back to the clearing and walked widening circles around the smoldering mess of Ezra's tent, looking for any indication of what had happened. She thought about Ezra's disappearance going parkwide over the radio. Everyone would be alerted, looking. They'd find him—hurt, cold—get him to a hospital.

Roberts had an occasional hookup. Apparently the woman slept with interp guys and law enforcement rangers as well. Roberts called her "Parkwide." He'd nicknamed his girlfriend the previous summer "the Bicycle." Everyone got a ride. Clancy had assumed he didn't want an audience when he talked to the Com Center, preferred that she and Nate didn't catch the shake in his voice and tease him about it later. But what if it was because he had something to say that he didn't want Clancy to hear?

She found three additional lengths of severed webbing fitted with grommets and staked to the ground. She left them where they were, figured Mack or whoever came to conduct the search would want to see them.

She stepped into the tall grass that edged the aspen. She couldn't see her boots and shuffled along. Had Ezra slept here last night? She sifted through the morning's details. If he'd stayed with Penelope to ride out the storm, he would have caught up with them by now. Had some trouble found him between here and the Atlantic Creek Campground? A bear, a fall, a twisted ankle? Clancy needed to search that trail. She suspected Ezra had not mentioned his plan to visit Penelope to Roberts and Nate. They would've given him nine kinds of hell. They all kept some things private.

What no one besides her parents knew was that Clancy was supposed to have been with her brother the day he died. She backed out on him because a river guide she had a crush on asked her to float the Middle Fork. She didn't suspect for a moment that Sean would go without her. He was afraid of heights. When they climbed, Clancy always led. Sean scaled mountains reluctantly. While he was usually glad he'd gone once they were home, he never planned a trip, never burned with the desire to be on top of a certain peak. Clancy couldn't help imagining his death, fear paralyzing his judgment, the fall something of a validation when it came. He'd been right all those times they'd been climbing and his leg had gone all Elvis as she talked him through a class 4 pitch. She should have been there to help him down. Instead, Clancy was drinking cheap beer and making out with a guy she hadn't seen since, a fellow dim enough to try to fondle her breast through her life jacket.

A small creature scurried through the underbrush. Dappled sunlight spotted the tall grass. It sparked off an object. She crouched and touched something cold, metal. When she lifted it out of the grass, she saw that it was a length of tent pole, gnarled and bent. Teeth had pierced the titanium. Sharp bits poked from the shaft. She scanned the area. A few feet away amid the aspen, Clancy spied a pile of bear scat.

She told herself it could mean anything. Things occurring at the same time—Ezra was missing, a bear had visited his tent site, and his tent had been shredded—didn't prove causality. Dear God, Clancy prayed it wasn't a bear that got him. Ezra loved grizzlies. She couldn't brook the thought that one might have killed him. Maybe

Roberts was right. Ezra had come up against trouble he couldn't find his way through and bolted farther into the backcountry after shredding and later torching his tent with their saw gas.

Clancy's dad had theorized about it before when, despite an extensive search, he couldn't find any sign of a solo backcountry camper who'd been mired in debt. The scenario went like this: Hike in with a load of cash, camp, survive, walk out the other side of the park a week or two later, and hitchhike your way toward a new life. Great idea, just not likely. And if it had been that bad, wouldn't Ezra have shown some sign? Clancy had spent the last seven days at his side. He hadn't said or done anything that indicated he planned to disappear.

Most everyone who went missing in Glacier turned up eventually, even if only years later and in scattered skeletal form. One summer a hiker filling his water bottle found a femur in a stream. It belonged to the bankrupt guy her dad hadn't been able to find three summers earlier. They'd never know if he'd offed himself, fallen, drowned, starved, or been attacked by an animal and killed. But they knew he was dead.

The thought made Clancy shudder. She looked up at the mountains, waterfalls streaking their craggy faces. Seeing Bad Marriage made her think of Penelope. The woman was obsessed with Ezra. He had signed the papers. He planned to tell her they were finished. Had Penelope flown into a rage and killed him? She could've pushed him over a cliff or into the frigid creek or both, but that didn't explain the tattered tent, the wretched smell, or the fire. There were loads of ways to die back here—mauling, falling, drowning, lightning, suicide—but odds were he hadn't. Odds were he'd show up with a broken ankle or a blown knee and a great story and they'd gather at the trails shed and drink. They'd drink until the alcohol diluted their fear, until, awash in relief and buoyed by endless bottles, they'd sink into a chemically induced joy easily mistaken for love.

CHAPTER 6

BIZARRE

Mack watched Layne hop out of the truck and sprint toward him, knees high and arms pumping. Mack turned his attention to the bear. It remained in site 7, though it dug less frantically. When Layne arrived, the young man kept his voice to a strong whisper. "I know who registered the site."

Mack pointed to the bear. "Take a look at him." He handed Layne the binocs. The bear had his head deep in the hole he'd dug.

Layne removed his flat hat and adjusted the lenses. "How can you tell it's a male?" He looked like a Boy Scout, binoculars raised and wearing his prepared-for-any-eventuality duty belt. Was that a Leatherman and a Swiss army knife? The breeze shifted, lifted Layne's blond curls back from his forehead, carried with it a fresh wave of stink.

"I can't know. Not for sure. But it's huge and doesn't have cubs." The smell—decay heavy with the stink of blood—had to be Liz's bait.

"I think I have an idea regarding why the bruin's here," Layne offered.

"Shoot." Mack realized Layne was armed and corrected himself. "I'd like to hear it."

"The people who registered site 7 were an older Canadian couple. They rolled out before well before oh six hundred." Layne shifted his weight from foot to foot like he had to pee. "But the person I saw here after they left . . ." Layne hesitated. "You're not going to like it."

Mack forced himself to speak kindly. "Try me."

Layne peered through the binoculars as though the bear might save him from whatever unpleasantness he wanted to avoid.

"For the love of God, Layne. Who?"

"Your partner."

Mack furrowed his brow with skepticism. He didn't have a partner. They didn't work in pairs. They weren't street cops or detectives. This wasn't *CSI*. He caught another whiff of the sharp, rank smell. "You mean Liz?" He reached out and gently lifted the binoculars out of Layne's hands. The young man looked scared.

"I'm afraid so, sir. That's who I saw on my way back from my initial patrol. I try to do a walk-through before anyone leaves, note the license plates in case I discover a violation after they've vacated." He lowered his eyes as though ashamed. "She had an unleashed dog with her. A Karelian if I'm not mistaken."

Mack nodded. "Muffy." The damn dog had killed a baby fox, so Mack had taken to keeping her tied and muzzled when Liz was gone. If Liz had discovered her precious pooch tethered and silenced—a handy snack for a mountain lion—she'd be livid. So why the proclamation of love on the machine? Unless she'd left the message and then discovered the dog. Or maybe she was trying to throw him off, get him thinking about something other than what she'd been up to for the last twenty-four hours.

Layne spoke slowly. "There's more."

Mack forced a wan smile. "More?"

"Our perimeter's been breached, sir."

"What are you talking about, Layne?"

"There's a vehicle just beyond the boundary fence." The young man told Mack that the occupants had attempted to conceal it downhill from the road. "I believe that despite my having posted the sign clearly stating that the valley is closed due to bear activity, people have entered." His earnestness pained Mack. Layne continued, "They have 38 plates, sir. Locals."

"Why were you back at the boundary?"

"Intuition, sir. Gut instinct." Layne went on to explain that he felt like he was being watched as he drove to the ranger station, so he checked the boundary gate. And sure enough, a Subaru wagon sat alongside the fence. "Apologies for the insubordination, sir. I should have cleared my plan with you prior to executing." He paused. "But you didn't answer when I attempted contact via radio."

Mack bit back a grin and shrugged.

"And..." Layne paused and looked down as though choosing his words carefully.

"And?" Mack prompted.

"Dispatch called my cell when they failed to reach you on the radio." He inhaled deeply. "You're not going to like this either, sir."

"You don't have to call me 'sir.'" Mack tamped down his annoyance, made himself look up at the mountains and take a long breath. "Tell me."

"Trail crew, the one gypsied up the valley, called it in. A fire, sir. In their camp."

Mack took a step back. That made no sense. Zero. "We must have gotten almost a quarter inch of rain last night. A few weeks ago this entire place was under snow."

"Lightning strike?" Layne offered. "Last night's storm lasted hours, sir."

"Maybe."

"And . . ." Layne hesitated.

"Good grief, Layne. Spill it."

"One of the trail crew members has gone missing, sir."

Mack's mind flew to Clancy. "Missing?" Her crew, the Two Med Crew, cleared the valley this time of year, spent ten days at the Atlantic Creek spike camp. Not another one of Truman's kids.

"They last saw him over thirteen hours ago."

Him. Layne had said "him." Mack closed his eyes with relief.

Patrick marveled at the meadows choked with wildflowers and drenched in sun, the smells of the ground warming, sap rising, mountains running with falls, their tops full of snow—all of it made even better by his companion. Rosie plopped down on a log. Spray from Atlantic Falls peppered their faces. "I need to eat."

"Your feet wet?" Patrick asked.

Rosie pulled a sandwich from her pack and nodded. "You win the dry sock contest, gaiter-boy."

"I'm right about your boyfriend, too." Patrick lifted his binoculars from his pack. Rosie looked exhausted. He decided to lay off the lecture. She could date whomever she chose, and he could love her. He didn't have to convince her of anything. The water rushed steady and loud, roiling over logs, braiding past boulders. Dippers danced on islands of rock. Swifts darted through the mist.

"Ezra said their camp is beyond this waterfall."

"That's something I'd love to find." Patrick poached trail crew gypsy camps whenever he could. He sat beside her. The breeze tossed mist lifting off the falls.

"Do you ever miss it?" Rosie sounded wistful. "The power, the prestige, the money?"

Patrick glassed the mossy rock on the far side of the cascading water. "Home, you mean? New York? Trading on the Exchange?" He lowered his binoculars and furrowed his brow. "God no. The vapid quest for more almost killed me. I do better out here. No one cares how much money I make or who my family is or that I clean vacation rentals for a living or look goofy in gaiters."

"Shane misses you."

"Your brother's made for that life. He's not an addict. Me, I couldn't handle it, the stress, the money, the easy access to controlled substances." The wind shifted, raced low in the brush.

"Smells like something scorched." Rosie wrinkled her nose.

"This time of year? Nothing's going to burn unless someone went to a hell of a lot of trouble."

Rosie's face twisted with concern. "We can't just sit here. Not when it smells like something's on fire."

Patrick tossed his jerky back in his pack. "Maybe it's a campfire at Atlantic Creek Campground—no view, biting flies in plague proportions, but it's one of the few backcountry campsites where the

Park Service allows fires. The place needed something to recommend it."

Rosie stood and shivered. "It's close by."

Mack charged the hill, anxious to get to the spike camp before trail crew trashed the scene. He'd seen Liz's work truck in the lot at the trailhead. She was back here. Layne breathed hard behind him.

"Aliens," Layne said. "I've heard several abduction stories."

"Which bar were you in?"

"How did you know I was in a bar?"

Mack glanced back. "Any other theories?"

"Someone murdered him and started a fire to destroy the evidence."

If only our job were that interesting. Mack smiled at the thought.

Layne hurried to close the gap. "What do you know about these trails guys?"

"Just that they're not going to tell us a damn thing."

Layne had his head down and a determined set to his jaw. He didn't need to know that Roberts puffed like a fiend and most of his crew probably did, too. Layne would want to arrest them all for possession and paraphernalia, and that would be bad for everyone—the stoners, the park, the trails, the visitors hoping to hike. "Clancy's our only hope."

"She a daddy's girl?"

"Not hardly. No better way for a chief ranger's kid to rebel than hiring on with trail crew."

Mack slowed a skosh. He didn't need to hyperventilate the kid.

"We have a missing trails laborer, a fire, and a possible bait spill that drew a grizzly to the car campground." Mack glimpsed a pine marten, saw its kitty-cat face as it scurried down a tree trunk and darted for cover. His questions for Liz, beginning with whether she was pregnant, drove him up the trail.

Mack wanted a family, and Liz Ralston seemed his only hope. In high school he'd had an affair with his English teacher—a woman merely seven years older. If they'd met as adults, no one would've batted an eye. She'd recruited him for the school production of *Our Town* and kissed him one evening when they were running lines. Mack was enough of a Catholic to know anything that felt so good had to be a sin, but he couldn't stop and didn't really want to. The girl who played Emily Webb caught them backstage after rehearsal when she returned for her forgotten mittens.

The teacher was fired. Mack's father resigned from the school board. His mother stopped attending mass. The basketball coach benched Mack. His teachers hardly looked his way or spoke to him. His best friend was suddenly too busy to hunt with him. The entire town treated him like shame might well be contagious, and distance proved the only antidote. For his last two and a half years of high school, when he wasn't in class, Mack took to the woods. The outdoors, with its utter indifference, became the one place he felt at ease.

Mack tried to date a bit in college and at the law enforcement academy and after he got the job in Glacier—the place drew smart, attractive outdoorswomen like ants to honey. But when the time came, as it inevitably did, he lost his enthusiasm. The shame returned and he could not bear to see those women again, but he almost always had to. They lived in park housing and worked in his district. They were in the entrance booth or patrolling the campground or giving naturalist talks. He could not escape them, could not avoid their pitying looks and the heat rising to his face, could not stand the mortification. So he stopped pursuing women, shuttered that part of himself.

When Liz came to St. Mary on a research grant, he invited her over in the depths of a brutal winter with no intention beyond human companionship while watching a wolverine documentary. She jumped him. As she undid his pants she said, "I don't have time for movies." Her swiftness hijacked his anxiety. The sex was impersonal and fabulous. He could have been anyone to Liz, and as anyone, he performed. She was somewhere in this valley. He needed to find her. And the missing trail crew guy. He picked up the pace.

CHAPTER 7

NETTLED

◆

Penelope trudged up the trail toward Triple Divide Pass, trying to keep Liz and her spastic dog in sight. They'd blown past the trail that led to Medicine Grizzly Lake, plummeting Penelope's mood further. She loved that lake. The hike was more level, and she had hoped Liz would choose a spot off that trail for the new rub station. As they gained elevation, time reversed. They climbed toward early spring—buttercups, douglasia, and fritillaries amid the expanse of green. Along the edge of receding snow, glacier lilies sprang from the cold ground. Penelope had made Ezra laugh by impersonating them—arms and head arched, reaching to meet the toes that she poked skyward as she balanced on one foot. Ezra had called her stance "Seussian." They'd had fun, dammit.

Penelope owed her balance and flexibility to years of dance as a kid. She hated ballet, but her mother had insisted. Dance lessons were a socially acceptable way to abandon your daughter. Her mom signed her up for all of them—jazz, tap, ballroom, sometimes several at once. Penelope's marriage to Ezra gave her mother a fresh excuse for distance. She did not approve of the union, told her, "I wanted better for you." *Better how?* Penelope wondered. At least Ezra didn't well up with disdain when he saw her, the way her mom did.

If you asked Penelope why she'd married Ezra—and it was not an infrequent question—she would lie. She answered the sometimes genuinely perplexed, other times downright rude queries with a wide-eyed accounting of Ezra's passion for wilderness and grizzly bears, his humor, his body taut with muscle, his mountain-man beard. Sure, he had demons to battle—drugs, alcohol, infidelity, rage—but that was part of his charm. Penelope was good for him. She was the one whose love could save him. Her presence, being married, reined in his destructive impulses.

All of that paled in comparison to the reason she never voiced. Penelope wanted desperately, more than anything, to belong in Glacier. When they met, Ezra had been working as a trail dog—that was how the trail workers referred to themselves, "trail dogs"—for six years. One more and he would get his "dog year." Glacier had embraced him. He had a standing invitation to Park Service potlucks, trail crew barbecues, and Boat Company parties. He just wasn't allowed to drink whiskey because it made him cantankerous and itching to fight. Lodge employees sought him out in bars to learn about trail conditions, climbing routes, and where to see grizzlies. When Penelope started sleeping with Ezra, she felt like she belonged. Belonging by transitive property: If Ezra belonged in Glacier and Penelope was at his side and in his bed, then by association, Penelope belonged here, too. She had found a person who rooted her in a place she wanted to call home. The summer they hooked up, her first in the park, she worked the Two Medicine entrance booth, and her heart swelled with love, love for the mountains and waterfalls, rivers and wildlife, flowers, trees, and sedges, and she mistook it all for love for Ezra.

Penelope landed a winter job at Big Mountain, a ski resort an hour and a half to the west. She worked once again in a booth, but this time selling lift tickets. When she suggested that they get married, she mentioned that as her spouse, Ezra would get a season pass at half price. As further enticement, when she told her father about the abysmal options for renting in Whitefish, he slapped a down payment on a one-story ranch with a full basement. It was little more than a box with a roof, but it was a box a few blocks from downtown Whitefish and on the resort shuttle route, which made it a treasure. One gray November afternoon with snowflakes drifting lightly in the air, she and Ezra grabbed a couple witnesses off barstools and hoofed it to the courthouse.

Now, headed toward Triple Divide Pass, Penelope ached. Her marriage was over. Liz set a mean pace, and save for an occasional glance at the flowers, Penelope stared at little more than her feet and tried to concentrate on something other than her failed relationship, her labored breath, and Muffy's butt.

Liz slowed. As the woman bent forward, she dropped her trousers. Compelled in the same way as a compound fracture, a horrible car wreck, or a maggot-ridden carcass, Penelope gaped. She did not want to see Liz's backside, not ever. Yet here it was obscuring the mountains and snowfields, krummholz, and spring flora that surrounded them. She beheld Liz's bare, bold, hideously pale bottom. The woman hoisted her pants and, glimpsing Penelope's expression, hooted. Her head fell back, her mouth opened, and she emitted a snorting sound that could just as easily have been a sob. Liz appeared joyfully unhinged.

"Our biggest problem is now behind us." She grinned at Penelope. "Get it? 'Behind.'"

Which problem? Penelope thought. All sorts of problems riddled Liz's study. It was barely statistically viable to begin with, so all the sabotage had to have it on the brink of ruin.

Liz shrugged out of her backpack. "You, my dear, need to remember this spot." She rummaged in the depths of her pack's massive main compartment. "I figured a gratuitous glimpse of your boss's bum might help. We leave the trail to take you to . . ." She flung her arms wide as hot-pink flagging streamed out of one hand. "Your new hair-snag station."

The gesture jostled the pack Liz kept tight between her feet, and an object tumbled free. She snatched it from the ground. But Penelope had seen the camouflage band of a headlamp. She'd swear on all her outdoor gear it was the one she'd given Ezra their first Christmas together. It was a joke, of course. Practically everything between them was a joke of one sort or another. Ezra didn't hunt. He would no more cause intentional harm to an animal than he would work for a land developer or vote Republican. If only, she'd thought more than once, he afforded the same courtesy to the humans in his life, refusing to cause them suffering as well. She told him the headlamp would be perfect for stealth as he monkey-wrenched his way across the wilderness, slowing human encroachment on roadless areas, the ideal eco-warrior tool.

"Where did you get that?" Penelope demanded. Liz stuffed it deep into the maw of her pack.

"It's a headlamp. Chill."

"That's Ezra's. Tell me where you got it."

"Are you crabby because that deadbeat husband of yours didn't show up last night?"

"I never told you he was coming."

"You talked about nothing but him all day, started primping and applying product when we got to camp, and walked around in that empty, doe-eyed daze you sink into when you're daydreaming about him."

Penelope stepped toward her. "I need to know how you ended up with his headlamp."

"Don't." Liz sounded exasperated. "Do not ask questions you don't want to know the answers to." She canted her head and lifted her mouth in a faux smile. She waited for Penelope's eyes to meet hers. "That is evidence in an ongoing investigation into sabotage and the destruction of federal property." The wind gusted hard. Muffy barked. Liz pushed at the contents of her pack, compressing the headlamp inside with vigor. She softened. "Trust me. Even though you can be a bit much, I like you. Knowing more than I've told you will only bring trouble. Let him go. You deserve better."

Penelope's heart pounded. "Give me Ezra's headlamp."

Liz pulled the drawstring with a sharp tug, snapped the Fastex clips, and shouldered her pack. "You shouldn't wear makeup in the backcountry. It makes you seem more shallow than you are."

"You know that people hate you? Loathe your study?"

"My work is important. I'm not here to make friends." Liz pointed down the hillside. "We've got to flag a route. One suitable for Grady and the mules."

"You didn't answer me."

Liz raised her palms like people did in church while praying, open to the divine, and shook her head, indignant. "I cannot allow other people's opinions to bother me. You shouldn't, either."

Penelope stared down the steep hillside dotted with krummholz that led to thick trees. She could glimpse the edge of Medicine Grizzly Lake, a bear haven. She shouldn't ask, shouldn't go there, but she needed to know. "What happened to your meeting this morning?"

"Let it go, Penelope."

"Where did you spend last night?"

Liz smiled a huge, self-satisfied grin. "In my office in St. Mary, working. Alone. No alibi." Sunlight caught in her hair. Her almond-shaped eyes shined bright green. It should have been beautiful, a beaming woman in front of a backdrop of ancient red rock, spring flowers bursting with brilliant yellows, blues, and purples, the smell of the earth awakening to the promise of sun and warmth. Instead, it caused Penelope to shudder.

Penelope followed Liz through a vicious stretch of nettles amid the evergreens. Welts swelled up and down her legs. She fought the urge to scratch, drag her nails deeply and with great satisfaction across her skin. "How. Much. Longer?" She clenched her teeth.

Liz turned and brushed aside a branch. "Are you not enjoying our hike today, my dear?"

"If we've got much more of this, I need to put on my rain pants." Penelope had told Liz she was allergic to nettles. If the woman had been closer, Penelope might well have kicked her. Leaves smacked her forehead. Muffy weaseled in beside her and breathed steamy dog breath against her irritated skin. "No pack string is coming through here. Not even mules would be this dumb."

"Don't you worry about Grady. He's quite capable. He'll probably come up from the Medicine Grizzly trail." Liz flashed an infuriating grin.

"You said we had to flag a route for him."

"I lied." Liz forced a laugh. "I do that. I suspect you do, too." She plowed ahead. Nettles slapped in her wake.

Penelope stopped. Had Liz found out she'd been feeding Ezra the hair-snag station locations? Had she flagged that spot off the Triple Divide trail to deceive Ezra, entice him into this nasty trek? Penelope told herself to keep quiet. There was no way Liz could know for sure unless she slipped up now and said something that confirmed her boss's suspicions. Liz was trying to goad her into confessing. Penelope and Ezra were the only people in on it, and Ezra wouldn't betray her. He relished destroying the stations. He wouldn't jeopardize the operation. Unless he'd told someone on his crew, someone like Clancy who'd narked to her dad who'd clued in Liz. Penelope shook her head to free the thought. Liz was baiting her now, manipulating her into an admission. She had lost sight of the woman completely. Penelope's entire being blazed with indignation and an all-consuming itch. Every step, every brush against the serrated edges of the spiky leaves caused the pain to worsen. This was ridiculous. As Penelope opened her mouth to quit, she caught a glimpse of blue sky. A clearing lay dead ahead. She tucked her head and pushed through the remaining tangle with a vengeance. Liz had her arm around Muffy as she sat gazing up at Triple Divide Peak. Penelope threw her pack to the ground. She had Benadryl in there somewhere.

CHAPTER 8

COLLABORATORS

❖

Patrick stopped short and held his arm out to signal Rosie. He gave her a wide-eyed look and brought his finger to his lips like a librarian shushing patrons. He pointed. A path had been trampled across a meadow. It led into a copse of trees.

Try as he might, Patrick had never been able to locate the Park Service Atlantic Creek spike camp, but he had a good feeling about the social trail in front of them. Just as Ezra had told Rosie, it was a bit beyond the falls. One of Patrick's many joys was locating gypsy camps. The crews used them ten, maybe twenty days a summer. The rest of the time they sat empty, ideal for clandestine, permit-free backcountry camping, complete with food hanging poles, food prep areas, and level tent sites. All of the ease of a designated backcountry campground with none of the tourists, none of the fees, none of the Park Service hassle.

They headed into the trees and picked their way through deadfall parallel to the social trail. Patrick stopped when he heard a voice. He raised his binoculars and glassed the area. The crew boss, a grizzled guy he'd met a couple times who'd work trails for eons, sprinkled tobacco into a rolling paper. His radio squawked incessantly. Patrick and Rosie were too far away to catch anything beyond garbled voices. He continued glassing, perused the area until he spied a tent, the food hanging pole, and the crew kitchen area covered with a tarp. Why was trail crew in camp in the middle of the day?

"Do you see Ezra?" Rosie whispered.

Patrick shook his head. He hoped Rosie would get to witness Ezra interacting with Clancy. Those two got along famously. A dose of their rapport and Rosie might realize that with a guy like Ezra, the fellow's wife might not be her only rival.

Patrick and Rosie picked their way toward the creek. It was impossible not to make noise. Twigs cracked underfoot, branches snapped, startled rodents scurried through the brush. Shortly after he heard the rush of water, Patrick also caught a sporadic *tink* and stopped. He raised his binocs and scanned until he focused in on a guy wearing glasses and a *Virginity Rocks* ball cap skipping objects into the creek. Patrick recognized him as one of Ezra's coworkers. The guy side-armed whatever he had in hand, sent it bouncing across the water. It hit a rock. *Tink.* Patrick grinned. He was tossing DNA study tree ID tags. Patrick had ripped enough of them down to recognize the metal disks. He felt giddy with relief. Trail crew sabotaged the study, too. No way Ranger Turner could pin it all on him.

"Where's Ezra?" Rosie asked. They pushed through brush and around trees as they headed back toward the main trail. Scratches crisscrossed Rosie's legs.

"That guy's hurling DNA study tags into the creek. Maybe Ezra doesn't want to be involved."

"Ezra hates that study."

"We all do. Montgomery Donaldson's no friend of bears, and anyone who pretends otherwise has a doctoral thesis to write or wants to shoot grizzlies dead." Patrick turned and held his hand out to Rosie as they navigated a stack of snags. Her touch sent electricity through his center. "Looks like trail crew's been doing their part to monkey-wrench it."

"Oh, the irony, one group working for the government rectifying the harm caused by another group working for the government." Rosie hopped down off the last log and Patrick released her hand.

They stepped up onto the main trail. Patrick couldn't wait to come back and set up a base camp. He could climb James and Triple Divide, Bad Marriage, Eagle Plume, and Mad Wolf, even McClintock and Morgan.

"Fire's out, right?"

Patrick nodded. "Trail crew's on it. Had to have been set. Maybe one of them burning love notes or something. You can bet the Park Service will launch an investigation. Probably a bunch of badges headed in right now."

"Patrick?"

He turned and looked at Rosie. Twigs had caught in her hair, poked from her pigtails. A sheen of sweat set her face aglow. She looked lovely.

"I want to turn back, head for the car. I'm tired and I've got a bad feeling. Let's take our time."

Patrick would have loved to continue, hike to Morning Star, nap beside the lake, watch the beaver that was often there shore up its lodge, glass for grizzlies, but he hadn't been mopping the diner at midnight.

Once they were back at the falls, they crossed the narrow bridge, two logs side by side planed flat, or as flat as planing with a chain saw could get them. A crude handrail fashioned from a peeled lodgepole ran along the upstream side, no fanciness. The Cut Bank Valley didn't get enough visitation to warrant the elaborate Swiss Family Robinson–esque structures trail crew erected for Virginia Falls and McDonald Creek. Patrick sensed Rosie losing her balance. Seeing the water rush beneath the bridge unsteadied people. Drowning killed more visitors in Glacier than anything. Bears, wrecks, suicide—nothing else came close. People found myriad ways to die here, but most often the icy water took them. Rosie wobbled. He reached out and she grasped his hand. Happiness coursed through him once again.

She jumped off the last step and wrinkled her nose. She lifted her boot. "Patrick," Rosie's face twisted with disgust, "I stepped in dog shit."

A ranger watching a grizzly tear up a campsite, comrades in sabotage, fresh poop at Atlantic Falls, and best of all, he was with Rosie. Wonders upon wonders. None of it made a lick of sense, but Patrick couldn't imagine a place he'd rather be on the first day of summer than the Cut Bank Valley.

Clancy found Roberts in their kitchen area, elbows on the rough counter, meticulously rolling a cigarette. She set the mangled tent pole in front of him and willed her voice steady. "A bear's been in Ezra's tent site." Anxiety thrummed beneath her ribs.

Roberts shook his head. His eyes flashed with anger. "I told you to stay away from there."

"He went to visit Penelope last night at the Atlantic Creek Campground." Clancy was kicking herself. She should have gone that direction as soon as she'd found his tent. Roberts had only slowed her down.

"In that storm? No, he did not. Not even Ezra's that wacked."

"He was desperate to end it and be done with her. That's why he volunteered to finish cleaning up. He didn't want any of us to stop him." Clancy tightened her pack straps. "I'm going to look for him."

"You made me call in the law." Roberts poked his cigarette at her. "You will be here to deal with them." He grabbed the tent pole and waved it close to her face. "You show me this and announce you're gallivanting up the trail." He threw it against a tree. "Not on my watch. I don't need more problems." He lit his smoke and took a hard drag. "Break camp. Marty's going to be pissier than his mules. Packers don't cotton to last-minute gigs."

"They're pulling us?"

"What did you expect? Law enforcement to camp out and protect us while we dig fill pits and place log checks?"

"We need to find Ezra."

"The brass is great at addressing threats that no longer exist. You get to return to your cushy cabin in the campground early while I'm stuck trying to reschedule the work we're not doing."

Clancy knew Roberts was best left to his tizzy. But why wasn't he worried about Ezra? What did he know? He'd said earlier that Ezra didn't want to be found. What made him think such a thing?

Liz used climbing rope to hoist herself into a Douglas fir. She trained her trail camera on the site she'd flagged for the new hair-snag station and affixed it to the tree with a thick cable. She ordered Penelope to move through the perimeter to test it. No wonder Liz wanted to lure Ezra to this spot. The camera would catch him in the act. Liz would have Mack arrest him. With every click, Penelope's belly twisted with worry. He was back here on a hitch. He'd see the flagging, follow it, and get busted. Penelope had to warn him.

She smelled the mules before she saw them, dank, vile creatures that they were. Muffy yipped, darted back and forth, and sprang straight up in the air. Liz screamed, "Grab her! Now!"

Penelope lunged at the pooch. Muffy darted down the hillside. From her knees Penelope cursed all domesticated animals. Muffy barked and bounced in a fit of canine obligation to right the wrongs of the world, which for her apparently included pack strings.

"Git!" Grady's voice rose gruff.

Liz rappelled down from her perch. Penelope hopped to her feet and followed her boss. The horse and mules—a smear of hooves, withers, tails, and taut haunches—wound in an ever-tightening circle. The cowboy lifted off the saddle, his feet secure in the stirrups. He wore a work coat and a Stetson, the spitting image of a Marlboro Man. He pulled a foot free and bounded to the ground. He held the reins taut in a gloved hand, patted the horse's neck with the other, and spoke softly. Muffy closed in, barking and frantic, seemed to reconsider, and retreated. Penelope watched as Grady issued some inaudible assurance, low and calm, his gloves easing up the reins. Muffy spun and ran full bore at the mules. Grady nailed her chest with the toe of his work boot. The blow landed with a solid *thunk* that made Penelope wince. Muffy sailed a few feet and crashed into the brush. Liz was on her like a shot. Penelope followed.

"You didn't have to hurt her," Liz said.

Grady patted the horse's flank and clucked his tongue. The animals seemed to relax back into themselves. "A dog you can't control has no business near stock." He led the horse and mules away from Liz and Muffy.

"Glad you finally made it," Liz called.

"Lot going on in this valley," Grady said.

Liz grabbed Penelope's hand and closed it around Muffy's collar. "Hold her." Liz stormed up to Grady. She spoke low. The woman was adamant. Her finger jabbed downward again and again. Penelope caught only snippets. "Busted . . . trust . . . end." Grady stood stock-still and stared at the ground until she was done. He looked up, his jaw set firmly, and nodded one time.

As Liz left his side, Grady loosened a knot securing one of the loads. His hands moved deft and sure. Liz led Muffy up the hill, collected the climbing rope, pulled out a lead, and clipped it to Muffy's collar. She struggled into her massive backpack. The dog appeared physically fine, though she ducked her head when Liz brought her back down the hill and past the mules. "You two can handle building the hair-snag station. Muffy and I are off to collect samples up Pitamakan and out the Dry Fork."

"You're leaving?" Penelope both wanted it to be true and felt uneasy.

Grady leaned a mantied box against a tree trunk. "That's over sixteen miles."

"Every inch is prime grizzly habitat. Muffy's along because we can no longer afford to squander two people's time collecting samples that may have been compromised." Liz barreled down the hill toward the Medicine Grizzly Trail with Muffy at her heels. She stopped suddenly and turned toward them. "Penelope, collect hair samples on your way out this afternoon." She issued rapid-fire instructions, told them that tomorrow Penelope needed to show Grady the rub trees and lure stations along the South Shore trail and up to Two Medicine Pass. Once he got the hang of it, she said, they should split up and Penelope could head to Dawson. "Grady, pick me up at the North Shore trailhead tomorrow at 5 p.m." She strode away, hollering as she went, "Get an early start."

"You're camping with a dog?" Penelope yelled.

Liz disappeared below the curve of the mountainside.

"I haven't forgotten about that headlamp!" Penelope screamed after her. She took a breath and turned to Grady. "What did she whisper in your ear?"

Grady lifted his hat and scratched his forehead which was shades lighter than the rest of his face. "What headlamp?"

"Liz has something that doesn't belong to her. What was she telling you just now?"

He brushed back his hair and replaced his hat. "I had trouble following most of it. Ms. Ralston doesn't strike me as a woman who cares to repeat herself. I caught that she's pissed." He shed his jacket and tossed it atop the mantied box. A handgun tumbled from the pocket and caught the sun.

CHAPTER 9

SUMMONED

◆

The sun felt warm, but cool air clung to the shadows. As Clancy rolled her tent tight, she caught movement out of the corner of her eye and glanced up in time to see Mack stride right past the social trail leading to camp. It was nothing more than trodden grass, easy to miss. Some guy she'd never seen before wore ranger gray and green and scampered behind him. Watching them hurry away, Clancy realized how a person kneeling a couple hundred yards off the trail could go completely unnoticed. She wasn't even trying to hide. What if, in her rush to get to Roberts and his radio this morning, she'd run past Ezra because she wasn't looking for him, because she already believed he was gone? She shivered. Roberts's voice boomed, "Clancy!" She startled, hated him for scaring her. "You best collect them before they wander all the way to Morning Star." She grabbed the mangled tent pole—evidence of a bear having been in Ezra's tent site, justification for summoning them—and jogged toward the main trail.

"And Clancy," Roberts hollered. She turned. "Remember who your friends are."

When she caught up to them, Mack introduced Layne, who squeezed her hand too hard and held it too long. She told them about Ezra's shredded tent. "The whole area stunk. It was horrible. I went for help, and when we got back, the tent had been torched." She offered Mack the bent and bitten titanium pole. "I found this."

Mack held it up. "Any sign of him? A note?"

She shook her head. Her throat ached with tamped emotion. She didn't trust herself to speak but did anyway. "Fresh pile of scat near his tent site."

"Should we tell her about our bear?" Layne asked.

Mack gave him a nod as he shrugged out of his pack and secured the pole with the elastic cords zigzagging its front.

"All morning, what we suspect is a male grizzly has been digging in site 7 of the car campground. Rank odor there as well. Our theory: a DNA bait spill."

It hit Clancy like a blow. Penelope. What if she'd poured study attractant on Ezra's tent to kill him? Murder by grizzly. The thought made her shake. Clancy wanted to retreat somewhere safe with sturdy walls, somewhere like her cabin in the Two Med campground with her woodstove and her book, somewhere without bears or ex-wives or anyone else. She made herself breathe. First she needed to find Ezra. "We have to search the Atlantic Creek Campground. Ezra planned to visit his soon-to-be-ex-wife. She camped there last night, works on the DNA study."

"Once I touch base with your crew." Mack nodded. "We'll divide into teams and be on the trail in no time."

Clancy led and took the spur that went straight to their kitchen area. Roberts and Nate had taken down the tarp and piled tents, duffels, and bear-proof boxes in a giant heap that awaited Marty and his manties. They used the huge squares of canvas to wrap the gear into tidy packages that Marty would lash to the mules. Mack shook Roberts's and Nate's hands, introduced Layne. It was like a flipping Elks Lodge convention. Clancy fidgeted. She itched to hit the trail. She needed to know if Ezra was at the Atlantic Creek Campground with Penelope or ailing somewhere along the way. She did not have the patience for niceties.

Mack asked what they knew for sure.

Roberts issued a huge sigh. "Our maintenance worker, Ezra..."

Vestiges of its military origins permeated every aspect of the Park Service. Even trails had a hierarchy. Crew leaders like Roberts assigned tasks, completed paperwork, and prioritized projects. Every crew also had a second in command, a maintenance worker who got paid more and usually had more experience than the lowly grunts, but everyone got the same dirt under their nails. They all hauled rocks and dug fill pits and shoveled and sawed and scraped scree off trails and made fun of each other.

When Roberts didn't offer anything more, Mack asked, "When did you last see him?"

"Last night between 8:00 and 8:30." Clancy explained that they'd gotten to camp late, the storm had blown in and Ezra offered to finish stowing their kitchen gear so the rest of them could hunker. Roberts and Nate nodded.

"What do you think happened?" Mack asked.

"No idea," Roberts said before anyone else could speak. "None of us know."

Clancy looked at Nate. Was he holding out on them? He met her eye and shrugged.

Mack asked for a description and Nate said, "Girls fall for him, lots of girls, but you'd never guess by looking at him."

"Five ten, one ninety, reddish-brown hair smattered with gray, hazel eyes, and a full beard," Clancy said. "One of his front teeth's crooked, overlaps the other."

"Any distinguishing birthmarks, scars, tattoos?"

Roberts said, "You'll want to check with his intimate acquaintances on that."

Mack sent Layne with Roberts and Nate. He told them to walk the camp perimeter in an ever-widening arc for an hour, slowly and arm's length apart. "Radio if you find anything, and if not, come back." Once the others started walking, Clancy tossed Mack the empty gas can. "Over half full last night."

"I need to see his campsite."

She pointed to the aspen grove. "He's not there."

Mack fake-smiled. "I know you want to get up the trail to that campground, but I need to see where you found the tent pole."

Clancy led him through the trees. The fire had burned fast and hot, and despite the stiff breeze, the charred smell and an undercurrent of rot still lingered. She covered her mouth and nose with the collar of her fleece. Mack kicked at the melted debris.

"What makes you think he went out in that storm?"

"Ezra always said, 'There's no bad weather, only bad gear.'" She told him how Ezra and Penelope's marriage had been over for a long time, but he'd just gotten the papers. He had a new girlfriend and was finally ready to follow through with the divorce. "He planned to break it to her last night. Wind and rain wouldn't stop him. He'd been out in worse, would've viewed it as an adventure, the final obstacle in his Herculean quest." She pointed to the stakes still sunk in the ground. "We think someone cut his tent free."

Mack crouched and examined a frayed bit of webbing. "When did you guys get back to camp yesterday?"

Clancy told him it was after 7:00. "The storm was coming. We could feel it."

"What time would Ezra have gotten here, to his tent?"

"We all stayed in the kitchen area and helped. We chopped veggies for stir fry, got organized for today. None of us went to our tents until after supper."

Clancy showed him the pile of bear scat and pointed out where she'd found the tent pole. Mack studied the area, asked why they'd gotten back late.

"Ezra and I cleared trail up Pitamakan. When we came back down, Roberts and Nate met us at Morning Star." She described how a logjam at the lake's outlet had backed up water and flooded the trail. "It took hours. We had to float the logs apart." Since they'd worked late, Roberts had told them they would get to knock off early the next day. "We planned to climb Bad Marriage, celebrate Ezra's divorce."

"I'm wondering when the tent was shredded, yesterday afternoon or sometime during the night. Did you hear anything?"

She told Mack that when they'd gotten to camp eight days ago Roberts had yelled, "You got a million acres. Spread the hell out."

"We pitched our tents out of sight and a good hundred yards from one another." Clancy shivered at the thought of a bear destroying Ezra's tent while she slept.

"Who would have known which tent was Ezra's?"

Clancy considered this for a moment. "Our crew, of course. Penelope—she gave it to him. His friends, anyone who'd camped with him."

Finally Mack tossed his head toward the trail. Clancy took off, relieved to be moving. "Who's the girlfriend?" he called.

"I don't know her," Clancy answered over her shoulder. "Ezra met her at the diner in East."

"What else was he up to?" Mack jogged to catch up to her.

"We're working. Same as always." Clancy hiked faster. "Roberts and Nate are replacing old log checks and filling in tread up toward Morning Star, and Ezra and I have been clearing deadfall, cleaning drains, scraping passes." They hit the main trail, and she all but ran toward the falls.

She dashed across the bridge they had built, a two-stringer consisting of crudely planed logs laid side by side and scribed to fit snug to its cribbing. "Like Lincoln logs," Robert had explained to her as he'd used the compass-like tool to draw the curve on each log. She'd peeled the bark from the spindly lodgepole handrails and thought that someday she'd bring her kids here, show them her work. That was before. Clancy's life had been cleaved in two—before Sean died and after. Now she couldn't fathom how people mustered the courage to bring children into the world.

"The DNA study's had some trouble." Mack sounded tired. "Ripped wire, destroyed hair-snag stations, errant hairs mixed in with the bears'."

Clancy laughed. The guys had been plucking short-and-curlies and wrapping them around Liz's wire. She'd wondered how long it would be before the DNA folks discovered exactly what they'd been collecting. She flashed him a quick smile. Mack grinned, too.

"I know you're a tight crew. If you could tell me who's responsible, it might help us find your friend."

"'We owe nothing to the facts and everything to the truth.'" It was another of Ezra's poet quotes, the Hugo guy. She rounded the hairpin turn off the main trail and onto the spur that would take them to the Atlantic Creek Campground. It forked again about a mile farther in. The lower trail led to Medicine Grizzly Lake, the upper climbed to Triple Divide Pass, where she and Ezra were supposed to have spent their day. Something about this junction carped at her, something she needed to register.

Before she could parse it free, Mack asked, "What is that supposed to mean?"

"Ever since we started this season, Ezra's been quoting a Montana poet. Hugo somebody." Trees hugged the trail. A chipmunk's chatter rattled from a high branch.

"The sabotage needs to stop." Mack sounded both adamant and resigned.

"That study's an abomination. That's the truth. The rest is just noise."

"I might agree with you, but that's not for public consumption."

"You think the DNA people retaliated against Ezra?"

Mack was quiet for a stretch. Clancy could hear him pulling air into his lungs. "I'd like your help figuring out what happened and why."

"You want me to spy on my crew?" Clancy glanced over her shoulder without breaking stride. "You're asking me to be a mole to protect Liz's study?" Anger fueled her as she notched up the pace. "Not going to happen."

"I know you don't like her and after what she pulled, I certainly don't blame you. But sabotage is only going to prolong the study."

Liz had shown up at Sean's memorial with papers for Clancy's dad to sign about the DNA project. Later, at home, Clancy's mom had gone off. "One day. One day to mourn our son without your job intruding. Who does that woman think she is?"

Mack's voice was gentle. "This has to be hard. I'm sure it brings up last summer and Sean's death, and I'm sorry for that." They hiked in silence. The air smelled of pine and damp earth. A Clark's nutcracker flew across the trail. "How are your folks?"

"Dad's okay. He's got work to distract him. But my mom, if you see her on the West Glacier bridge, well, don't assume she's out for a stroll." The bridge spanned half a city block above the Middle Fork of the Flathead. Clancy's mother had lost weight she didn't have to lose. Her hair had grayed. Her eyes held a vacant look. She spent an inordinate amount of time in Sean's room.

"I'm sorry." The breeze rustled the pines.

"I shouldn't have said." Her dad would not want his coworkers to know or treat him differently, try to protect him from the job that helped him hold it together.

"It won't go any further."

Roots crisscrossed the trail. They were almost at the campground. "Start with Ezra's ex-wife. She's nuts and she's obsessed with him." Clancy told Mack how this spring during training in St. Mary, the crew had driven through the Park Service compound. Penelope stood outside the break room and watched their truck roll past. She leveled a look at Ezra so full of disdain, it made all of them squirm. Roberts said, "I don't know what you did to her, but you had best take it back."

Clancy told Mack how Penelope had hired on with Liz so she could work the same valleys as Ezra. "She's got access to the bait they use. Ezra owes her money, lots of money, for their house in Whitefish. Once she realized he was divorcing her, she could have poured bait on his tent, drawn a grizzly to get back at him."

"That's extreme."

"She's bitter. And crazy."

"The sabotage?" Mack sounded frustrated. "Did Ezra have a hand in it?"

If Penelope or Liz had hurt Ezra, Clancy was going to rip their study shit down herself. "I'm the wrong person to ask about that." Clancy couldn't keep a secret to save her life, but the way her crew despised Liz's study was common knowledge. She only had trouble keeping juicy tidbits to herself when she was the sole bearer of the information.

"Who should I talk to about Liz's materials?"

"You're a smart man, Mack. You'll figure it out."

The Atlantic Creek Campground was nothing more than a cleared hole in the trees with swarms of flies. "Ezra!" Clancy cupped her hands and called again and again, louder each time. Puddles in the food prep area reflected blue sky. Vole tracks crisscrossed the mud. With dread building in her belly, Clancy started toward the tent sites.

"Slow down." Mack smiled kindly. "If he's here, we'll find him."

Mack studied the ground, found more prints. He identified boots and sandals, none of them large enough to be Ezra's.

"Look at these." Mack crouched and pointed to tracks showing four teardrop toes and a pad.

"Coyote." Clancy shrugged. The air had gone still. Birds chirped. The sun beat down. "Rain could've washed away Ezra's boot prints."

She followed Mack to the tent sites. The first one held nothing but a rectangle of dry dirt where a tent must have deflected the night's rain. Probably where Penelope had camped. Small branches and rocks littered the others. They hadn't been used in a while, if at all this season. Clancy's heart fell. She'd been so sure this place would hold answers, but she'd come up empty once again. He wasn't here. And there was no way to tell if he ever had been.

"Whatever else, Penelope keeps a clean camp," Mack offered.

"Someone poured bait on his tent." Saying it out loud loosened the knot in Clancy's belly.

Mack furrowed his brow. "Without him knowing it? Nobody would climb into a tent covered in that stuff. And no one would stay in a tent that reeked like that." He headed down the trail to the outhouse.

"What if he was already asleep?" Clancy asked. *Or,* she thought, *stoned out of his mind on his secret stash?* "Penelope could have followed him back to our camp, to his tent, waited."

Mack tilted his head and gave a small shrug, like *possibly*. The hinges on the outhouse door squealed as Mack yanked it open. Nothing inside but pit-toilet stink. A wave of exhaustion rolled over Clancy. She inhaled and started back toward their gypsy camp, telling herself to go slowly, keep her eyes peeled. Ezra could be anywhere.

Clancy heard Layne midway down the social trail. He and Roberts sat on stumps in the kitchen. Roberts saw her and rolled his eyes toward Layne. He took a drag from his cigarette. Layne hopped up and gushed, "Mack, you've got to see this. It's an outhouse without the house. No odor, a view. It's brilliant."

"Find anything?" Mack asked.

Roberts shook his head. "Didn't expect to."

"Where's Nate?" Clancy asked, the sting of anxiety building in her belly. They'd learned nothing.

Roberts blew smoke out his nose. "On his way."

"Why'd you split up?" Mack asked. He sounded miffed.

"He took off saying he'd see us in a few. I figured he needed to use the facility, but your boy here's so taken by the low rider, Nate had to find an alternative."

Mack's jaw clenched. He was not happy. "If you had to guess, what do you think happened to Ezra?"

"Our friend led a messy life, Mack. You understand it wouldn't be right for me to discuss it with you. Not yet."

"I just want to find him."

"Me too, Mack. Me too."

If that was true, why had Roberts stalled? Clancy wondered. Why wasn't he out looking instead of smoking a cigarette and listening to Layne prattle on about the shitter? And why, when Clancy had asked about Ezra borrowing money, had he gotten so defensive?

CHAPTER 10

BETRAYED

◆

Mack had no beef with Roberts. The guy had been working trails in the Hudson Bay District when Mack hired on as a seasonal and had spent more time in Glacier's backcountry than probably anyone alive. Almost thirty years on trail crew will earn you those kinds of distinctions. But the man was not making his job easy. Mack had seen what were most likely Muffy's prints in the Atlantic Creek Campground. He might as well get to the hard questions.

"Do you know who's been messing with Liz's study?"

"Could be anybody." Roberts shrugged. "No one likes that project, and even fewer people like Liz." He ground his cigarette under his boot and then reached down and fieldstripped it. He motioned to Mack, and the two men strolled away from Layne and Clancy.

Once they were out of earshot, Roberts said, "She went over your head, Mack, straight to Dyer and then up the chain. The bosses called all us trails leaders in, told us to make it stop." Roberts's raised an eyebrow and dipped his chin. "Liz is gunning for us, Mack. And now Ezra's missing. His tent might have been drenched in bait. It got torched. Our gas can's empty, and none other than your girlfriend's working this same valley."

Mack wanted that not to be true. He knew she had been frustrated with him, ratted him out to Dyer. Still not satisfied, she had gone to the superintendent. Surely Liz was too smart to jeopardize her career by pouring bear lure on a Park Service employee's tent. But she could be rash, impulsive. The woman had a temper. He had experienced Liz's fury, her irrational behavior. Like the time she had gotten bad news about a grant proposal and thrown the phone. Mack helped her replace the shattered office window. He told himself he couldn't allow his suspicions about Liz to blind him to other possibilities. "Clancy told me to check out Ezra's wife."

Roberts shook his head. "Negative. She's harmless. Nuts, but harmless. If Penelope was going to kill Ezra, he would've been dead a long time ago. The woman loves drama. If she knew anything, had any inkling about what happened, we all would've heard from her by now."

Mack watched a narrow seasonal stream tear through the meadow, the water running urgent, desperate to be somewhere else. "Where'd Nate go?"

"He knows things about Ezra that you and I never will. I thought it best to give him his head. See what he could find." Roberts drew a long blade of grass from the ground and chewed the root. "That picture Liz has on her wall, or at least she used to, the one of her in a Girl Scout uniform full of badges," Roberts said. "She's still like that, an achiever. She'll never let anything, or anyone stand in her way."

Mack knew the picture. Liz must've been eleven or twelve, her hair tamed with a half-dozen barrettes, the green sash draped across budding breasts complementing her eyes. She wore a proud grin. "The two of you?" The photo had hung above her bed when she lived in West Glacier. "When was that?"

Roberts gave a small smile. "She's been kicking around the park for years. You thought you were the only guy to have a poke?"

Mack felt heat rise, radiate from his face. He swallowed, watched the water rush past. Roberts was fit and good-looking and possessed a certain *je ne sais quoi* just for being Roberts. Why was Mack shocked?

"Hah. You didn't take me for her type. Even Liz, all educated and full of herself, gets less picky at bar time."

"Who set the fire?"

Roberts shrugged. "Liz? Ezra? One of his girlfriends? Hell, it could've been Clancy for all I know, but I doubt that. You're the lawman." He clapped Mack on the back. "Let it go, my friend. It was a long time ago, probably even before she started sleeping with you."

Roberts started back toward the kitchen and Mack watched him go. Why had the man told him he'd slept with Liz? Was Roberts trying to rattle him, put him in his place? Distract him from Ezra's disappearance? Mack studied Bad Marriage. Sunlight beamed off the snow covering the peak. He thought about the test in the top pouch of his pack.

In college he'd learned about the physicist who imagined a cat in a box with radioactive material. As long as the guy didn't look inside, the cat could be alive or dead. Mack's life could be changed forever by the test results or go on like it had been. He moseyed back toward the others. Mack had never been big on change. Clancy walked in at the same time and added her bundled tent to the mound of gear.

"Still no Nate?"

"Want me to go after him?" Layne asked, jumping up and pulling on his pack.

"He must have found something," Clancy said.

Nate crashed out of the brush. "Ezra vaporized." He pressed his glasses up to the bridge of his nose. "No sign of him between here and Atlantic Creek or all the way south to Cut Bank Creek."

Mack eyed his boots. They were sopping wet. The young man kept his gaze low, didn't meet anyone's eye. He could've discovered a clue and decided to keep it to himself. It was why Mack had people search together. They kept one another honest. Maybe he knew something he didn't want to say in front of Mack. Maybe he'd tell Clancy. She was still his best hope with these people.

"We should be looking for Ezra." Clancy told Mack he and the rest of them could go and search along the trail on their way out. "I'm happy to wait for Marty,"

Mack and Roberts were both shaking their heads before she finished.

Layne chimed in, "I'll stay, too."

Mack tried to consider the request. It would be more efficient. Layne had a gun, which was likely to make any situation more dangerous. If Clancy's brother hadn't died, if her dad wasn't Mack's boss, and if he had any idea what they were dealing with, then maybe. He said, "Negative. We stick together."

Penelope sat in lotus position and daydreamed about a bubble bath and a Q-tip. The hair-snag station had come together quickly, with the motion-sensor camera clicking away. The storage card would be full before animals or Ezra had a chance to find it. Liz was probably less interested in images of bears than photos of saboteurs. Grady leaned against a tree. Had Liz planned to spy on her and Grady all along? Penelope doubted it. It seemed a misstep to train the camera on the lure station before they'd constructed it. Liz had been in too much of a hurry. Off her game, that one. Penelope and Grady would enjoy a break, pour the bait, and hit the trail.

"Quite the reaction," Grady said, pointing at her angry red legs. "You allergic?"

"Nettles." Penelope nodded as she pointed up the hillside.

"She led you through that?" A lopsided grin lit his face. "What'd you do to piss her off?"

"Let's see," Penelope blew a breath that riffled her bangs. "I suggested we got to use the park mules because she's sleeping with the district ranger. I hate her dog. My husband's headlamp fell out of her pack and made her totally defensive. I know her study's statistically shallow and barely viable because most of the stuff we've put up on the east side has been sabotaged. And largely I'm okay with that because my husband says this study's ultimately bad for grizzlies." She stretched her legs out in front of her and dug in her pack for the pink-and-white pills. "Other than that, even though she's rude, I admire the woman. She's a strong female excelling in a male dominated field."

Grady cocked his eye skeptically. "You're married?" He tore off a hunk of jerky and tossed it to her. "Try some. It's dry meat." He bit into a strip and chewed. "Where's the ring?"

Penelope was mostly vegetarian, but the smell of the meat made her salivate. "The diamond industry's evil."

Grady cocked an eyebrow. "He could've at least sprung for a band. A tiny Montana sapphire. Something."

Penelope was not going to discuss Ezra's refusal to purchase a symbol of their love with this bumpkin. She'd given it considerable thought, tried to convince herself that Ezra was simply frugal, saving his money for outdoor gear, but she knew it was more than that. Before anything can be real, a person has to believe it's possible. For Ezra, a long-term, monogamous relationship was akin to Santa and unicorns. She knew she should have known better, had no one but herself to blame. Penelope needed to change the subject. "Mack and Liz have been together over a year." The jerky tasted like blood, and she feigned a nose wipe with her kerchief to slide it from her mouth. Liz had suggested Grady would make a good boyfriend. Hah! The woman was definitely having an off day.

"Liz has a man. Good for her."

"Relationship of convenience for both of them. Not a lot of people winter here. If you ask me, it's not so much that they like one another as that they dislike each other less than their other options." She offered Grady her bag of gorp.

He shook his head. "Squirrel food."

"They don't have much in common. Liz is driven. She's got big plans for herself and her career." Penelope tossed back two antihistamines and swallowed them dry. "Mack seems really content working in St. Mary and will probably stay district ranger until he dies or retires." Penelope pulled a hacky sack from her pack. "Do you hack?"

Grady's eyes narrowed. "Do I look like I hack?"

"I got good during my NOLS course. It's fun."

"Your what?" Grady pulled his hat brim low over his eyes and eased against the tree as though preparing for a nap.

"NOLS—National Outdoor Leadership School. It changed my life. Before my parents sent me, I'd never spent the night outdoors before, let alone backpacked. Now I spend most of my summer in the backcountry."

Grady grinned again. "That's what they taught, walking and pitching a tent?"

"Leave no trace, food storage, starting a fire without matches, orienteering, self-defense. It covered everything." Penelope smiled. "How to camp without a gun."

"You paid money to go to camping school?"

"Why bring an illegal firearm?" Penelope felt pressure below her belly and a familiar spreading warmth. Great. Now she had to deal with her period, but at least it explained her state of hyper-annoyance. She tugged her pack onto her lap, started digging for her supplies.

Grady gave her a strange look, like he had something to say but thought better of it.. Finally he said, "Just because I feel safer back here with a gun doesn't mean you're better than I am." He took a long swallow from his canteen. "If you'd seen what I have, you'd carry a firearm, too." He gazed up at the wall of red rock that ringed Medicine Grizzly Lake. "Wonder if they found that missing guy."

Penelope stopped rifling through her pack. "What missing guy?"

"I smelled smoke. Ms. Ralston had told me trail crew was camped in the area, so I went looking for them to report it. Turns out one of their workers didn't show up this morning." Penelope tried to tamp the dread rising in her gut. Grady told her the girl he'd met on the trail had been worried, so he'd helped her get to her crew. "Wish I could've stuck around and helped, but I didn't figure Ms. Ralston would appreciate me being any later."

"Who? Who is missing?" Penelope had never once considered that Ezra hadn't shown because something had happened to him. She'd simply assumed he'd flaked just as he had so many times before. Her heart clenched. Liz had his headlamp.

"The guy with the beard. Redhead," Grady said.

"She's hurt my husband." Penelope shot to her feet. "Is that what the two of you were whispering about?"

Grady's eyes flew wide open. "That guy's your husband?"

"She told me she doesn't have an alibi." Penelope's stomach lurched. She thought she might be sick. Liz had retaliated against Ezra. Penelope made herself breathe in through her nose, out through her mouth. She curled a length of hair around her finger, chewed its end for a long moment. Calmer, she tried again. "What did Liz do to Ezra?"

Grady stuffed what was left of his lunch into his saddlebag. "Liz doesn't answer to me."

Penelope turned her pack upside down. Stuff sacks, clothing, and plastic bags poured out. "She has his headlamp. He carried it with him everywhere. My husband's missing. I just got my period. And I'm sick of this study." She snatched at the pile of gear, tossing items aside. "I'm going after Liz and she's going to tell me what she did to Ezra. She can pour her own damn bait. I'm done."

Grady's face darkened. He stood and shifted his weight from one boot to the other. "Maybe they found him. Ride out with me. You shouldn't be wandering through bear country, not now. Not on your moon."

Penelope took another long breath, thought about telling him the menstrual-blood-as-bear-attractant theory was bullshit, just another sexist myth, but felt too tired. She found what she needed amid the moisturizer and makeup in her ditty bag—tampons and a plastic bag of baking soda.

Grady tossed his chin. "They teach you that in camping school?"

Penelope nodded. "No odor, no attractant." Her abdomen cramped. She headed into the brush for privacy. How had it come to this? She'd sunk so low that riding out of the backcountry with a string of mules and an armed redneck proved her best option.

Clancy followed Marty and his string of mules. The animals moseyed at a leisurely pace. She figured if she had a bear-proof box, a two-burner camp stove, tents and sleeping bags and gear strapped across her back, she wouldn't move fast, either. She respected their power, had witnessed their unpredictability, and gave them plenty of space. It was a relief to be alone with her thoughts while Marty was a mere shout up ahead.

Mack had them scour Ezra's tent site again, all of them inching forward a couple feet apart. They found nothing more, not so much as a second scat. Marty arrived and loaded the mules, and despite Roberts's prediction, he seemed in a better mood than the rest of them. Roberts and Nate went first, then Layne and Marty and the pack string. Clancy followed behind them and Mack behind her. He'd sent her on ahead while he updated the Com Center.

She came to the trail junction where the spur led toward Atlantic the Creek Campground, Medicine Grizzly Lake, and Triple Divide Pass. Clancy felt the weight of a gaze and shivered. She swore someone was watching. She stopped and turned in a slow circle. A distant meadow rampant with shooting stars and balsam root, arnica and mariposa stretched back toward the creek. The mountains lifted skyward. Birds flitted through the stand of lodgepole, called from high branches. A golden-mantled ground squirrel darted across the trail. All was as it should be. She tried to shrug off the sense that someone had their eyes trained on her. She needed to stay alert for any sign of Ezra. He could be anywhere. Nate was wrong. People did not vaporize. What if it was Ezra watching her? What if he'd borne witness to the aftermath of his own disappearance all day? As she rushed to catch up, get within sight of the last mule, sunlight stuttered through the trees. Clancy heard barking in the distance. She wondered if it was the same animal from this morning. Some coyote wasn't having a day that loved him, either.

CHAPTER 11

FRONT COUNTRY

◈

As Mack pushed his chair back from the table in the Cut Bank Ranger Station, he glanced around Layne's tidy quarters. The railroad had built a network of chalets in the early 1900s. Travelers would detrain in East Glacier and explore the park by horseback, riding up over mountain passes from one chalet to another. Multiday horseback tours were a thing of the past, but many of the Swiss-inspired buildings, all dark brown, all sturdy, most of them log, still stood. Mack loved the feel inside them, solid with history. They held the comforting smell of decades of wood fires. The Cut Bank Ranger Station, one of his favorites, consisted of three rooms—a bedroom, an office/kitchen/sitting area, and a bathroom the Park Service had added sometime in the '60s. It sat well inside the park boundary and three-quarters of a mile from the primitive campground and the trailhead, about as private as it gets in the front country of a national park. Mack would have loved to live here instead of his '70s ranch-style house smack in the middle of the St. Mary housing compound, but his job required that he reside within five minutes of the district office, and the Cut Bank Ranger Station was too far on a good day. Motor homes, wildlife, cattle, road conditions all tacked time onto the drive.

"I wish I had tomatoes, cilantro, and fresh jalapeños." Layne washed dishes. "Some fruits and vegetables keep longer than others." Despite lacking easy access to a grocery store, Layne had created the best tacos Mack had ever eaten. The young man toasted corn tortillas in a cast-iron skillet; added ground turkey and black beans spiced with cumin, chili powder, and garlic. He topped it all with aged white cheddar cheese, glacier lilies, and dandelion greens. As a finishing touch, he squeezed fresh lime.

"Where did you learn to cook?" Mack set his plate on the counter, grabbed a kitchen towel decorated with moose, and dried the dishes Layne washed.

"Our housekeeper. She and I spent a lot of time in the kitchen together."

"I didn't realize glacier lilies were edible."

"I read a book about foraging." Layne asked Mack if he wanted a mug of nettle tea.

Mack shook his head and tossed Layne his towel. "Time to check site 7."

"The bear's gone, sir."

"We're interested in what it left behind. Bring some baggies." Mack resigned himself to the "sir" and let the screen door bounce closed behind him. He heard Layne scrambling into his boots. The porch looked out on a meadow full of flowers, a stretch of blooms in yellows, reds, blues, and purples, drenched in honey-colored light. Mad Wolf and Bad Marriage began a chain of snowy peaks. The sky and mountains stretched forever and harbored every wild creature indigenous to the Rockies except woodland caribou. Nothing more than a long drive prevented him from being right here every evening. He shook his head at the shame of it.

As he'd anticipated, trail crew had refused to provide Mack with leads. But they'd all be back in the morning to search. He hoped to catch each of them alone. Roberts and Nate would hold out until they were sure Ezra wasn't going to waltz back into their lives, angry about any betrayals of confidence. Clancy would help find Ezra, but no way would she confess to any knowledge of the sabotage culprits. Who knew, maybe she'd wrenched Liz's work herself. Mack hoped the guys had opened up to Clancy during their drive back to East Glacier.

Layne wore his "be prepared" duty belt and his flat hat with the head strap fastened under his chin like a bonnet. He carried a box of sandwich bags.

"Take off the hat, Layne." The young man looked perplexed but removed it. "Here." Mack showed him how to secure the strap behind his occipital lobe. "We can't have you looking like a Sunshine Girl, now, can we?"

Red blotches lifted on Layne's sculpted cheeks. "No sir."

As they walked the gravel road to the campground, the sun angled golden over the mountains. A breeze shuddered the brush. Mack inhaled the cool air, fresh with the damp of early summer. The smell from earlier in the day had dissipated to an occasional pungent whiff. Number 7 looked more like the dirt phase of a construction site than a place to camp. Rocks large enough to bludgeon someone had been excavated and tossed, the dirt churned loose, the vegetation decimated.

"They told us in bear training that grizzlies bury carcasses so that they'll develop maggots and increase the available protein. They create what amounts to a larder."

Mack sighed. The Park Service was big on training which easily warped into a highly efficient means of spreading misinformation. "My understanding is grizzlies eat as much as they can as soon as they can." He spied what he was after and started toward it. "If they leave a food source, they might conceal it to discourage birds and other scavengers, but I think burying carcasses has more to do with being stingy with their prize than any long-term plan regarding nutrient consumption." Mack reached for a baggie.

"You're collecting feces, sir?"

"We've got bears acting strangely, a controversial DNA study, a torched tent, and a missing person." He pushed the bag inside out and gathered as much of the fresh scat as he could. The smell forced him to turn his face. He fastened the Ziploc, pulled a Sharpie from his shirt pocket, marked it "#1," and handed it to Layne. "Next time," Mack shook his head, doubting there'd be a next time, "bring gallon-sized bags. Grizzlies don't take sandwich-size dumps." Mack collected another horrible-smelling scat. "We need to get you on the road or you're not going to make it in time."

"Sir?" Layne held the bags at arm's length.

"You're going to drive to East Glacier and overnight these samples to the lab. You need to stay at the Mercantile until the shipping company's driver arrives and personally hand him or her the package. If you have questions or run into problems, call Sandy at the Com Center. She'll help you."

"And you, sir?

"I'm going to greet our DNA research friends as they come off the trail."

Penelope tried not to look up at Bad Marriage, avoided it like it might curse her further. She refused to put her arms around Grady. She clutched the saddle behind her bum, had for miles. Her arms throbbed while millions of needle pricks stung her hands. By the time she could see the top of the stock truck poking above a rise, fury had hijacked her entire being. The last of the Benadryl had worn off, and her legs burned. The muscles of her lower abdomen twisted and cramped as though being wrung like a dishrag. Her throat ached with the effort of keeping her emotions in check. She felt angry, a flip-out-and-scream-at-the-top-of-her-lungs like she'd done that morning when Muffy and Liz had scared her kind of angry. Two miles back, she'd said something about ranchers not having the savvy to protect their interests without enraging every environmentalist in the Pacific Northwest, and Grady had stopped speaking to her.

Mack Savage stood in front of the stock truck. He waved and called, "Is Liz with you?" Penelope scowled at him. The horse closed the distance between them.

"Mrs. Riverton?" Mack asked. Grady hopped from the horse and tied the reins to the hitching post. Mack offered Penelope a hand. She leaned on him as she worked her stiff limbs free.

"Have you found Ezra?" She slid from the horse. "I never took his name."

For a moment, Mack appeared nonplussed. "We meet at 6 tomorrow morning." His voice, his expression, registered concern and capableness. "Teams will be on the trail and searching by 7. We're doing everything we can." Grady climbed into the stock truck. It bleeped a steady warning that seemed to echo off the mountains as he backed to the loading ramp. Once both the truck and the sound stopped, Mack asked, "How did you find out, Ms. . . . ?"

"Keller," she said. "Penelope Keller."

"How did you learn your husband's missing, Ms. Keller?"

"You need to talk to your girlfriend, Mack." Penelope spoke through clamped teeth. "Liz has Ezra's headlamp. Told me to 'let him go.' Said I deserved better." She inhaled through her nose.

"You believe Liz hurt Ezra?"

"She said she'd taken matters into her own hands, claimed the sabotage would now stop, and said she didn't have an alibi. You need to arrest your girlfriend."

"My relationship with Liz will not impair my ability to do my job. Should you see or experience anything that causes you to believe otherwise, I'd appreciate you letting me know." He tossed his head toward the trail. "Ezra's crew told me he was headed to see you last night."

"Never showed." Penelope fought to keep her emotions in check. Mack asked where she'd been the evening before. She told him, "I don't have an alibi, either. I was alone in that storm." She balled her hands into fists. "Liz did something to Ezra. She left yesterday afternoon as soon as we got to the campground. Said she had a meeting this morning."

"I'll look into it." Mack pulled a pen and pad from his shirt pocket and made a note. "Who all would have been able to identify Ezra's tent?"

Penelope clenched her teeth. She forced her voice even. "Liz attacked him while he was sleeping?"

"We don't know what happened."

"I told her." Penelope closed her eyes for a moment, pushed away the image of Liz stalking Ezra like a shadowy figure in a horror movie. "I described his tent when I tried to convince her to get me one like it for work."

Mack jotted something in his notebook. "Can you think of anyone besides Liz with reason to harm your husband?"

Penelope spoke low, not wanting Grady to overhear. "You might want to talk to his girlfriend."

Mack's expression betrayed nothing. Penelope couldn't tell whether he'd heard about the other woman already. "Where can I find her?"

Penelope lifted a condescending eyebrow. "She and I are not close." Penelope knew perfectly well where to find the floozy, but she planned to get to her before Mack. During the long ride out, she'd been gripped by a shuddering thought. What if Ezra had intentionally left his headlamp where Liz would find it to implicate her as he faked his disappearance and ran off with his girlfriend? He could have been letting Liz know that Penelope had fed him the locations of study materials, ensuring that she'd be fired while he and the girlfriend drove into the sunset and a new life. The idea made her want to cry.

Mack nodded and pointed to her legs. "Looks painful. Can I help?"

That was all it took. She'd held it together for five and a half interminable miles, miles passed at mule pace, with a view of a mountain named, of all things, Bad Marriage. For the entire journey, she'd swallowed her sorrow, made sure her mascara didn't run. Now, her emotions released in a torrent. Grady, who had been dealing with the mules, came over and eased her pack from her back. Mack retrieved the keys from the gas-cap compartment of her government truck and started the vehicle. Grady set her pack on the passenger seat. Mack held open the driver's-side door and closed it behind her like a valet. No more questions, just kind, efficient support with the singular goal of getting her and her messiness on the road.

As she settled behind the wheel, Penelope cranked down the window. "Liz was acting strange all morning. She mooned me." She had Mack's attention and shifted into reverse. "She's done something, something to retaliate against Ezra. Arrest her." She backed onto the road.

"Where is she?" Mack hollered over the engine noise.

Penelope ignored him and threw the truck into drive. She had her own questions and needed to find the woman who could answer them. In her rearview mirror, she saw Mack watching as she rumbled down the washboard gravel. High clouds stuttered overhead, a mirror image of the bumpy pattern that riddled the road.

Penelope's truck shrank in the distance, "You know anything about spilled bear bait over in site 7?" Mack really wanted to know about Liz, but he needed to go easy, earn this fellow's trust.

Grady led a mule up the ramp into the back of the stock truck. He hopped down and strode back to the animals. Mack followed. "Liz seems pretty careful with that stuff. All kinds of protocol. Told me it was too risky to load on the mules." He patted an animal's flank, clucked his tongue. "But then," the young man seemed to grin despite himself, "I hear you know her better than I do."

"When did you last see Liz?"

Grady told him she'd left them a few hours ago. Mack asked him how he'd spent his day and he accounted for it thoroughly, from seeing smoke to finding Clancy, delivering her to her crew, meeting up with Liz and Penelope, Liz taking off, building the hair-snag station, and convincing Penelope to ride out with him.

"There's something you're not telling me." It was Mack's ace-in-the-hole technique. Over the years it had led to a naturalist turning in her female lover for embezzling grant money, an addict ratting out his mom, who dealt pills, and a poaching confession. Most people, when given the chance, unburden themselves. Mack remembered the relief when he and the teacher had gotten caught and he'd confessed to his parents. The trouble no longer belonged to him alone.

Grady tugged the last mule's lead. "I know you and Liz are," he searched for the right words and came out with "a couple." He looked away. "I don't want to make things difficult."

"There's a man missing, Grady. If he's not dead, he's facing a cold, damp night alone. Most likely his second. I need you to tell me what you know."

Grady disappeared into the truck. Mack waited while he finished with the animals. The squeal of metal scraping metal pierced the air as he swung the doors closed. The birds fell silent. "She's headed up the valley, over Pitamakan. Told me to meet her at the North Shore trailhead late tomorrow afternoon." He met Mack's eye. "She has her dog with her. That's all I know."

"Muffy." Mack nodded. Images of deer chased to exhaustion, cowering foxes, and furious bears flashed before him.

Anger lit Grady's eyes, twisted his mouth. "The Karelian without manners. Could've gotten someone hurt, chasing the mules."

"Why would Liz take her dog into the backcountry?"

"She believed she knew who was sabotaging the study."

"Why didn't she call law enforcement?"

"Her evidence was circumstantial and, no offense, I don't believe she considered the park rangers effective. She was frustrated." He hesitated, studied his boots a moment. "Mostly with you."

He nailed that. "Who? Who did Liz think was wrenching her study?"

"She found a headlamp at a destroyed hair-snag station. Initials were scratched in the battery cover."

"Those initials implicated someone she already suspected?"

Grady nodded, drew his lips together in a tight line. He seemed to wish things were different. "Ezra Riverton."

Mack kept his expression neutral, didn't allow himself to react. "I need you here tomorrow morning, six o'clock."

"Ms. Ralston told me to work on the study in Two Medicine."

"For now, you answer to me. Count on that until we find Ezra."

Grady climbed into the truck. As he pulled onto the road, he lifted his fingers from the steering wheel by way of goodbye. Mack watched the truck disappear behind a cloud of dust. His mind reeled. Penelope's demand rang in his ears: *Arrest your girlfriend.* The pregnancy test in the top pouch of his pack would have to wait like a possibly dead cat in an unopened box. Liz's truck sat empty, the only vehicle left in the lot.

CHAPTER 12

VISITORS

Clancy accelerated out of the sharp curve above Froggy Flats, anxious to get home to her cabin in the Two Medicine Campground. Thoughts of a shower, a beer, her bed pressed her foot to the pedal. The truck shot down the hill toward the bridge. A cow the color of night stood in her lane. Clancy braked, honked, inched forward, encouraged the bovine across the highway into the borrow pit. Bone-tired and grimy, she felt aghast that Roberts had kept them at the shop till 4:00 on the dot. He'd forgotten about the time they'd put in clearing the logjam, hours he'd promised to make up to them. Neither Clancy nor Nate was brave enough to remind him.

As he'd pulled onto the highway and pointed the truck toward East Glacier, Roberts had suggested they'd find Ezra stoned on Nate's pot, waiting at the trails shed. The man then cranked the Stone Temple Pilots, putting the kibosh on any further speculation. Clancy studied the mountains and imagined they'd toss back beers while Ezra spun a tale of grappling with wind and rain, cold and mud, a bum knee or bad ankle as he fought his way back to them.

Their collective mood plummeted when they swung into the lot and there sat Ezra's old Ford in the shade of the pines, still and waiting with the rest of their vehicles. No Ezra at the shop. No Ezra in the park housing that Roberts and Nate shared. Even Nate, usually chipper and easygoing, turned edgy. Roberts asked how long he planned to sharpen the adze end of his Pulaski, which he was doing only to kill time, and Nate flung his file into a mound of shovels, the clamor enough to raise the dead in the cemetery up on Kittson Hill.

Now Clancy banked her truck around the curves of Highway 49 and saw the sign for the tribal campground. Her peppermint soap and down comforter would have to wait. She swung off the main road onto the gravel. Clancy needed to check Ezra's camper.

Red Eagle Campground hugged the shore of lower Two Medicine Reservoir and boasted a view of Rising Wolf, the biggest mountain in the Two Medicine Valley. A craggy mass of purple and green with a circumference of twenty miles, its top resembled a massive shoulder blade. It took its name from Hugh Monroe, a Canadian fur trapper whom the Blackfeet had adopted into the tribe. The story naturalists told on the boat tour was that the man would emerge from his tepee stretching and yawning, his mouth wide as a wolf's. The story Clancy had heard at Kipp's Beer Garden from a descendant of Hugh Monroe who may or may not have been hitting on her was that Mr. Monroe had emerged from his tepee with his manhood as prominent as a wolf's. Glacier's best stories got sanitized for public consumption.

She parked at the entrance, hoping a walk would unfrazzle her nerves. Anywhere else in the country within baseball-throwing distance of a national park and she'd be amid throngs of tourists all shopping, dining, attending yoga retreats, and extolling the virtues of forest bathing. Instead, thanks to reservation economics, nine months of winter, gale-force winds, and no running water, the place was deserted.

Ezra had parked his camper at Red Eagle for as long as Clancy had known him. Rent was cheaper and there were fewer rules than in Park Service housing, plus no law enforcement neighbors to smell marijuana smoke. He filled five-gallon jugs at Roberts's and Nate's place and said he didn't mind conserving water, called it "a lesson in appreciation." Earlier in the summer, Roberts had accused him of having two of everything: two homes, two girlfriends, two lives. Ezra had corrected him. "One of those women is my wife." Now Clancy wondered about his second life. Why had he borrowed money from Roberts, the last person to whom any of them would want to feel beholden? No trails worker in their right mind gave their boss, especially if their boss was Roberts, something to lord over them. And what had Roberts done to have money to lend? Given his defensiveness, nothing good.

Ezra's camper sat tucked beneath trees. Skirted for warmth, it looked snug, protected from the wind, and shaded from sun. A couple times, when his old Ford was on the fritz, Clancy had given Ezra a ride into East Glacier and the trails shop, where the crew met every morning when they weren't on a hitch. She called his summer home "the womb" and knew he probably kept a key stashed outside somewhere. He didn't bother with bourgeois trifles like carrying keys.

After a few minutes of poking around, turning over rocks and running her hands along the wheel wells, she spotted a hummingbird feeder dangling from a branch. Ezra would never have risked attracting bears or the water mildewing and poisoning the birds. That was one of the many things that stuck in his craw about the DNA study. One afternoon he'd ranted while they'd eaten lunch, leaning on their packs and soaking up the view of Old Man Lake. Ezra jangled the ID tags he'd pulled from rub trees and pointed out that for decades bear managers had preached about keeping bears safe by eliminating attractants. Now Liz Ralston and her army of Patagonia-clad wildlife biology majors desperate for scraps of scientific work marched through the park stringing barbed wire and pouring attractant. It upset Ezra, humans tinkering with wildness, the disrespect of luring bears to a spot with the smell of something they'd love to eat only to disappoint them. "They're altering the movements of a threatened species. That should be illegal." Clancy countered that the study was less invasive than darting bears with tranquilizers and affixing them with radio collars. Ezra said, "They can only afford so many collars and helicopter flights, but they've got enough rotting fish and cow blood to manipulate every bear in the ecosystem. Those bears should be eating. How do you study the impact of that?"

Clancy unscrewed the base of the hummingbird feeder. Voilà, the key. As she swung the door open, the smell of mildew poured from the camper. "Ezra?" Weak light filtered through curtains. The bed was neatly made. She knew him well enough to realize that meant he was sleeping with someone and, given that it was Ezra, possibly more than one someone. Behind the door leaned Ezra's Pulaski and a pair of hiking boots, laces tucked neatly inside. Clancy's heart drummed in her ears.

Last winter she'd been in Costco when a woman had run frantically down the main aisle calling, "Southern. Southern." The name vexed her. A direction? A region? A school of literature? She watched as the mom found her toddler. The woman did not draw the child into a hug or shower him with kisses. She yanked him up by the arm and swatted his backside like a tetherball. The mother was angry—angry that she loved what could be lost, that his existence made her vulnerable to that sort of pain. Clancy understood. If Ezra was here, she was going to kill him. She tore through the trailer shouting his name, stuck her head in the bathroom, ducked inside the back bunks Ezra used for storage. They held clothes, boxes, plastic bins. No one was here. Her anger ebbed, and dread rushed in to fill the void.

Clancy started with the stack of papers on the table, not knowing what she hoped to find, maybe some indication of his state of mind, some clue to what might have happened. She didn't buy that he'd walked away, but why were his Pulaski and boots behind the door? Timing-wise, he could have walked up and over Pitamakan Pass, come out at Two Med, and either hitchhiked or walked here. But why? And where was he now? What would he be running from? He had a job he loved with winters off to ski, a girlfriend, a camper, and a house in a resort town. Plus, he was on the verge of ending his nightmare of a marriage. He wasn't going to suddenly decide to chuck his whole life because someone had thrown bear bait at his tent. Was he? She spotted some legal-size papers protruding from either end of the stack and yanked them free. The long-overdue divorce. Clancy skipped the gory details and flipped to the last page. He'd signed and dated the papers before they'd gone on their hitch. The line above Penelope's name remained blank.

A slick sheet curled from the pile. She put the divorce papers on top and pulled it free. It was a photo that had come off a roll. A medical scan, black-and-white. A tiny arrow pointed to a smear. The top corner held a name she didn't recognize and was dated May 29. For all Clancy knew, it showed a ham sandwich. People had scans for all kinds of reasons, but the most familiar was pregnancy. Were Ezra and his girlfriend pregnant? Was that the impetus for him to finally divorce Penelope? Or, was that what had caused him to flee?

A car door slammed. Another. Louder, harder. "People don't just disappear." The guy was angry. "Not when they owe me money."

"What are we looking for?"

Clancy knew that voice, the second one. But she couldn't quite place it. Her mind flew desperate, like a bird trapped in a room. Her brain refused to function again, just when she needed it most. Her feet moved before her mind registered that they should. She dashed into the bathroom, inserted herself between the toilet and the flimsy wall, and pulled the door closed, yanking till she heard it click. Weak sun dappled by pines leaked through a skylight.

The front door squeaked. Clancy felt as much as heard the footfalls that rocked the camper. Whoever they were, these were not delicate people.

"Did he even pick them up? Do we know?" the familiar voice asked. She heard high-pitched scrapes, imagined drawers being pulled open. Metal crashed, sent tremors through the floor. "This is between the two of you." Glass shattered. Clancy pressed her teeth tight. Stayed silent.

"You know it's not that simple." Cupboards slammed, banged against their frames. The camper shook. Something scraped across the floor. Her fists ached. Her limbs pulsed with the pounding of her heart. *What had Ezra gotten himself into?*

"Where the hell is he?" Angry Voice shouted. His rage rocked the trailer.

"That's it. I'm done." She was sure she knew that voice, those words.

"Something's got to be here." A crash echoed through the camper.

Clancy needed to pee. The lip of the toilet seat dug against her knees. She told herself she and Ezra would laugh about this later. The irony. Ezra loved irony.

"I need the shipment or the cash." Angry Voice was right outside the bathroom door. Clancy's mouth went dry. Sweat rolled from under her arm, tickled down her side. The door flew open. She pushed back so hard against the bathroom wall, she feared the pressboard behind her would give way. Her heartbeat throbbed in her ears. He was right there. She could feel the man's heat.

"When I find him . . ." A hand reached in and groped along the wall for the light switch. The nails looked manicured. A silver cuff gleamed from the wrist.

"Here," Familiar Voice said. "This what you're after?"

The hand disappeared. "He's trying to scam me." The man stormed toward the back bunks. "Beat me at my own game."

Clancy fought the impulse to reach out and grab the knob, pull the door shut. She listened hard. What had they found amid the boxes and bins? The more she tried to identify the voice, the further the name retreated into the recesses of her brain.

"How much was in there? Enough to make a break for it? Start over?"

"Not hardly," Angry Voice scoffed. "That's from the first one. Wouldn't get him past Spokane. The second shipment, that's another story."

"We found everything there is to find." Familiar Voice pushed the bathroom door closed as he bounced down the narrow hall. Clancy unclenched her fists. "He's been in the woods. It's probably still at the post office."

More pounding footfalls. The front door slammed. The wind gusted, rushed through the trees, tossed shadows in the tiny bathroom. Car doors *thunked* closed. She heard the engine roar to life, the crunch of tires on gravel. She started to shake. They were gone. Clancy was safe. But Ezra, Ezra was mixed up in something ugly.

CHAPTER 13

NO VISUAL, NO FOUL

Don't let Ezra be with her. Don't let him be with her. Penelope pressed through the diner crowd. Weeks ago she had heard from a frenemy that Ezra was seeing someone. She drove to Red Eagle Campground and, using binoculars, spied on his trailer. On her third trip she spotted a woman inside. Penelope hid in the trees and watched as they ate falafel, the only dish Ezra knew how to cook, at his picnic table. She asked around and discovered that the unremarkable female—light brown hair, neither short nor tall, not heavy or terribly thin, just a plain old other woman—worked as a server in the diner in East Glacier and hailed from some swanky New York suburb. When the other woman wasn't at Ezra's, she lived in the housing above the East Glacier Mercantile. It was the woman's first summer in Glacier, and Penelope could imagine her smitten with Ezra for the exact same reasons she had been. And now Penelope spotted her in the tiny diner kitchen washing dishes. Relief washed over her. Ezra had not run off with his girlfriend. The woman wore her hair in pigtails. Her cheery smile revealed perfect teeth. *Who smiled while doing dishes? It was too much.* She approached. "I need . . ." Penelope started but then stopped. She needed her husband.

The pigtailed woman pulled plates from the sink and arranged them between the rungs of the drying rack. She explained that it was actually her day off. She'd just popped in for dinner and seen how busy they were. So she was washing a batch of dishes to help them catch up. "I'll find the server. She'll help you."

"Where is he?"

The girlfriend cocked her head. "You're looking for someone?"

"You." Penelope could not abide the false innocence. "You are screwing my husband." Penelope hadn't meant to yell. A hush settled over the restaurant.

"Out." The girlfriend pointed at the back door and wiped her hands on her apron. Depicted on it were houseplants, some sort of ivy, an African violet, a watering can, and the words *I wet my plants.* Penelope almost found it funny. She maneuvered through the maze of tables. As she stepped outside, she breathed deep the sweet scent of the sticky cottonwood seeds. The girlfriend extended her hand. "Rosie."

Penelope fought the urge to slap her. "I need to know where he is." This wasn't a diplomatic mission. No need for handshakes. They were not going to be friends.

"Ezra's on a hitch. He comes out the day after tomorrow."

"Ezra is missing." Penelope told her no one had seen him. Every minute worsened his chances.

The girlfriend took a step backward. Her face went pale. "The rangers we saw . . . My friend Patrick and I hiked to the spike camp.

We hid from a couple rangers because they'd closed the valley." She shook her head. "They must've been hiking in, going to look for Ezra as we were hiking out?"

The girl was clueless. Penelope was wasting her time. "He'll do the same to you, you know. Cheat. It's who he is. Don't go thinking you're special." She started for the alley behind the diner. "He'll never be the man you need him to be."

Whatever else Mack knew about Ezra Riverton—and it wasn't much—he had disappeared from a stunning valley. The broad creek rushed between glacially carved peaks, curved through broad meadows pink with prairie smoke and shooting stars. Lynx, coyote, moose, bear, mountain lion, elk, and pine marten thrived here. With the campground closed, it seemed to Mack as close to perfect as a place could get. He'd told Layne to make the most of town, go ahead and fuel the truck, pick up mail, grocery shop, have dessert in a restaurant, enjoy himself.

Mack doubted that the scat analysis would be done in time to help find Ezra, but it was worth a try. It was the worst-smelling bear scat he'd ever encountered. What had that critter been eating? Had it ingested some of Liz's bait? Had it fed on a human? Or did fresh bear scat simply smell worse than the stuff he usually encountered? Liz would know or at least have a theory. Add it to the growing list of things to ask her.

The air cooled as the sun dipped below the peaks, shooting bands of white light. He privately called it *God light*. When he was a kid, he'd noticed that planks of sun often appeared in the Jesus paintings hanging in hospital chapels and nursing homes. Mack admired the artists for trying. Depicting this time of evening couldn't be easy—the grasses and trees aglow, waning sunlight throwing shadows with the promise of the coming dark. When they'd been leaving the office late one evening, Vera had told him the Blackfeet believed the lengths of light were Old Man's gaze as he looked back over his shoulder. "Old Man?" Mack asked. She said a word he didn't catch and then "the creative power of the sun." Mack loved that phrase. He repeated it to himself then and now. Every time he saw planks of light, he thought of the divine, how no one had a corner on it, it was available to everybody like sunlight, God light. Hopefully, wherever he was, Ezra was watching it, too.

Mack's boots crunched gravel, and a squirrel chattered a rebuke. He walked slowly, without purpose or destination. Ezra had disappeared sometime between 8:00 p.m. and 8:30 a.m. The hard rain had probably obliterated any footprints or other tracks. In addition, the fire that torched Ezra's tent had incinerated any evidence there. Only Clancy had visited the site before the fire. Mack pulled his notebook and pen from his uniform pocket and made a note to ask her about it again. Who could've started that fire? Ezra was a distinct possibility. What might he be hiding? Liz could have done it. Had she intentionally spilled her bear bait on his tent and in the campground? Using bear attractant as a weapon and a diversion would jeopardize her study and carry a charge of reckless endangerment, but what better way to occupy law enforcement, the same people she'd decided she did not need to meet with that morning? And why had she brought Muffy illegally into the backcountry?

Had she hiked out for the meeting as she'd told Penelope, discovered Muffy tethered like a Scooby snack, and done all this to get back at him? He didn't like Muffy, and Liz wouldn't be able to forgive him for that. Was she pregnant? Were hormones contributing to her erratic behavior?

Had Ezra surmised that a bait spill would implicate Liz and pulled off the ultimate sabotage? He might have acquired a bottle of the stuff from Penelope, framed Liz, and doomed the DNA study before going on the lam. If so, he'd won.

After the cursory search for Ezra had yielded nothing, Mack had radioed dispatch to get hold of Ranger Turner and have him check Ezra's camper in the Red Eagle Campground. It seemed odd that he hadn't heard back. He'd have Layne check with dispatch from his charmed corner of cell reception when he returned. The scat should get to the lab tomorrow, but the analysis would take time. That smell—surely it held some sort of clue. Mack would know a lot more after a day of searching. People disappeared, sure. But they didn't dissolve into the ether. Nate had used the word *vaporize*. Mack knew, with the same certainty that he knew the sun would set and rise again in the morning, that Ezra had not simply vanished, nor had he been abducted by Layne's theoretical aliens. Tomorrow would hold the key.

Mack loved this work, feeling needed, like his skills could make a difference, save people. It made the mind-numbing meetings, the thick policy binders, the endless Park Service rules and regulations worth it. What he couldn't know was that in the years ahead, he'd view the search for Ezra as pivotal, the event that would upend his trajectory and set him on a fresh path.

Mack stopped short. His heart flipped. Roberts stood still as a stone, watching him. Adrenaline stung down his limbs. The man wore a full backpack and held a can of Schmidt in one hand and a hand-rolled cigarette in the other.

"Figured it out yet?" Smoke shot from his nostrils.

Mack shook his head. Smiled a slow smile. "This valley's closed. You know that."

"Couldn't do it, couldn't curl up in bed, all warm and comfy listening to tunes, while Ezra's out here somewhere." He took a drag and dropped the smoke, ground it to smithereens under his boot. "Wish to hell I could." He reached into his jacket pocket and handed Mack a photo.

The smell of alcohol rolled off him. "You drive here?"

Roberts narrowed his eyebrows. "Even I'm not that dumb. No visual, no foul." He nodded in the direction of the photo. "Figured you could use that. It's recent as they come, trail crew barbecue right before this hitch. Thought you could blow it up, plaster it from here to Miles City." The picture showed a ginger-bearded twenty-something grinning wide, his crooked front tooth on full display.

"You going to help me pair folks up for the search?" Mack asked. Roberts's eyes swam bright with booze. "You know the trails people, their strengths, who's sleeping together, who's not speaking."

Roberts scoffed. "You need my help like a fish needs a bicycle. Isn't that the T-shirt?" He handed Mack his empty. "Recycle that, will you? I gotta git."

"Closed, Roberts. You can't go back there. I can't allow it. We got a missing man, bears acting weird, a torched tent. The last thing I need is another person to worry about."

Roberts started toward the trailhead. "Then stop me." He tossed a smile over his shoulder. "You don't want him out there without another soul around, either." He kept walking.

Mack turned away before he saw him set foot on the trail. No visual, no foul.

CHAPTER 14

CALLUSED

Penelope leaned against the porch rail of the Mexican place, sipping her blended margarita and waiting on her veggie burrito. Several off-duty St. Mary rangers stood in a tight knot and regaled one another with tales of visitor encounters. "I told him I'd have to ask my supervisor. I didn't know the precise elevation where deer become elk."

Usually, Penelope would've joined in. She had some visitor gems stowed away herself. A group of Germans had complained to her about the view from Scenic Point, "Vee couldn't see a thing, Rising Wolf vus in the vay." But she didn't have the energy. She'd resupplied on Benadryl at the Mercantile and swallowed two immediately. Her legs still itched, but the tequila made it so she didn't care.

"Guys." A handsome blond dressed in Park Service green and gray took the porch steps in a single bound. "We have ourselves a SAR."

Penelope turned back to her drink. He looked too soap-opera beautiful to last in Glacier, high cheekbones, strong jaw, Roman nose, blond curls. The meaty-complected rangers would ridicule him out of the park, drive him back east to the Liberty Bell or Lincoln Memorial, someplace where people didn't view looking like an underwear model as a character flaw.

"Trail crew stoner. Gone. Disappeared."

Penelope narrowed her eyes. The guy's blatant enthusiasm for having the scoop made him less good-looking—way less. "Mack and I suspect him of sabotaging the DNA study." The rangers went feral. They chimed in about trail crew bums and the study and who'd get overtime for the search, whose turn it was to ride in a chopper. The pretty boy raised his voice over the din, "Someone from the DNA study—probably Liz or the guy's estranged wife—spilled bear lure in the car campground to divert us from their nefarious activity." He explained that they'd adversely conditioned a bear, interrogated trail crew in their spike camp, and performed a cursory search. Mack had sent him to town to overnight grizzly scat for analysis. "We'll know if the bear fed on a human."

Penelope's fury mounted. Ezra deserved so much better than a bunch of bored pseudo cops capping on his disappearance to give their lives some purpose, to break them out of their sorry food-storage-violation, speeding-ticket-writing routine. Pretty boy headed inside to order. Penelope sucked the rest of her margarita through the tiny straws, down to the sloppy remnants. As the ranger burst back out the door, she flung salty slush in his lovely face. "That 'stoner' is my husband. Find him, you loser."

Water so hot it stung shot from the nozzle, just the way Clancy liked it. She soaped and rinsed, shampooed and scrubbed, and repeated. As much as anything—camping with a full-sized pillow and hardback books, the work, watching bear cubs slide down a snowfield, the laughs and comradery and climbs—she loved trail crew's backcountry stays because of the pleasure in returning home. She relished feeling clean, sleeping in a bed, eating tomatoes, cucumbers, and oranges bright with freshness. She planned to burrow beneath her down comforter and escape into the 1940s Montana of *Perma Red*. The whole time Clancy unpacked, hung her tent and sleeping bag on the line to air, and stowed her gear, she tried to put a face to the voice she'd heard in Ezra's camper. She told herself it would come to her while she slept and tried not to try so hard.

Her cabin in the Two Medicine Campground had been built before the advent of indoor plumbing, and the bathroom was a separate structure. Having to traipse out the front door and around back made Clancy careful about consuming liquids before bed. Not the worst thing to limit. When she overindulged, her bladder forced her out from under her blankets and into her clogs to scamper through grizzly habitat and the chilly darkness. Constructed of hand-hewn logs, the cabin had running water, bunk beds, a woodstove, and a kitchen table that doubled as a cupboard door until she unlatched it and the hinged legs swung out to meet the floor. It sat tucked amid the pines in Loop C.

The water pouring from her shower nozzle cooled. She felt clean. After toweling dry, Clancy donned what her brother had dubbed her "marm robe," a "one-size-fits-most" fuzzy monstrosity. She twisted her hair in a towel spa-style, shoved her bare feet into her hiking boots, and grabbed the pile of stinky clothes, locking the bathroom door as she left. Campfire smoke hung in the air. She rounded the corner of the cabin. Perched atop her picnic table in his Stetson and work coat sat Grady. He hopped down, grinning his crooked half grin. "I thought I'd take you to dinner at Daniel's, the Mexican place." He pointed his chin at her head. "But you look ready to turn in."

Disappointment stung Clancy's center. She would have loved to tuck into a shredded beef burrito smothered in caramelized cheese, green sauce, and sour cream. She would have enjoyed sipping a margarita across the table from Grady and finding out more about him. But he was right, it'd been a hell of a day, and she wasn't up for going anywhere except to bed. "You want to split a beer?" The first blue of twilight seeped into the sky behind him. He'd seen Clancy flat on her ass twice, and now he was privy to her dressed like Cousin Eddie in *Christmas Vacation*.

Grady removed a disk of chew from his back pocket and slapped it against his palm. "I'll be right here."

Inside, Clancy tugged on layers and wool socks and twisted the towel to squeeze water from her hair. Mercifully, the cabin lacked a mirror. Hell, it was almost dark, and he'd already seen her after a week without a shower and sprawled in the mud, so what did it matter that her hair hung lank, giving her the look of a drowned animal? At least it was clean. Still. Clancy donned her stocking cap. Huge help, she was sure.

She grabbed a bottle from the fridge, pried off the cap, found an almost clean jelly glass in the sink, and stepped into her clogs. Her whole body hummed with anticipation. He was at her picnic table. A pang of guilt stabbed at her glee. Somewhere up the Cut Bank Valley, Ezra suffered, cold and alone. But hey, if anyone would understand the fun of a romantic prospect, it was Ezra. *Go on*, she heard his voice in her head. *What are you waiting for? An engraved invitation?* The hinges on the screen door squeaked. The evening air was cool and smelled of woodsmoke. "Glass or bottle?"

He sat on top of the table and reached for the bottle. He studied the label. "Dead Guy?" His brow furrowed. "Seems kind of," he hesitated, "unfortunate."

Clancy laughed. Her laughter struck her as wildly inappropriate, and that made her laugh harder. Grady started to laugh, too. She caught her breath. "It's just good beer. Try it." She climbed up next to him and studied Rising Wolf, hoping to spot the dun-colored dots of bighorn sheep backsides or the lumbering figure of a grizzly.

Grady poured the glass full and took a tiny sip from the bottle. "That's no Schmidty."

"How'd you find out where I live?" She enjoyed a big swallow. The beer tasted bitter, hearty, and dark. No Schmidty, indeed.

"People like to know stuff. Most times all you have to do is ask." He turned and spat. "Marty's helpful."

Clancy was flattered that Grady had gone to the trouble. She was fond of Marty, and the fact that he seemed to like Grady boded well. A breeze rustled the pines, kicked up their scent. "My great-aunt came from Baltimore to visit. When we took her over the Sun Road, she said, 'Just look at all these damn trees, and they're making us recycle.'"

Grady laughed. "The woman's got a point."

They watched the mountain change from brown to gray in the fading light. "I went to his camper." Clancy said it without thinking, and relief flooded her. Grady's eyes looked darker than they had this morning, less cream in the coffee. She told him about seeing the Pulaski and boots right inside the door and how it galled her to think Ezra might be fine and had simply spent the day hiking home while the rest of them worried.

"There's more than one Pulaski in the world." Grady scraped the edges of the label with his thumbnail. The back of his hand was mottled with a bruise. "That goes for boots, too."

Clancy shook her head. "He could be cheap." A chill crept down her neck. She drew her feet up to the top of the table and wrapped her arms around her shins. "He didn't spend a lot on his gear." She thought about his orange four-season tent, upended and tattered. "Any fancy stuff he had, Penelope bought him. She grew up wealthy." Grady was right. The boots could have been spares, but their presence still nagged at her. "It looked like they were waiting, like any minute he'd step into them and head out to raise some hell."

An owl hooted, and Clancy felt Grady tense. "You don't like owls?"

"My mom's got stories." They were still, the air between them electric with possibility. Clancy wished he'd elaborate but didn't want to push. Owls called back and forth. Campfires popped, shot sparks against the twilight. A raven flew so close Clancy could hear its wings beat the air, a steady, rhythmic *whoosh*.

"I found the papers. He was definitely divorcing Penelope."

"Can't blame the guy for that."

As darkness settled in the trees, Clancy told Grady how Ezra always said he'd married Penelope for the spouse's half-price lift ticket at Big Mountain. But of course the truth was more complicated than the one-liner. "Penelope loved him like she wanted to devour him, and Ezra enjoyed being adored." She told him that Ezra had been homeschooled by his hippie Idaho parents and seemed to play by a different set of social rules.

"Is that your way of saying he was a total hound?"

Defensiveness rose in her chest. "His moral compass ran wonky, for sure. But Penelope messed with him on multiple levels." Clancy struggled to explain Ezra's attitude toward women. "He loves the women he sleeps with, he's just not *in* love with them." She glanced at Grady, who had one eyebrow cocked skeptically.

"When Penelope wanted to get married, Ezra saw it as a way to make her happy. It's hard for me to fathom, but to Ezra it was like, why not create happiness? Why wouldn't he make her dream come true? He thought he was being compassionate." The sky's dark blue deepened toward black. She told him Ezra wasn't realistic, but Penelope wasn't, either, and the marriage imploded. "He's tried to be kind, help her understand that they're over. But the more he insists, the more obsessed she becomes with winning him back." The breeze shivered the tops of the pines. Cool air swirled.

"Do you think she knows?" Grady asked. "About the papers? She seemed really upset when I told her he was missing. I don't know how it works, but it would be strange for him to divorce her without her having any idea."

"He was going to tell her last night. That's why he went out in the storm. They have to sort out the logistics. The house is in both their names, but as I understand it, her dad paid for the bulk of it." Clancy took a drink, swallowed the emotion threatening to surface. "I wish I knew if Ezra returned to camp."

"Penelope told Mack Savage he never made it to her." Grady turned and spat. Clancy heard it hit the ground.

"It gets weirder. I also found an ultrasound. Before I could figure out what that was about, a car pulled up." She drained her glass and pulled her hands into her sleeves. Clancy told Grady how she hid, how she heard two guys arguing about something Ezra was supposed to have, something valuable that they eventually located part of in the back of the camper. Her voice shook. "They sounded so mean."

Grady's arm came around her like a wing. Clancy leaned into his warmth, breathed in his smell, woodsmoke, a tinge of mint, a bit of dusty animal.

"Liz Ralston was pretty upset with your friend."

Clancy wanted to stay right where she was, warm and comfortable, but she couldn't let that go unanswered. She straightened and Grady dropped his arm. "A lot of people have a problem with that study. Ezra wondered, and I do, too, at what point we will have collared and studied and harassed the wildness out of bears. It's the same for wolverines and wolves and lynx, pika and all the rest. Why can't we leave some of their mystery intact? Why can't we just let them be?"

Grady chewed his bottom lip. Clancy leaned closer.

"She asked me not to say anything, but given the circumstances, I think she'd understand." Grady reached for her hand. Clancy pushed it free of her sleeve, and he wrapped it lightly in his. His palm felt warm and rough. Calluses lifted the base of his fingers. "Liz found Ezra's headlamp at a destroyed hair-snag station. She believes he's the main culprit. She also knows if she has him arrested, the entire trail crew will retaliate, and her project is toast."

"What did she do?" Clancy studied Grady's face. His eyes looked sad.

"She doesn't tell me everything." He smiled his half grin. "How are your hands so cold?"

"Warm heart." She laughed. "My mom claims that's what cold hands mean."

Clancy thought Grady was going to kiss her, but he looked away, studied the sky. "What do you think those guys in his camper were looking for?"

"He needed money. He smoked pot. A lot. All I can come up with is that maybe he invested in a large quantity to sell. But I have no proof. Nothing for sure." Clancy twined her fingers in his. "Will you search tomorrow?" she asked.

"Mack said I answer to him now." Grady wrapped his arm around her shoulders again. "He's pissed at Liz. Tried not to show it, but I could tell." His eyes met hers. He smiled, and the right side of his mouth lifted, pushed at his cheek, lined the skin at the corner of his eye. "I should let you get to bed."

Clancy did not want him to go. "You didn't drink your beer."

"You can have it."

She wondered if Grady was Native. He spoke with a reservation lilt, but anyone who lived here a while picked up the local cadence. He had those beautiful dark eyes, but not the coal-dark of a lot of Blackfeet. His complexion betrayed nothing. Could be Native American or Greek, Bulgarian, or Turkish. She decided to just ask, "Are you Indian?"

To her relief, he smiled again. "Not enough to count."

Clancy waited. Figured he'd tell her more if he chose. A sliver of a moon hung high in the night sky.

"My mom's enrolled, but Dad's white. My grandpa on my mom's side's traditional and speaks Blackfeet. My grandma's a fluent speaker, too, but she's also a Romanian Jew. We're all Blackfeet." He gave a laugh. "You follow that?"

Clancy shook her head, bewildered. They both grinned. "The upshot is my sister, Josie, and I don't have enough blood. We're deemed descendants. We don't get to vote in tribal elections, and we don't qualify for the same benefits as most of our cousins. It's a shame. We could use a per cap payment, Josie especially."

"Doesn't seem right."

Grady shrugged. "What are you going to do?"

"Why don't you drink?"

"I guess like your friend, I have the one-liner and the real reason." He rubbed his thumb across the back of her hand. "Which do you prefer?"

"Both." Clancy stared up at Rising Wolf. It lifted solid, made her feel protected, safe.

"I don't drink because I can." He brought his lips close and whispered, "That's the line." He locked his gaze on hers. "Not drinking is an option for me. That's not the case for everybody. I don't drink because alcohol's cost me and my family too much, and I'm not willing to risk it taking more." His palm cupped her jaw. "I don't drink because I'm better without it."

Clancy closed her eyes. Grady's mouth met hers.

CHAPTER 15

WANING CRESENT

Mack reclined in a willow rocker on the porch of the Cut Bank Ranger Station. He appreciated the tasteful forest-green cushions Layne had added. Had he used his days off to travel to the west side for home decor? Mack held a pen and a legal pad. He had a search to organize. For tomorrow he planned a grid search originating at the spike camp while at the same time sending teams up each of the trails to scour the valley for any clues.

He began pairing searchers and kept hiccupping on one name: Clancy. For good reason, he never allowed close friends or loved ones to search. Any rescue could turn into a recovery operation. No one should see the body of someone close to them once it had been set upon by carnivores, scavengers, birds and vermin.

Mack harbored hope that Ezra was out there, some fascinating, nonfatal mishap having waylaid him. He toyed with the idea that the young man had made a break for it, destroyed Liz and her study for good with the bait spills, and left his ex-wife and troubles behind. The guy worked trails and was more than capable of hiking the fifty miles north into Canada, where he could start from scratch. He also could've hoofed it up Pitamakan Pass and either out the Dry Fork to Two Med or up over Cut Bank Pass. That route would drop into the Nyack. From there he could have left Glacier, crossed Highway 2, and disappeared into the Great Bear and Bob Marshall. Nothing but wildernesses for miles upon miles. It held an appeal, that scenario. It was just damn near impossible to pull off. Besides, Ezra already lived life on his own terms: seasonal, outdoor employment, as many women as he could get away with, loyal friends. Why walk away? Maybe he had his reasons.

Mack's money was on finding Ezra, ailing or dead, within a mile of where he had last been seen. That's what the odds indicated, and barring any new information, that was probably how it would play out. He did not want Clancy to be the one to find him. He decided to make her part of Incident Command, put her in charge of logistics, keep her busy organizing meals and lodging, procuring sports drinks and energy bars. No way was that young woman, still grieving her brother, going to have to endure discovering the body of her friend.

Headlights pierced the distance. *About time,* he thought as he glanced at his watch. Layne had made the most of that errand. When the young man climbed the porch steps, he did so with his head down. "I messed up," he said. He carried tote bags full of groceries. "Big time."

"The scat?" Mack asked anxiously.

"I was just so . . ." Layne's voice trailed off as he looked up at the mountains. "For once I was not the most clueless law enforcement officer on the planet." He set down his bags, plopped into a cushioned rocker, and told Mack about what he'd said, not realizing Ezra's wife stood three feet away.

Mack leaned forward. "You made a mistake you'll never make again. Doubt there's any real harm done. You ready for your list?"

Layne whipped a Smokey Bear notepad from his shirt pocket and had his pen poised and at the ready before Mack could find his notes.

The knowledge that Penelope should not be driving proved intermittent, a thought illuminated periodically by a roving mental searchlight. Two double yellow lines appeared in the center of the road. Penelope closed one eye. The searchlight vanished along with one of the double yellows.

When she opened the door to Ezra's camper, she couldn't quite recall how she'd arrived. The place was trashed, seriously trashed—probably someone looking for his stash. Penelope held her headlamp and waded through piles of silverware, kitchen utensils, and broken dishes to check his hiding place behind the toilet. She shined her light. Taped to the back of the bowl was a baggie. It held marijuana, a lighter, and a film canister. Penelope popped the container's lid. Vicodin—just what a gal with a missing husband and an allergic reaction could use. She swallowed one. It gave Ezra the heebies when she took pills without water.

She swung the beam of light and surveyed her husband's summer home. The detritus of years of camper living lay strewn across every surface. Shards of glass glinted from the floor. It was impossible to walk without stepping on batteries, camper cushions, and bungee cords. She spotted a pile of papers.

She breathed the musty camper smell and found what she dreaded. An ache throbbed in her chest. She flipped to the last page. He'd signed. It was over. She fought through the fog to remind herself of what she'd decided this morning. It was over for her, too. Maybe Ezra's disappearance was just the universe helping her stay strong in her resolve to be done with him. Another sheet caught her eye. It felt heavy and slick. She trained her headlamp on an ultrasound. She'd seen an image like this before, a smear of white on black.

She and Ezra had been married two months. She felt the heady rush of love and everything she wanted falling into place. She had a husband, an almost outdoor job, and walls she could paint. Her appetite evaporated. She skied every day. She caught a cold and took antibiotics. That was what her doctor said had done it, rendered her birth control pills ineffective.

Penelope saw babies everywhere. They sat snug in car seats at the coffee shop, slept in strollers as proud parents pushed them through downtown toward the library, lay bundled in slings as their moms coached older siblings on the bunny hill. It looked doable—more than doable, it looked warm and joyful, like a family. Penelope and Ezra kept to their routine. Other than big, sore boobs, an increased aversion to the smell of Ezra's dirty laundry, diesel exhaust, and instant noodles, and the sudden ability to sleep for twelve hours solid, not a lot changed.

One evening, after a day skiing, they soaked in the tub together. Penelope leaned against Ezra's chest, marveling at her stomach, still flat but rumbling with gas. He laid his hand low on her belly and said simply, "I'm not ready."

The ultrasound had been her last attempt to yank him into the cocoon of family. In hindsight, it had been a terrible idea. The baby became more real to her while causing Ezra to withdraw. He turned cold, distant. She knew she couldn't have them both and scheduled the appointment. She'd cried when she first heard her baby's heartbeat, and she cried when she knew it had stopped.

Back home and bereft, Penelope took to the bed. Ezra climbed beneath the covers and curled his body into hers. He pulled her close and said, "We'll have a baby someday. Someday when we're both ready and it will be the best baby and we will love it and each other and be a family." She clung to that "someday" like a lifeline that kept her tethered to Ezra, to the image in her mind of the three of them in Glacier, exploring wild places, their baby, their dear, charmed baby, camping where no baby had camped for hundreds of years, if ever.

When Penelope spotted a child the age that hers would have been, sadness welled up, pressed heavy on her chest. One of the things she appreciated about the backcountry was its utter lack of toddlers. She stared at the tangle of bedding piled atop Ezra's mattress. The possibility of recovering her irrecoverable loss had disappeared along with Ezra.

Penelope read the name at the top of the scan, the name that should have been hers. She did not know this person, the woman who carried the child she wanted and who'd had an ultrasound at the end of May. She sifted through the mound of drawer contents on the floor until she found a pair of scissors. She sliced a strip off the top, removed the name. It would be easier to pretend this way, to live for a while at least in a world that turned out the way she'd hoped.

She tossed back another Vicodin, grabbed the lighter, the divorce papers, the length she'd cut from the scan, and made for Ezra's firepit. He'd find his way back to her. She had believed it for so long, she couldn't stop now. As she stepped outside, she looked up at a crescent moon. High in the sky, it looked to be winking, welcoming her in on a secret.

"And," Mack handed over the photo Roberts had given him, "take a picture of that with your cell phone and see if it will send to the Com Center. The courier will get the original to headquarters tomorrow. They'll issue the BOLO and distribute the picture. Also, have them run that 38 plate so we can find out who came through the campground after we closed it." The Be on the Lookout would alert every law enforcement agency in the region.

"You suspect malfeasance?"

Mack stifled a laugh. "I just want to know who it is and if they saw anything that might be helpful."

"Yes sir. But they entered a campground clearly marked 'CLOSED.'"

"They had driven miles of bad gravel intent on hiking or climbing," he said gently. "It is their park."

Layne looked crushed. Mack tried again. "I need Turner's report on Ezra's camper. We can't completely discount the possibility that the guy engineered his own disappearance and pulled off the ultimate sabotage of Liz's study."

"I'm on it. Anything else?"

"Contact the permit desk and find out if any visitors camped at Morning Star last night. And not because they're felons, they just might have seen or heard something helpful."

Layne looked at his watch. "They're closed, sir."

"Good point." Mack checked items off his list. "See if the Com Center can access the permits. Get the names and numbers of the campers and give them a call."

Layne closed his notebook with satisfaction. "I'll be in the corner where my phone works." The door closed gently behind him.

Bats swooped through the twilight, lifting and dipping in long arcs. Mack's thoughts turned to Liz. He could hardly list all the questions he had, starting with whether she was expecting. Why had she called off this morning's law enforcement meeting and told him she loved him? Except for Layne's magic corner inside his residence, the Cut Bank Valley didn't have cell reception, so she must have called from somewhere else. What time had her call been recorded on his voicemail? He made a note to check that. When had she grabbed Muffy from outside his house? Why would she take her dog into the backcountry? Had she poured bear lure in the campground to keep them occupied while she torched Ezra's tent? Where, exactly, and when had she found Ezra's headlamp? Was that the entirety of her evidence against him? She had a lot riding on this study. If it had gone well, she'd have had her pick of bear biology jobs. Since it hadn't, she'd be relegated to the ever-growing pool of well-educated scientists clamoring for scraps of wildlife work. He told himself Liz hadn't always been the sort of person who would hurt someone to further her own career. Tremendous pressure accompanied the support from Washington. Once the funding had come through, little else had gone Liz's way.

Mack eyeballed his list, hoping something would jump out, but he arrived at the same conclusion every time. Barring a frame job requiring tremendous cunning from Ezra, Mack's girlfriend was his number-one suspect. When she came off the trail tomorrow, he'd be there to meet her.

Layne let the screen door slam behind him. "Good news or bad news?"

"I always want good news, Layne. Nothing but good news."

"The Subaru is registered to one Patrick Hughes. The dispatcher knew of him. He's been cited for numerous infractions, including camping without a permit, unlawful campfires, and—as we're well aware—hiking in a closed area. He has never paid the fines. Dispatch said he's an avid mountaineer and year-round resident of East Glacier. He's got a sheet, pled guilty to possession but never served time. He went to treatment, did community service, and hasn't been in felony trouble since."

And, Mack thought, *he's the guy Liz described as the charismatic climber who enlisted all his east-side buddies to rip down her barbed wire.* "Interesting. What do you say we recruit him for our search?"

"If you don't mind my saying so, sir, he flaunts regulations and has repeatedly demonstrated a lack of respect for the Park Service and our mission."

"He knows the park. Chances are he knows Ezra. He may have seen something when he was back there this afternoon, and if he did, we're more likely to learn what it was if we make him part of the team than if we interrogate him." Darkness had fallen in earnest.

The air was cool. Mack looked forward to climbing into his truck and blasting the heater. "What else do you have for me?"

"Ranger Turner, sir, dispatch can't reach him. He's off duty, has been since fourteen hundred. They sent a backcountry permit writer by his residence, but he's not home."

Probably on one of his dates, Mack thought. *And more power to him.* Maybe if the guy could find love, he wouldn't be such an insufferable jackass.

Turner's standard operating procedure was to make things worse. The balding man had once pulled a vehicle over for speeding and discovered a carload of Native teens who'd been huffing nail polish remover. Instead of quietly giving them a lift home, as Mack would have done, Turner arrested them. That action required five additional rangers and two additional vehicles to transport them all to the jail seventy miles away. It also caused untold heartache for the kids' parents and grandparents, a ream of paperwork, and a large financial outlay in overtime that came directly out of Mack's budget.

By far, Turner issued more tickets than any other law enforcement ranger in Glacier. His favorite trick was to check the Running Eagle Falls parking lot for coolers in the backs of pickup trucks. He issued food storage violations to vacationers who'd entered the park a mile back and had not yet read about bears or proper food storage. He also confiscated their coolers and made them retrieve their property directly from him so he could give them a lecture.

Layne reassured Mack, "Dispatch plans to get Turner over to Ezra's camper first thing in the morning. I have the names and phone numbers for the backcountry campers, but given that it's after 11 p.m., I'll wait and call tomorrow."

Mack clapped the young man's back. "Nice work. Get some sleep."

"You're leaving?" Layne sounded disappointed.

Mack had considered staying the night. He was pretty sure Layne would've volunteered to take the futon and given him the bed, probably even provided fresh sheets, but he needed some distance from the Cut Bank Valley. "You'll hardly have time to miss me."

The Milky Way stretched like a path across the sky. A fingernail shaving of a moon lifted above the peaks. Mack hoped that somewhere, not too far away, Ezra gazed up at it, too.

PART II

FOUND

Tuesday, June 22, 2004

CHAPTER 16

BEST OF ALL

Vera Fisher had news. She worked as Mack's administrative assistant and served as the official timekeeper for all incidents on Glacier's east side. She bounced along the dirt road that would take her to Cut Bank—the ranger station, not the town. She drove the washboard gravel slowly, admiring the hillside, a stretch of dusty pink thanks to a good year for prairie smoke. Vera was late, but there wasn't much she could do about it now. She'd had to run her mother-in-law to Browning for dialysis. Tardiness irritated Mack, but the guy they were looking for would probably still be missing when she got there. All the vehicles would be backed into parking spots in case anyone needed to "respond." These white people believed themselves very busy and important, but not a one of them would get paid if it wasn't for her.

While Vera didn't get all excited about search and rescues, she also didn't mind them. Her family could use whatever money she earned. Luckily for her bank account, the park created its own problems. Steal the land from Natives starving to death because you decimated the buffalo herds, designate a wild place full of vicious animals for all the American people, create a bunch of laws to protect the place and the animals from all the people, hire and keep hiring rangers—mostly white men—to enforce the laws, hire people like herself capable of meticulously completing the federal paperwork that the law enforcers didn't possess the attention span to handle, and then get all distraught and excited and mount expensive, elaborate searches when the people got lost, fell off the mountains, met with weather, or got attacked by the predators.

They were all out walking around in the bears' living room, clawing their way up mountains, fording raging rivers. What did they expect? It seemed to Vera that some of the appeal of striking out into Glacier's backcountry must be the adventure. So why, when the hikers and climbers sought out difficulty, danger, and adversity, was there all the shock and sadness and hullaballoo when the poor fools found exactly what they were looking for?

Last summer, when Truman Dyer's son had gone missing and been found dead, Vera had felt for his family. Dyer had always been kind. His daughter was, too. Vera knew well the dark hole in one's heart created by the passing of a loved one. But most of the folks who met their end inside the park didn't need her sympathy. She'd save that for her family, her community members, people with real problems like failing kidneys, trailer homes wracked by wind, no dependable rig to get around the million-and-a-half-acre reservation.

Compared to a lot of the ways to make money in the area—ranching, cleaning motel rooms, dealing drugs—Vera considered her job working for Mack downright cushy. Though she looked forward to the day he dumped that vile woman he was seeing. She knew exactly what they had been up to in his office, of all places. She recognized the flush of the freshly screwed. When Liz strode past her desk with her impeccable posture and that bulb of a chin in the air, Vera fought the urge to stick out her foot and trip her. Given what she'd seen the night of the storm, Vera could tell the woman had gotten herself in some sort of pickle. No one on the straight and narrow grabs a wad of cash from an ATM in the middle of the night. Vera and her family were headed home from a barbecue. They'd waited for the storm to pass before setting out. The kids were all asleep in the back. She spotted Liz, pointed out the snitty woman to her husband as he pumped five dollars of overpriced fuel into their minivan. "Hardly smiles, that one," she told him. "She's got money, a fancy education, a job. What's she got to be so pissy about?"

Liz Ralston reminded Vera of the lady who had adopted her and her sister, a Missoula lawyer with a spineless husband. The day they arrived, they sat at a long glass table, the girls on one side, the wealthy couple on the other. The woman wore her hair short. It framed her narrow face just so. She ate only salad. Bowls of the stuff sat on the table in front of each of them. The woman perched on the edge of her chair and enunciated as though the girls were foreign or dim. She told them, "You may," she pinched the corners of her mouth upward. "Call me," she brought her palm to rest above her tiny breasts. "Mommy." They sat still and quiet, touching their stocking feet to one another's beneath the table, staring at the leafy greens. "Or Tori." Then she told them they could call her husband "Daddy" or "Oliver." The girls didn't call them anything. Tori was busy lawyering, and Oliver tiled kitchens and bathrooms under tight deadlines. Vera and her sister tracked in mud, left handprints, and did not eat salad.

Tori bought them expensive matching clothes. The pants that fit around Vera's tummy were too long and bunched painfully inside her snow boots. One morning, as Tori frantically tried to get them ready and out the door, Vera pulled off the pants the lady had just made her put on and said, "I won't wear them." The woman slapped her. Vera did not cry. She knew then, the worry building in her belly like a ball of snow pushed across the yard for a snowman, that the woman would be unable to accept that she had hit a child. Tori could handle her dislike of the girls. Angered by their presence, she would storm through the house with a rag, scrubbing traces of them from floors and doors, tables and glass. As they untangled from their beds, the woman recoiled from the smells of their warm bodies and heavy breath. But Tori would not be able to tolerate that she'd sunk to violence. It didn't square with who she wanted to be.

That night Oliver read them some story about a boy who'd been punished and sailed to a land of grand adventure until he decided he wanted to return to the one who loved him best of all. The man slowed as he read that part. He seemed to realize it might hurt the girls' feelings. He knew they had no one like that. To make up for it, he granted their wish to sleep in the same bed even though Tori forbade it, calling it "unnatural."

Tori was still at work or the gym or, as Vera thought of it now as she bumped along the bad dirt road, drawing up the papers to fix her mistake. That night, the night that followed the morning slap, Vera curled into the warmth of her little sister and told her they had to be good, sit up straight, eat the salad, wear the clothes, and complete their chores or the people would send them away. And the girls tried, oh how they tried, for days they did their best to behave and be helpful. Vera wore the uncomfortable pants and clamped her teeth at the way they rubbed inside her boots. But still. After Saturday-morning cartoons, the woman sat in front of them and opened her hands to show them two batteries. Oliver stood off to the side and looked at his shoes. She said, "Like these batteries, we've run out of energy." The batteries were the brand that advertised with pink bunnies beating drums. The commercial claimed that they kept going and going. It showed the bunnies scooting along beating the drums until they swiftly changed direction and headed back the way they had come. Vera realized the woman was like that. She just kept going, and if she encountered something that didn't fit with her version of how life should be, she turned on it. Vera never forgot the airy desperation of those few days full of nothing but trying to be unobjectionable.

The drive home to Browning had felt long. Snow piled higher as the car rolled north. Cold pressed the windows. Her stomach roiled as the road curved through the mountains. She learned that day how to tuck the most precious bit of herself deep inside, safe from rejection, away from fear, to be the one who loved her best of all. She settled her forehead against the cool window. She could smell the trees. During that ride she felt the release of what she feared, and fought to avoid, having happened. She tucked into herself, rolled all that was really her into a tight brightness at her center. And when the man hugged her goodbye, she bit the inside of her lip and did not hug him back, did not so much as look at him.

They spent the first two nights with the family who ran the Methodist church. Neither Vera nor her sister spoke. Social Services located a great uncle out in Babb. He and his wife were old but kind and quick to laugh. They served the girls hangover soup and candy and didn't mind a whit if they slept together on the couch or in blankets on the living room floor. Even though Tori had painstakingly folded the clothes she'd bought for them and packed two Strawberry Shortcake suitcases, Vera never touched them. Instead, she wore her great-uncle's T-shirts, miles too big and incredibly soft.

Vera despised having to interact with Liz, the severe, driven woman Mack had taken up with who pounded her drum in one direction till she ran out of options and then swiftly changed course, plowing past whatever stood in her way. Vera would have bet her overtime that Liz had initiated the sex in Mack's office, the manipulative vamp. Why had she needed a stack of cash in the middle of the night?

Sun poured down as she pulled into the parking area. Indeed, the three-quarter-ton trucks and Crown Vics were all backed in and poised at the ready. She stepped from her car into the sunlight. She tugged on the hideous yellow button-down they insisted she wear over her T-shirt. Vera did not like being told how to dress. She taught personnel to fill out their red dogs, the official incident time sheets used for search and rescues or fires. She organized all the paperwork, didn't actually search for anyone, didn't really need to don yellow. Social Security numbers, routing and account numbers, overtime hours—she tracked those down, found them all. But missing people she'd leave to the folks who got all worked up about it.

The searchers huddled in groups. The law enforcement folks stood serious with their mirrored glasses and the .357s on their hips. The entrance station staff, giddy at the break in routine, bounced with enthusiasm. Backcountry permit writers and trail crew clustered in their own knots.

Mack dashed to meet her. "Glad you made it. I need a favor. Can you put Clancy Dyer to work around the command post?"

She nodded. "Never a shortage of paperwork." Vera noticed her boss looked tired. She wanted to tell him what she'd seen the night before, but she didn't want to be overheard. "Where's Liz?"

"Mack," one of the searchers yelled, "where'd you hide the wheeled litter?" Her boss strode away.

If they'd been actual friends, she would've told him. She would have said, "Find somebody nice. Jokes." And he would've known she wasn't joking. But they simply worked together. She lugged her tote of files up onto the porch.

Layne bounded up the steps and offered to help. She told him she could use a table and a few rocks to anchor the papers. He was back in a flash, hauling a card table. Minutes later he pressed a mug into her hand. She could taste the cream and sugar. Without her asking, Layne told her she could use his private bathroom. Vera abhorred outhouses. He led her inside his tidy cabin to show her the way. For years she and Layne would retain a soft spot for one another in the way of two people who have little in common beyond that they don't quite belong.

"The evidence points to Liz," he whispered. "She's on the lam."

"I saw her," Vera told him. "Last night. Late. She was at the ATM in St. Mary."

"Anyone with her?" Layne's eyes brightened.

Vera sighed. "It was dark. Had to be almost midnight. Looked like she withdrew a lot. Her dog was in her truck."

"Useful intel." Layne nodded. "I'll inform Mack."

She stepped inside Layne's sparkling-clean bathroom and thought of that long ride back from Missoula and the smell of the trees. She remembered the relief she'd felt that evening as they climbed out of the car in front of the church in Browning and the wind tossed her hair. What she'd dreaded had happened. She was free of it, free of that hard woman. These days, when she got home after work, she was greeted by a houseful of people—her children, nieces, nephews, husband—who loved her best of all. She hoped that whatever mishap had befallen the missing trails guy, whatever that dark-hearted woman had done to him, he too had known the relief of what he dreaded having passed and been freed from fear.

CHAPTER 17

IMPLICATED

High clouds curved across the sky. Clancy reached for her yellow Nomex shirt and shivered. The last time she'd worn it, they'd been looking for her brother. Not that Mack had actually allowed her to search. He had better not pull that today. Clancy had slept badly. After Grady left, she felt wired, physically exhausted, but the day's events bounced in her head—Ezra, Grady, the angry-voiced man, the guy whose voice she knew she knew but couldn't identify. She'd been tempted to ask Grady to stay, but she'd promised herself. She was done with one-night stands. Inviting a guy she'd just met to bed wouldn't lead to anything real. At some point in the wee hours, she must have dozed, but the shallow sleep left her exhausted.

She stood in sunlight that didn't yet hold warmth. Ezra had last been seen over thirty-three hours ago. Clancy knew the rule: three minutes without air, three days without water, three weeks without food, three months without joy. It was all a human could survive.

They had some time, but not much. Every hour that passed exponentially decreased Ezra's chances of being found alive.

"Clancy!" She jumped and Nate stepped around the truck. He looked stricken. Behind his glasses, his eyes were bloodshot and puffy. "Sorry to scare you."

"Anything? Anything on Ezra?"

Nate shook his head. He was about the funniest person she knew. She'd once picked him up when he was hitchhiking holding a sign that read, "Axe Murderer." Another time, they had crossed the border together on their way to Waterton to deliver tools to the Goat Haunt crew. When the Border Patrol officer asked if they had any weapons, Nate said, "I could light my camp stove and throw it at you." They'd been asked to pull over so Border Patrol could search the truck. When Roberts once dunked his head in a stream and then flipped his hair back and it puffed up from his forehead, Nate quipped, "Eddie Munster: Where are they now?" He described Ranger Jed Turner as "the pro bowler–looking dude." And indeed, with his bushy mustache and bald head, the guy appeared fresh off the tour.

It disarmed her to see Nate look so stern. He'd ditched his *Virginity Rocks* hat for a plain old Park Service ball cap. He wore what Ezra had dubbed "birth-control glasses," thick black military-issue-looking frames. His Nomex shirt was untucked. "I need your help," he said. Any hint of the jokester Clancy knew was gone. "Can we talk?" She nodded and followed him down the road, past the ranger station and its gathering crowd. They headed toward the campground. "I'm not sure how to say this. I don't want to offend you." Nate paused.

"You're as serious as a heart attack, Nate. What's up?" Clancy could see Bad Marriage and Mad Wolf, the peaks aglow in the morning light. If all had gone as planned, she and Ezra would be sore and exhausted this morning from having dashed toward the top, climbing as high as the snow would allow. Roberts would be grousing around about work as a priority and the maintenance schedule and how they'd better not slack or he'd put the kibosh on after-work climbing.

Gravel crunched beneath their boots. "You think the best of us, Clancy. You like us for who we are." He pushed his glasses into place. "It's why we love you. Love having you on the crew."

Clancy felt a "but" coming. A swallow flew across the road, dipped in front of them as though by way of greeting.

"But . . ." There it was. She smiled to herself. Nate continued, "There's another side. Guys like us, Roberts, me, Ezra, we didn't grow up with two parents, a nice house, supper at 6." He paused, "Roberts's mom was a stripper."

"He told me she taught belly dancing."

"Precisely," Nate said. "You get the tidy version. The story we think you won't judge."

The last thing Clancy needed was a guy who worked all of five months a year and skied the rest telling her how great she had it while he suffered in the "real" world. He knew nothing about how she'd grown up. Her dad worked constantly. Her mom suffered from depression. Her brother was dead. No one's childhood came without struggle, and certainly not Clancy's. "Your point?"

"We need each other. Because of your family, your dad, you're going to have access to people and information that I don't. And I'm going to know things you can't." He drove his fists into the pockets of his green pants. "Let's keep each other in the loop."

"Hold up!" Mack Savage jogged toward them, another of Nate's points proven. "I need a word."

Nate kept his voice low. He seemed desperate not to be overheard. "Together we can figure this out."

Yeah, Clancy thought as she watched him peel away and stride toward the campground to dodge Mack. *We can start with what you were doing trashing Ezra's camper last night.* No wonder the voice had sounded familiar. She'd been listening to it crack jokes for the past two summers.

Mack caught up to Clancy and watched Nate dash in the other direction. That guy was avoiding him. He'd have to find out why. Later. He'd been dreading this conversation. He told Clancy he was glad she was here. "Do you know Ezra's family?"

Nate reeled back around and strode their way, propelled by barely contained aggression. His jaw jutting, he said, "You asked if we had any idea what happened to Ezra. You need to talk to Penelope."

Mack nodded. "I've heard that from others as well."

Nate's glasses eased down his nose, and he poked them back into place. "I hoped he'd show back up with some crazy story. I don't like blabbing people's personal lives to law enforcement, airing his dirt to someone who up until yesterday didn't know his name."

Mack gave another nod. "I appreciate the information."

Nate shifted, leaned toward Mack. "Penelope has access to the bear bait. She's crazy. Ezra's done with her, and she's desperate to change that."

"Thanks for the suggestion."

Nate turned and strode down the road, back toward the ranger station and the crowd of searchers.

Mack watched him go. "Who knows, he may hold the key." He turned to Clancy. "Do you really think Penelope's capable of hurting Ezra? She seemed genuinely upset."

"Like Nate said, she's not stable." A breeze rattled the leaves. "I told you yesterday she was obsessed. And angry. Ezra was breaking it off for good." Clancy raised her voice to be heard over the a gust of wind. "Penelope had cause. The house in Whitefish, money he owed her, Ezra's new girlfriend." She thought about mentioning the ultrasound she'd found in Ezra's camper, but she agreed with Nate about keeping personal lives private. She needed time to figure out what all Nate and Ezra had gotten mixed up in with the angry guy.

Mack started to walk, gestured for Clancy to accompany him. "This is a complex young man we're looking for."

"Why'd you ask about his family? Do you think they had him killed?" She grinned.

Mack laughed. "I hadn't considered possible mafia connections."

"I met them once. They were nice enough, but a little . . ." Clancy searched ridgetops as though they held the right word, "odd. I could see where Ezra got his passion. He told me they'd 'dropped out' in the '70s."

"Hippies?"

"Peace, love, pot, no trust fund." Clancy nodded. "The real deal. Abhorred the idea of 'working for the man.'"

Mack reminded her that she was the only one to have seen Ezra's tent before the fire. "Describe it for me."

Clancy shuddered. She recounted the nasty smell, the tattered orange nylon flapping in the breeze.

"Have you ever smelled the bait Liz uses?" Mack asked.

Clancy told him she'd managed to steer clear.

"I'll need you to do me a favor—take a whiff, see if you recognize it. I need to verify our assumption about the odor at Ezra's tent site." He stopped walking and forced a smile, exhaled. "We need to talk about your duty assignment."

Clancy stopped, too. She shot him a narrow-eyed look.

"I need you in the Command Center. No one here is more familiar with this place and the guy we're looking for than you are. I need you coordinating logistics."

Clancy let loose a high-pitched "Hah!"

Mack ignored it. "I need your help."

"Don't pull that bureaucratic BS. Vera's been keeping time and running logistics on searches practically as long as I've been alive. I would only be in her way." She took a step toward him. "Man up, Mack. What's the problem?"

Mack pursed his lips. "It's you, Clancy. I can't risk it. Not after Sean, after all you and your family have been through."

"I thought you might pull this. I know my father at least as well as you do, and he would want me to do the right thing, which is not to cower in some office arranging per diem meals at Daniel's Mexican Bistro."

Mack grinned despite himself. "Layne already tried that. No go. They don't want to deal with the paperwork. Said it's too much trouble trying to get paid from the feds. It's the diner for us or nothing." Wind flashed the aspen leaves. They spun verdant in the sun. "Have you talked to your dad?"

"I got busy last night. The ranger station was closed when I got back to Two Med. I couldn't have called him if I wanted to." She started walking. "That's one of the reasons you have to let me search, Mack. I know these guys. Something strange is going on. I haven't figured it out yet, but I won't have a chance if you banish me to office work. Vera's got that under control. And no way will Roberts and Nate open up if they think I'm blabbing everything to law enforcement."

Mack shook his head. "Now it's my turn to call baloney. You got too busy to talk to your parents after you'd been in the woods for eight days and your best buddy went missing?" Mack cocked his head. "What's going on?"

Clancy studied the ground. Rocks, red and green and purple, cobbled the road. "This is difficult, Mack. You said so yesterday. It brings it all back. I'm having a hard enough time dealing with my own emotions. I'm not ready to come up against theirs." She bit her bottom lip for a moment and went on, "It's the worst part. I miss Sean, yeah, but I can deal with that. What gets me is the way my mom still can't say his name without breaking down, still hasn't gone through his clothes and books, the way my dad covers his mouth with his hand when he cries." She met Mack's eye. "I couldn't call them. Not now. Not with this."

"I'll make you a deal." Mack set a firm hand on her shoulder. "If your dad says it's okay, you're in. You're searching. The condition is that you keep me apprised. I need to know everything that you know. I'm not looking to hurt people, Clancy. I'm not out to bust any of your buddies for smoking pot or ripping Liz's wire. But I need all the information I can get." Mack extended his hand. Clancy shook it.

Layne burst around a curve, running full bore. His flat hat flew off his head and bounced against the gravel. "We've got a body."

CHAPTER 18

THE STINK OF MONEY AND LIES

◆

Patrick felt twitchy with nerves and coffee and the possibility of another encounter with Ranger Turner. He swung his vehicle into a parking spot. Rosie sat in a heap beside him. Last night, when he'd gotten the phone call, Patrick had thought one of his buddies was cranking him, but it really was the Park Service. The ranger recruited him to help search for Ezra. He would not have predicted that, not ever. The guy on the phone said they could use his expertise, which made a weird kind of sense. Who would want to turn a bunch of desk jockeys loose in the wilderness? Shortly after he'd hung up, while he was debating about whether to call her, Rosie called him. She'd heard about Ezra from Penelope, of all people. They discussed the fact that the rangers they'd hidden from on their hike out must have been headed into the backcountry to look for Ezra.

Most of the other cars and trucks had backed in, a weird Park

Service practice. "Ready to respond," Patrick mocked their Dudley Do-Right narcissism. "The catastrophe is here, folks. You don't have to peel out to save someone."

"They mean well." Rosie was, in a couple of words, a mess. Her hair hung haphazardly from a clip, crimped from yesterday's pigtails. Her eyes puffed and her face was splotched with red. She wore a trails sweatshirt Ezra had given her that read DURT MAKES ME CUTER. It looked slept in.

"Should I tell them about Ezra and me?" She wiped her nose with a kerchief.

"If you do, they won't let you anywhere near someplace you'll actually find him." Patrick reached into the back seat and tugged his pack onto his lap. "No way do they want a loved one finding . . ."

"You think he's dead?" Her voice quivered around the words.

Patrick kicked himself. "He's a capable, resilient guy. If anyone could be out there injured and survive, it is your man." He meant it to be reassuring but the word *man* came out caustic. "Don't worry. Penelope probably already told them about you. They'll put you to work handing out protein bars and electrolyte drinks, but you're here. You're going to know he's okay as soon as we find him." Patrick smiled broadly and pulled a plastic hand from his pack. Each of the twenty-seven bones poked precise and accurate. It worked. Rosie laughed.

"You are a sick, sick man."

"Gotta make sure everyone's paying attention." Patrick stuffed the hand back into his pack.

"You going to tell them about the guy who claimed to be Ezra's high school buddy?"

"First chance I get." They headed for the cluster of screaming-yellow shirts in front of the ranger station. "That guy stunk of money and lies."

"Nobody leaves," Mack hollered as he climbed into his truck. "Everybody stays right here." Jed Turner had found a body. Great. Mack needed details. He wanted facts, and he didn't buy that Turner's radio wasn't transmitting. No way the grandstander couldn't call or have the Com Center relay. Turner had information, and he was never one to relinquish whatever morsel of power he managed to come by. The initial transmission had been garbled and then Layne's phone had dropped the call, but the young man had caught that there was a body in Ezra's camper. Turner was on his way to brief them.

Mack had been about to instruct Layne to use his cell phone in the magic corner and get the scoop when he realized what he needed to do. This had to be handled in person. No way was Mack going to allow Jed Turner to waltz in and commandeer his search.

"Sir, wait." Layne ran up to the truck.

Mack lowered his window. "Yes, Layne?"

"There's been a sighting from somewhere out east. A man called to say Ezra bought gas there yesterday."

"Let me guess—the Town Pump in Shelby."

Layne checked his notes. "That's correct, sir."

"He sees everyone who goes missing in the park. Good guy. A bit touched. Used to work maintenance until his addictions took over and the place ran out on him. You can cross that one off your list."

"Ran out on him, sir?"

"Glacier's a powerful place. Sometimes it's done with people, collapses out from under them. They're forced to move on. I like to think it culls the riffraff."

Layne looked bewildered and lifted his hand. "One more thing."

"Yes, Layne."

"Vera saw Liz last night at the ATM outside the grocery store. She said it was around midnight."

Mack held his breath.

"Liz had made a withdrawal. Vera described," Layne consulted his pocket notebook, "what 'looked like a lot.'"

"Why would Liz need cash in the backcountry?"

"Difficult to fathom, sir."

Had she paid someone to pour bait on Ezra's tent? He was about to take off when an idea struck. "May I borrow your phone?"

Layne pulled it from his pocket and handed it through the window slowly.

"What is it, Layne?"

"My mom usually calls about now."

Mack reined in his smile. "I'll probably let that go to voicemail."

As Layne stepped back, Mack gunned the truck. Gravel roostertailed. The road bisected a meadow. Prairie smoke grew thick. The breeze rushed the tall grasses, causing them to lift and dip in waves. He'd have cell reception on top of the ridge. Sandy was working the Com Center. She'd tell him anything he wanted to know. And since he'd be on a phone and not the park radio, he could control exactly who knew what instead of everything going out parkwide to every ranger station, volunteer, and anyone with a scanner.

Dear Sandy would also light a fire under the lab tech analyzing the bear scat. She could get a commitment to tackle that the minute it came through their door. Turner finding Ezra's body where he had raised at least as many questions as it answered. How had he gotten back to his camper, and why? Had he hiked or found a ride? Had he been injured? How had he died?

Mack swung the truck off the gravel and onto the highway. He accelerated. The vehicle scaled the hill toward Red Blanket Ridge, the site of Blackfeet tree burials for countless generations. Spooks ran rampant up there. Strange things happened. Mountain lions dead with no sign of what had killed them. Osprey nests tattered on the ground. Distinct tracks, animal and human, pressed deep into the mud until they suddenly stopped as if whatever made them had shape-shifted and flown away. The thoughts shivered Mack's spine. He pressed the pedal harder.

The sun lifted high enough to fend off the morning chill and wash the mountains in white light. Patrick marveled at how, even with everyone dressed in yellow shirts and green pants, he could still identify the groups clustered in front of the cabin. The Native admin woman wore street clothes with her Nomex shirt unbuttoned and patiently walked searchers through completing their red dogs. Aviator shades obscured the eyes of the law enforcement rangers. They all sported Park Service–issue Nomex over their Kevlar vests, heavy-looking duty belts with guns and tools and expandable batons known as ASPs, and don't-mess-with-me expressions. The men wore buzz cuts. The women threaded smooth ponytails through the backs of their Park Service ball caps. Patrick fought the urge to approach them and say, "Can I touch your ASP?"

The backcountry permit writers and entrance station folks, pseudo rangers who packed nothing more deadly than a tuna sandwich, buzzed with happiness at being included. Patrick caught snatches of their conversation: "I hope I get to ride in a chopper." "I've never seen a dead body." "What if a bear ate him? Consumed him. We might never know." The trail crew folks looked weathered, hungover, and somber. Patrick spotted the trails guy who wore glasses, the one he'd seen flinging tree ID tags into the stream. He stood next to his boss, the legendary Roberts. The two men fidgeted. Patrick figured they itched to get hiking, and he could relate. He watched Clancy skirt the crowd, her mouth taut and downturned, her eyes bright and sad. She was short, maybe five feet, and probably didn't weigh much over a hundred pounds. When she approached, he instinctively put his arm around Rosie as if he could shield her from whatever news had Clancy looking so bereft.

Clancy did not extend her hand. Patrick saw how it quivered at her side before she clasped her palms together in front of her as if in prayer. She opened her eyes wide and said, "You and Ezra were . . ." she paused a moment, "together."

Rosie attempted a weak smile. "He's getting divorced. It's all working out, except," her voice wavered and she bit her bottom lip, "now this."

Clancy stood tall, breathed in. "The Park Service found his body." She kept her voice flat, her face blank.

Rosie shrank into Patrick's arms, buried her face in his shirt. He held her, rubbed his palm across her back.

Clancy said, "Mack left. He'll be back with the details. I thought you should know." She tugged her sleeves down over her hands. "I hate to have to ask, especially now." She kept her voice low so none of the others would hear. "Do you have any idea what might have happened?"

Rosie breathed out through her mouth, in through her nose. "He needed money, a lot of money, to pay Penelope for the house. The woman is nuts. I know she'd threatened Ezra. She hated him because he didn't love her. He had the papers. On this hitch, he planned to talk to her. Tell her he'd signed. They were over for good. He was ready to put her and the whole mess behind him."

Clancy nodded. "Penelope's not stable. Mack knows."

The shock hit Rosie anew, and she curled against Patrick. As he wrapped his arms around her, he felt the sun against his back and tried to channel the warmth into Rosie.

CHAPTER 19

DECEASED

◈

Mack swung into a pullout just over the top of Looking Glass Pass and flipped open Layne's phone. To his relief, Sandy was the one who answered at the Com Center. Mack made her repeat the deceased's name.

Beyond his windshield spread the Two Medicine Valley and its chain of azure lakes. Snow-drenched mountains stretched into the distance as far as the eye could see. Sandy agreed to contact the lab, get them to prioritize the analysis of the scat.

Mack needed answers, and he needed them from Liz. He had checked his office voicemail when he'd returned to St. Mary the night before. Liz's message had been received at 9:00 p.m. Caller ID indicated that she'd phoned from her office in St. Mary. Penelope had told him Liz had left the Atlantic Creek Campground soon after they'd arrived. Why would Liz leave camp only to cancel the whole reason for her hiking out in the first place? It made no sense. Liz made no sense. She hadn't since she'd secured funding for her study. And Vera had seen her at an ATM around midnight. Why would Liz need cash?

If only Mack could contact her by radio. That was his fault, too. Liz's request for a park radio had irritated him, another ploy to make her study paramount in his operation. He couldn't help but think about all that the Hudson Bay District could do with the money allocated for her study—outdoor education for reservation schools, snowshoe trips, geology expeditions for university students, a recycling program, more law enforcement rangers, bear management personnel, and on and on. Liz was not a Park Service employee and had no business with a radio. No way did he want her monitoring their communications. So he'd allowed her request to languish on his desk until all the radios had been allocated to law enforcement, backcountry rangers, permit writers, fee collectors, campground hosts—anyone he could find who might actually need one. But if he'd gotten her the darn thing, he'd have a way to contact her now. He knew what he had to do. Ranger Turner wouldn't like it, but that was why Mack earned the big bucks. Hah!

As though he'd conjured him with his thoughts, Jed Turner's patrol car flew past. Mack hit his lights and siren and whipped onto the road. Turner locked his brakes and swerved into a pullout. Mack was right behind him. The man jumped out of his patrol car, looking angry. "They were supposed to let you know I was on my way. Did you not get the message?"

"What exactly did you find?" Mack left out the *twelve hours after I asked you to check on Ezra's camper.*

"Rock-star death is my guess. Beautiful blond, swallows pills, alcohol, then pukes and chokes. Asphyxiation by stupidity. Too bad about the baby."

"Baby?"

"She'd trashed his place. I found her on the bed clutching an ultrasound. Bet she killed him and couldn't live with it."

Mack willed himself to stay still, not shake his head. Turner could believe whatever he wanted. Penelope had been adamant that Liz was responsible for Ezra's disappearance. Maybe she'd sought oblivion and taken too many meds, drunk too much alcohol, and died accidentally. But because she missed him, not because she'd killed him. "I've got a mission for you. I need Liz found and questioned."

"Shouldn't you do that?"

"Go. Get packed. Come to Cut Bank prepared to spend the night in backcountry."

"I need to write my report. I just found a body."

"You're burning daylight, Turner." There had to be more than one way to keep a ranger from taking over a search, but the best way Mack had found was to assign that individual an impossible task.

Clancy paced the length of the dirt parking area, glad to be away from the cluster of searchers. Her shakiness subsided when she moved. She kept her gaze trained on the meadow, pink with prairie smoke, willing Mack's truck to emerge.

She pressed her arms across her chest and moseyed back toward the ranger station. Her legs felt loose, like they might give. Once Layne had told Mack about the body, the two of them had run like scalded hounds. Clancy watched them go. After she found Rosie—the girl deserved to know—and broke the news, Clancy realized that if she tried to speak, she would sound on the verge of tears. She spotted Roberts and Nate milling about. Nate waved her over, but she needed to be away from people.

The shaking had started with what she had come to think of as "After." It struck anytime she visited her parents, anytime she was overcome with emotion. "Oh honey." Her mom's cold hands had clasped her trembling ones. "How much are you drinking?" Clancy wished the shaking was alcohol related. That would be a simple fix. But it had little to do with beer or whiskey. The edgy tingling had flooded her when Sean died and never truly subsided. The world was not safe. Catastrophe lay around every corner. She drank too much at times, sure. But just to find relief from the dread. She tried to tell herself she was fortunate. At least she'd had years with Sean, fun times, companionship, their family whole. But the good memories just made the magnitude of what she'd lost more apparent.

One drunken night at Kipp's, Roberts had gotten philosophical. "You get to live long enough, it's going to happen. Someone you care about will wind up dead and you'll never be the same."

Clancy nodded and sipped her beer. "But why did it have to be him?" she asked. Her boss shook his head slightly and shrugged.

On this sun-drenched morning, she realized her turn had come around again. From this point forward, her world would be different. And why did it have to be him? Why Ezra?

Clancy hadn't been able to see her brother's body. He had spent too long on the side of the mountain before they found him. Her mom had begged, but the funeral home director had said, "I can't let you do that." The sight of him could not have been worse than what Clancy imagined. Beyond that were the dreams—dreams that Sean was alive and playing a trick, the dreams that left her shattered all over again. Clancy had lost her brother. It was who she was. The dreams rattled her, cracked the foundation of her identity all over again.

Because she had not seen Sean dead, Clancy saw him everywhere. She'd be hiking, lulled by the motion, calmed by the birds, trees, and sunshine, and look up only to catch a glimpse of a young man, thin and of average height with a big head of dark wavy hair, and for an eternal moment, she'd believe it was Sean. Her chest would lift with recognition and relief. And for a breath or two, her world would feel whole once again. The elation lasted until reality rose like a building wave and washed her back into loss.

Sean had managed the hard part of the climb up Going-to-the-Sun, leapt the chasm below the summit, signed the register, and started his descent. Fear must have paralyzed him, made it impossible for him to leap the expanse, a couple feet of empty air, on his way back down. It had taken searchers days to find his body because it was not where anyone expected. Instead of hopping the chasm and heading for the scree field he could boot-ski and descend in a matter of minutes, Sean had attempted to downclimb northeast of the usual route. The ledges narrowed and the pitches steepened. Glacier's crumbly rock must have given way, and he'd plummeted. In the end, he experienced what he most feared. Clancy liked to imagine a freedom in that fall. She needed to believe the blow was swift and total, that his head dashed rock and death came before the pain could register.

When Mack returned, Clancy was going to tell him she needed to see Ezra's body. She needed to know in her gut, know in a way more certain than being told, that he was truly gone.

Sun glinted off a windshield as a vehicle crested the last rise in the road. It was bigger than Mack's. As it barreled closer, she recognized the washed-out green Park Service stock truck. Grady drove like a man on a mission.

Watching him bound down from the driver's seat sent Clancy's center aflutter. The space below his bottom lip bulged with chew. He grinned his lopsided grin. Above the band of his Stetson ran a jagged white line where sweat had soaked and dried. It mimicked the contours of mountains. "There now," he said, removing the kerchief from around his neck. "It can't be that bad." The silk was soft as he pressed it against her cheek. His arms wrapped around her.

"They found him." She felt numb, saying it again out loud. Grady pulled her closer. "I need to see him." Clancy bit the inside of her lip. She told herself she was not going to cry. Not now, not here.

"I'll go with you."

She pulled keys from her pocket. "Will you drive my truck?"

"Where is he?"

"Turner found him in his camper."

Grady stepped back. His face twisted with skepticism. "The camper you visited last night at Red Eagle? That's where they found him?"

A vehicle tore up the road, spewing a cloud of dust and gravel. "Mack's here," Clancy pointed. "He'll have the details."

Grady cracked a wan grin and mumbled something about lousy timing.. "I wanted to ask you to supper before you donned your robe."

A wave of exhaustion tinged with anticipation flooded her. The day already felt long, and it was going to get longer. At least now she had something to look forward to, a bright spot to move toward.

Mack was surprised to see the stock truck. Grady had brought the mules? Mack realized he must not have been clear. Not the end of the world, especially not in light of everything else. He walked toward Clancy and Grady slowly. "Penelope," he said. "She's gone. Turner found her at Ezra's clutching an ultrasound." He swallowed. "Apparently she was pregnant."

Grady's face flushed, pulsed with heat. He shook his head. "She was on her moon."

Mack thought about the pregnancy test in the top pouch of his pack. Someone was pregnant. Who'd the ultrasound belong to? "Maybe Penelope miscarried? Or possibly Ezra's girlfriend is pregnant?"

"Oh, man." Clancy looked stricken. "I thought it was Ezra. I told Rosie a ranger found his body."

"Ezra had a girlfriend, too?" Grady asked, clearly aghast.

"He had moved on. More than once." Clancy turned toward Mack, "I thought Rosie should know that Turner had found Ezra. I'm sorry. I didn't think. It never occurred to me that it might not be him."

Mack closed his eyes lightly and gave a small nod. "Didn't dawn on me, either."

"You should know, like a lot of folks, Rosie believes Penelope's responsible for Ezra's disappearance," Clancy said.

"You really think she was capable of that, hurting him, killing him even? Yesterday she seemed genuinely distressed, shocked by his disappearance." Mack nodded in Grady's direction. "Do you think she did something to harm Ezra?"

"I barely knew the woman." Grady said. "But given the right circumstances, we're probably all capable of doing something horrible."

"She was nuts, Mack, a bona fide lunatic obsessed with a guy who wanted free of her. She could've poured Liz's bait on his tent so a bear would . . ." Clancy gazed out at the meadow.

"Except," Grady interjected, "she was with either Liz or me all day yesterday."

"But not the night before, the night he disappeared," Mack countered. "She told me she didn't have an alibi."

"Rosie said Penelope had threatened him," Clancy said.

"Threatened him how?" Mack asked.

Clancy shrugged. "Ezra and I are friends. Close friends. We joked about his love life. The whole crew did, but it wasn't really funny. Those women didn't deserve to be reduced to anecdotes and one-liners to make Roberts and Nate laugh. Ezra knew I disapproved. There are things he doesn't tell me. He knows I won't always take his side." Clancy added that the first thing Roberts had said when she'd told him Ezra was gone was that the guy owed him money. "It didn't sound like a bummed twenty at the bar. More like real money."

Mack nodded. "Roberts headed into the backcountry last evening. He probably spent the night at your gypsy camp. Keep that under your hat. I'm hoping he found something."

Clancy told him that Roberts had hiked out. He was here, with Nate in front of the ranger station.

A ranger vehicle flew over the rise, lights flashing, dust billowing. "That'll be Turner." Mack sighed. "Say nothing about his pregnancy assumption being wrong. He's going to enjoy spreading that tidbit, and it might just prove helpful. Someone must know about the ultrasound." Mack started toward the cluster of searchers and then turned on his heel. "Clancy, I need you to take a sniff test."

CHAPTER 20

THE MISSION

The mountain behind Liz blocked the sun. Cool air hung in its shadow. She filtered water out of Katoya Lake into Muffy's collapsible bowl. Glacier's waters often contained giardia, a parasite that caused gastrointestinal distress. It was futile, she knew. Muffy would drink from whatever pond, puddle, or brackish fen they happened upon when she was thirsty, but the rhythm of the work calmed Liz, and she would do just about anything to reduce the chances of sharing her tent with a giardia-stricken dog. The bowl was full. Liz bit a fingernail. She was over six miles from the Cut Bank car campground, where Muffy had managed to spill half a bottle of bait. Off trail with her dog, Liz was as alone as she'd ever been.

When Grady came to pick her up this evening at the North Shore trailhead, Liz would not be there. He was a capable chap. He'd figure it out. No way was she showing up in the front country, not yet. Not for a while. This would all blow over in time, but it would not be wise to answer Mack's questions today. He could tell when she was lying. Not because of any special bond or sixth sense, intuition, or investigative acumen, she just didn't lie well. She would need to work on that.

Muffy finished a handful of kibble and lapped up water. Liz dumped what was left and stowed the bowl. Despite her layers and purple hat, she felt cold. Hiking would warm her. She pulled on her pack and started walking.

Weeks ago, when the sabotage began, Senator Donaldson's office had put Liz in touch with a local ranch owner, a friend and supporter of the senator's who they thought might kick cash her way for supplies and trail cameras. As she was visiting with the man, Ezra's name came up. It was a small world, and Glacier's was even smaller. "The enemy of my enemy is my friend." Even before she knew the extent of his involvement in the sabotage, Liz knew that Ezra Riverton was destined to get what he had coming.

He had messed with the wrong biologist. What Ezra didn't understand, nor any of the rangers or bear biologists, all the good ol' boys who thought they knew better, scientists who for years had flown and darted and collared, was that Liz's study was revolutionary. Handling bears had always rattled her. On more than one occasion she'd sensed that a grizzly she'd collared recognized her when she encountered it in the woods months, or even a year, later. It gave her nightmares.

One of the things she loved most about her DNA method was that they could estimate the population, track movements, and never interact with the bears. Yes, she had to kiss up to a conservative senator to secure funding. And yes, he might want to hunt grizzlies. He might advocate for his rancher pals being able to shoot predators harassing their livestock without stressful investigations and hefty fines. But what Liz was doing was bigger than all of that, bigger even than grizzly bear recovery. Her methodology would transform the field of wildlife biology. And she would not allow pathetic punks suffering misguided environmental savior complexes to wrench her work into statistical oblivion. Liz was not the bad guy here. She was the victim of ignorant people who did not understand science. It shouldn't be this hard. She just wanted to do her job.

As she started up the switchbacks to Pitamakan Pass, Liz wished she had a park radio. Her actions were bound to have resulted in a barrage of Park Service pseudo action. Mack and his ilk were best at planning and wasting time on reactionary meetings and not getting a damn thing done. It would have been helpful to hear the morning's radio traffic. The sense that someone might be pursuing her propelled Liz up the switchback.

Add the radio to the list. One more thing she thought Mack could make happen for her that he simply hadn't. Sure, he said he cared, claimed he supported her, but he never came through with what she really needed. She suspected that instead of working to find and cite the saboteurs, he sympathized with them. That day in his office, she'd been so upset. He'd just sat there making excuses until she offered him some incentive. People she trusted had turned on her and her study time and again. Without Penelope feeding hair-snag station locations to that ignorant hippie of a husband of hers, there was no way Ezra could have found the one above Atlantic Falls where Liz had discovered his headlamp. It wasn't even a week old. He had ripped all the wire.

After she found the station destroyed and Ezra's headlamp, Liz hiked to trail crew's gypsy camp. In their kitchen, her tree ID tags hung on a thin branch. A stob held her barbed wire. The sight sent her into a rage. She acted without thought. Penelope had told her about Ezra's tent—orange, four-season, pricey.

For the duration of her hike out of the Cut Bank Valley, Liz questioned whether she'd gone too far. She was scared. She needed help. She needed Mack. She still hadn't gotten her period. She chalked that up to all the stress, the hiking and skipping meals. It would be good to know for sure.

Frantic, she drove the gravel road and then the winding highway. She spent an interminable hour behind a struggling motor home. When she finally reached St. Mary, she went straight to Mack's house. She planned to spend the night, figure out her next move. But what she found changed everything. She had been betrayed for the last time. She knew now that her only true ally was her dog.

Liz and Muffy crested Pitamakan Pass and beheld the northwest side of Rising Wolf. The mountaintop jutted into a fat cloud. Far below her, the deep blue of Old Man Lake glimmered like a jewel. She turned from the view. Muffy scampered along beside her. Liz knew she would triumph. Somehow. She always did.

A couple miles from the trailhead, almost halfway to Atlantic Falls, Patrick stopped. He couldn't see Turner. He stepped off the trail and peed. Still no Turner. He took off his pack and pulled out an apple. He gnawed the core down to a nubbin, then ate that, too. He glimpsed the top of a Park Service ball cap. Turner plodded up the trail. As he approached, Patrick saw him blinking fast as if in pain. Sunscreen-tainted sweat was probably irritating his eyes. When the man finally reached Patrick, he leaned forward, pressing his hands against bent knees, and drew rasping breaths. "You win," Turner said.

"Didn't know it was a contest." Patrick swung his pack onto his back. "I'm just hiking."

"Those legs of yours, practically two strides to my one." Turner breathed hard through his mouth. "You're in better shape for this than I am."

"Riding around in that car all day's not doing you any favors." Patrick's attempt at teasing fell flat. Turner looked annoyed. Patrick tried again, offered a verbal olive branch. "Like Mack said, Liz will stop to riddle the wilderness with man-made materials and bait her stations. We'll catch her."

"I get paid for an hour of PT every shift I work, buddy."

Patrick laughed. Jeez, Turner was crabby. He was probably dehydrated, but how do you tell a prick to drink water? It had the ring of a bad riddle. Patrick's answer: You don't. "PT?"

"Physical training."

"You feel good about that? The American people's tax dollars going to try to whip your sorry ass into shape?"

Turner reached for his water bottle but couldn't quite grasp it. Patrick softened. Water would help. The guy was an ass, but Patrick didn't need to grind him into the duff, at least not all day. He pulled the bottle from its pouch and handed it to the guy, waited while he gulped half of it down, and then stowed it for him. Turner did not say thank you. Patrick stepped off the trail and swept his hand ahead in a magnanimous gesture. "Your lead."

Turner nodded, deliberately placing one foot ahead of the other. "Fool's errand, this one."

Mack had pulled Turner and Patrick aside and told them that their sole mission was to catch Liz. She had a big jump on them, but Mack reasoned that she would work along the way, collecting hair from rub trees and bait stations, affixing barbed wire and ID tags. Their orders when they caught her were to report in via radio and escort her out of the backcountry. Turner asked what she'd done. Mack said he didn't know for sure, but he needed details regarding Liz's whereabouts last night and the night before. He said Patrick and Turner would make a good team given how they brought "divergent experience and skills" to their task. "She has her dog, a Karelian, with her."

Turner started for the trail. Patrick waited till he was out of earshot and told Mack about the bracelet-wearing dandy who claimed to have known Ezra during his nonexistent high school years. "He asked where Ezra lived, offered me money to show him." Mack scrawled notes on his clipboard, thanked him, and pointed him toward the trail.

Patrick found the whole situation odd. Liz had her dog with her? Mack must suspect her of more serious infractions as well or he'd just wait to write her a ticket when she came out of the backcountry. Had Liz discovered trail crew was wrenching her materials and retaliated against Ezra? If she'd done something illegal, it could mean the end of that blasted study. Patrick grinned at the thought. Whatever the case, he was thrilled that the Park Service was paying him to hike.

"Mack's sending us to track down his girlfriend because he wants me out of the way." Turner had caught his breath and walked steadily.

"You still planning to arrest me?" Patrick asked. Turner continued in silence long enough that Patrick realized he wasn't going to answer. "Sunscreen stinging your eyes?" Still nothing. He tried a different subject. "Liz and Mack are together?"

"He might come across as the perfect ranger, a class A do-gooder, but he's got an ego just like the rest of us."

The man could not resist talking shit about his boss. "How long have they been a couple?" Did Mack know Patrick and his buddies had been wrenching the DNA study? Had he sent him back here with Turner as a setup?

"I know how it happened. Mack wants me out of the way so he can get credit for solving the case."

"How what happened?"

"The dirty trail dog disappearance. It was a murder-suicide. Possibly both accidental to some degree. The guy, what's his name, Riverton? His wife's pregnant. He's not happy about it. They argue. She pushes him off one of the thousands of cliffs back here. He crashes into Cut Bank Creek or down some rocky chasm, never to be found. Fewer than twenty-four hours later, she kills herself."

"Penelope's dead?" Patrick stopped. He had assumed the report about the Park Service finding a body was plumb wrong.

"Found her myself. Already cold." Turner turned to look at Patrick. "She'd ransacked her husband's place, dumped out drawers, emptied cupboards. It took a tortured soul to go on that kind of rampage. She died clutching an ultrasound. Tell me that's not related to her husband's disappearance."

Patrick was tempted to say, "That's not related to her husband's disappearance," but given that he and Ranger Turner would get to spend the whole day melding their "divergent experience," he went with "Ezra's girlfriend is going to be pissed." He thought about the bracelet wearer. Maybe he'd found someone to lead him to Ezra's trailer after all? Had Penelope surprised him? Had he killed her and made it look like suicide?

Turner looked back and almost smiled. "See. The woman had cause. Her husband had a girlfriend. Mack wants to take his sweet time, run a SAR, ramp up his out-of-the-office duty, pad his paycheck with overtime. But in the end, we could save ourselves a lot of time and trouble and declare the guy dead. The body's bound to turn up sooner or later. It's a waste of resources to search when we could just wait till a member of the public stumbles upon the remains." Turner picked up his pace. "But Mack won't do it, not until it's his idea and he can find a way to milk the glory. Always has to be the hero, that one. Does all the stuff no one else will, hires the good-looking city kid with no experience, works with the Indian assistant who takes four days off for funerals several times a year, dates Liz. The man's insufferable."

"How'd Penelope die?"

Turner shrugged. "Like a twenty-seven-year-old. Too many substances. Aspirated on her own vomit. No way for me to gauge intent for sure. The coroner will tell us more." The trail led up a hillside and Turner slowed. "You're going legit now? Helping law enforcement?"

"Man, you can be a dick." Patrick spat. It landed with enough force to raise dust. "Yes. I am trying to help locate a guy who is missing. I am not his biggest fan, but it could be any one of us out here, a turned ankle, a bad bear encounter, an unfortunate misstep on a dark night in the rain. And if it were me, I would want people to set aside their petty squabbles and find me. That means me telling law enforcement what I know. That means me hiking with you. And if you're not human enough to see that, you're going to have big problems being gay."

The man spun sharply, angry. Patrick grinned wide. A smile slowly lifted the corners of Turner's mouth.

Sun poured from the sky. The harsh light flattened the colors and contours of the peaks. Questions bubbled one after the other for Clancy. Who was the angry guy who had been with Nate, and what business did he have trashing Ezra's camper? Why was Nate helping him? Ezra must owe him money, too. Had the angry man come back, found Penelope, and killed her? Clancy decided to keep quiet about all of it until she had a chance to talk to Nate. The exchange she'd heard in the trailer indicated that Ezra had gotten mixed up in something dicey, and when they found him, she didn't want him having to answer to Glacier's law enforcement about it because of her. Mack kept information to himself. He hadn't told Nate he already knew Penelope was nuts, and he didn't want people aware of Roberts's camping trip or that Penelope wasn't pregnant. If he could hold his cards close, so could Clancy.

Mack carried a Nalgene bottle full of bear bait at arm's length across the gravel lot. He'd retrieved it from the locked toolbox in the back of his truck. She and Grady stood in the shadow of the stock truck. The sky spread blue interrupted only by wisps of high cloud. Grady asked, "How'd you get hold of that?"

Mack ducked his head sheepishly. "Liz must have changed the lock on the shed we designated for bait storage. My master key didn't work this morning, but my bolt cutters did." He loosened the lid. A stink, rank with iron and rot, lifted from the container. Mack winced in disgust. The breeze shifted, blowing the stench toward Clancy. Her stomach seized. She gagged and dropped to her knees. A cool hand pressed her forehead. Waves of heat washed through her as she heaved onto the gravel. She clamped her eyes and saw Ezra's orange tent upside down. The wind teased lengths of nylon, fluttered them like remnants of a flag. Clancy nodded at Mack. "That's it. That's the smell." Grady pulled her to her feet.

"It's also what kept the bear at site 7 and Layne and me busy." Mack placed a hand on her shoulder. "Take a day, Clancy. I have three of you going to Triple Divide anyway."

"Who else?" She thought of her bed, the down comforter, a steaming mug of Earl Grey, her book, an entire day of lounging in her marm robe.

"Rosie and Layne. I'm hoping she knows something and it'll come out during the hike."

"Good God, Mack, Rosie's a basket case, and I doubt Layne's hiked more than a hundred yards without checking a manual. Those two couldn't find a sign of Ezra if it bit them."

Mack's eyes were kind, his voice firm. "Our deal stands. Talk to your dad, Clancy. If he okays it, fine. But think long and hard about whether you really want to be out there looking for your friend, if that's really what's best for you."

"I'll go with her," Grady said. It had been his hand on her forehead.

Mack thanked him but said he had him slated for a different assignment. He took a deep breath. "We don't usually bring stock on search and rescues."

"Bet there's something you'd appreciate having hauled in, a few items you'd prefer not weigh down a pack."

"You don't hike, do you?"

Grady smiled and gave a small shrug. "Not if I can ride."

Mack tossed Clancy a cell phone. "Get that back to Layne when you're through talking to your dad. It works in a corner in the back of his cabin. If you can't find Layne, Vera can show you."

CHAPTER 21

NEW NORMAL

◈

Trail crew veteran Marion Roberts sat on the steps of the Cut Bank Ranger Station, popped two ibuprofen, rolled a cigarette, and waited. It wasn't a bad morning for it. Sunlight poured through the trees. Swallows dipped. Pollen rimmed the puddles. He watched Clancy and Ezra's girlfriend head down the gravel road toward the trail. The newbie ranger followed behind them in his Smokey Bear hat. He must not have gotten the memo that it was okay to hike in a ball cap. At least the kid had quit fastening the strap underneath his chin.

Roberts had not slept. He'd returned to where he'd last seen Ezra stowing their kitchen gear in a metal bear-proof box. As he pitched his tent, he realized that while he spent most of his summer nights in Glacier's backcountry, he did not do so alone. Camping with his crew, he wouldn't have jumped at the sound of an animal crashing through the brush, a mule deer that looked shocked to see him. He sat on a log in their kitchen area and smoked a bowl in the gathering dark, trying to quell the anxiety that rattled beneath his ribs. He hoped Ezra would show, but the place felt empty. He was alone.

He couldn't shake the notion that the money he'd lent Ezra had led to this trouble. Roberts figured it was cursed. He had a buddy who worked as an orderly in a morgue and lucked into gold, some rings and watches but mostly what he extracted from teeth. For a cut, Roberts fenced it all in Spokane. Flu season had been rough in the Flathead Valley. They'd had a lucrative winter.

He broke camp before dawn and kept his headlamp trained on the trail. His gut told him that when they found Ezra, if they found him, it would not be good. No way was he going looking for that by himself.

Roberts lit his smoke. Clancy and the others disappeared around a bend in the road. Mack wouldn't send them where they were likely to find anything more distressing than a meadow full of wildflowers and a waterfall. Mack broke free of the searchers and made for the porch. Roberts stood. "Hey, Mack." Exhaustion rimmed the district ranger's eyes. Roberts figured he probably looked about the same. "Ezra borrowed money from me. Quite a bit. I figured you should know. It might be a factor. Could have contributed to the situation."

Mack continued up the steps to where his pack sat by the door. "How might money figure into his disappearance?" He waved goodbye to Vera as she organized the day's ream of paperwork.

"You be careful," she commanded. "I am not training a new district ranger."

Mack hoisted his pack. It looked to weigh at least forty pounds. "Not exactly a member of the 'fast and light' movement, are you?" Roberts said. They bounded down the steps. "All Ezra told me when he asked for the loan was that he needed money for an investment."

"Let's see if I can keep up." Mack buckled in, yanked his pack straps tight. "What kind of investment?"

Roberts shook his head. "He promised to pay me back with a generous show of appreciation." The mass of searchers stood ready. "You know who started that fire, don't you?" Roberts had watched Clancy's bear-bait sniff test.

"I have a strong, if disappointing, suspicion." Mack waved Roberts in front of him and hollered orders as they went. "Let's go, people. Time's a-wasting. Our objective is to find Ezra. Today. Grady, wait till everyone's on the trail, count to a hundred or so. Then ride." Roberts had watched Mack pile extraneous items for Grady to load—spotting scope, sleeping bag, front country first-aid kit, and some electrolyte drinks. Mack made sure everyone felt needed.

Fastex clips snapped into place. The crowd grumbled and shuffled. Voices rose, some laughter. Roberts could hear Mack right behind him, practically in his ear, keeping up just fine.

Mack hollered, "We meet in the meadow. No one goes near that spike camp without my okay and their search assignment. You need to know which patch of ground you're covering. It's a grid search, people, not a picnic."

Roberts set a pace that would have them there in a little over an hour.

Patrick knelt to examine tracks in the mud. Trees blocked the sun. Moisture seeped from moss-covered rock and pooled in a low spot on the trail. Turner's face was blotched red with exertion. Now that they'd stopped in the shade, he shivered. Patrick wanted to give the guy a bit of a rest without rubbing it in. "My guess, she spent the night at Katoya Lake, her dog weighs thirty-five to forty pounds, and they have about a three-hour jump on us." He made up that last bit but thought it sounded good.

"Can we catch her?" Turner breathed deep.

Patrick nodded. "She's going to be stopping to vandalize the park with her barbed wire. You and your ilk would arrest and cite any of us who damaged the flora. But Liz gets paid to ruin the place." He started up the trail, forcing himself to walk slowly. "Do you know Ezra?"

"Riverton? Yeah, I know who he is. I work the same valley as Roberts and his crew, but as you might imagine, law enforcement and trail dogs aren't exactly tight."

"He's dating a friend of mine. I'd like him a lot more if he weren't."

"Well, this should all work out just fine for you."

Patrick poured power into his legs. They started up the switchbacks in the scree bowl below Pitamakan Pass. He was going to leave Turner behind, treat himself to a little alone time. He wished it hadn't crossed his mind, how things would be with Ezra out of the picture, how he might have a shot with Rosie. But his rule was to at least be honest with himself. Screw the rest of the world, but to stay sober, he had to connect to his true motivations. Hearing Turner say it made him feel awful, like his worst impulses were entirely transparent. Even a thick-headed law enforcement officer who didn't like him, batted for the other team, and barely knew him could read him like a children's book.

Her pack warm against her back, Clancy felt better hiking up the trail toward Atlantic Falls than she had all morning. Her thoughts came in the breezy way they did when she hadn't eaten. She felt bad about Penelope—what a waste—but hopeful about Ezra. She told herself that one death in her corner of the park was plenty. To her mind, Penelope's demise bettered Ezra's odds.

Lodgepole grew thick. Sun pierced the gaps. A squirrel rattled its incessant protest at their presence. Clancy had done as Mack asked and crouched in the magic corner of cell reception. Her dad talked about establishing a "new normal." He'd been reading books about grief. She wasn't sure exactly what a "new normal" without Sean consisted of beyond a gaping hole filled with loss, but if it helped her dad, great. Clancy listened as long as she could and finally told him, "When someone goes missing, we look for them. Just like Ezra and all the others did for us. For Sean." He agreed.

A robin swooped low over the trail. Pinedrops poked up through the duff. Clancy loved them. They had no chlorophyll and gleaned all their nutrients from the forest floor, tough little stalks of hard-won beauty, indicators of forest health.

"What was he like?" Layne called.

Great. Layne was going to use her and Rosie to pseudo investigate. He was like a little kid playing ranger. "Present tense, please," Clancy called.

"Yeah," Rosie chimed in. "It was bad enough *thinking* he was dead. Let's not act like it."

"If you had to describe him in a word, what would it be?"

"Passionate." Rosie sounded upbeat, hopeful.

"Oh, really." Layne snickered like an adolescent.

"Don't be an ass. You can't do that. Ask about someone who's missing and then mock the person willing to tell you." Clancy yelled to make sure he could hear. It felt good.

Rosie blew an exasperated breath. "I meant that he cares deeply about the environment, about grizzlies and wildness. He's an intense guy. But he's also dedicated and funny and . . ."

Stoned, Clancy thought.

"Married," Layne said. "I've heard that from several sources."

"They're over," Rosie said. "Getting divorced. He's signed the papers. It's good as done."

Clancy shot a smile over her shoulder at Rosie. "I called you guys his 'sister wives.' Penelope was 'Nutty Wife.'"

"How many of us are there?" Rosie sounded hurt.

Clancy wanted to shrink into the trees. She should not have said that. "He told me things to get my goat, rile me into a rant." But she knew some woman had fed him those lines of poetry. Ezra wasn't a big reader. Why did women like Rosie think men like Ezra would be different with them? It baffled her, the naive belief that a guy who'd betrayed previous wives and girlfriends would suddenly turn faithful. Women who believed themselves the moral saviors of badly behaving men rankled her. If only females were as kind and understanding toward each other as they tended to be with males of the species. The shitty way men treated women was nothing compared to the wrongs women perpetrated on one another.

Clancy bounded up the hill. The trail to Atlantic Falls gained elevation in only a couple spots. No one spoke. She pushed the pace, needing to stay well ahead of the throng of searchers headed in behind them. She and Mack had checked the Atlantic Creek Campground yesterday, and despite the area Mack had assigned them, she had no intention of hiking in that direction today. Even if Ezra had gone to visit Penelope, Clancy highly doubted they'd find anything beyond the campground where the poor woman had spent her last night on earth. She didn't believe Ezra would have become so disoriented that he'd hiked past the campground in that storm. He would have been anxious to get to Penelope's tent. Mack didn't think so either, he was simply trying to protect them. More likely Ezra had been waylaid by some catastrophe on his way to visit Penelope. And that was where Clancy was going. She planned to start at his tent site and search painstakingly toward the falls, retracing his steps. She hoped to find something before Mack and the grid searchers arrived.

"Who was it?" Rosie asked as they crested the rise and peered down at the wide, roiling creek. "Whose body did they find, and why did they think it was Ezra?"

Layne piped up, "That information's classified."

"Stop being a dick," Clancy called. This guy needed help figuring out where he ranked, where all new seasonal Park Service law enforcement ranked: somewhere below those who wintered in Montana and a skosh above visiting Boy Scouts. "Nothing around here is 'classified,' you dork. We're not the CIA and besides, it probably went out over the radio and every park volunteer from here to Canada knows. There's no reason why Rosie shouldn't." Clancy stopped and turned to her. "It was Penelope. Jed Turner found Penelope in Ezra's camper. When word came that they'd found a body, I assumed it was his. I wish I hadn't said anything to you about Ezra. I feel horrible." Clancy couldn't take the stricken look on Rosie's face and dropped her gaze. "I'm sorry. The news about Penelope is awful. It's a relief and it's awful."

Rosie's eyes went wide. "She caused a lot of trouble. But dead?" She shook her head slowly. Clancy started hiking. The horde had probably hit the trail by now. They walked a ways and Rosie issued a sharp laugh. "I can't wait to tell Ezra. We're free. We can be together."

Layne's voice was gentle. "We don't know how she died, but we know she was pregnant."

Clancy glanced back. Rosie had stopped. Her eyes welled. "Ezra was always saying, 'We owe nothing to the facts and everything to the truth.' I'll wait on the truth about that. From Ezra."

The temptation to tell her it wasn't the case, that Penelope hadn't been pregnant, ached in Clancy's throat. Mack had asked her to keep that bit under wraps. She could do a lot of things—hike all day with a chain saw over her shoulder, climb class 4 mountains, bake a huckleberry pie with an all-butter crust, close down the bar and be at the trails shed by 7:00 a.m.—but she could not keep secrets. She'd told her brother what she'd gotten him for Christmas every single year, told her mom when her dad had picked out a diamond necklace for her as an anniversary present, confessed to her dad the very afternoon that she and Sean had skipped school and spent the day inside the Alberta Visitor Center in West Glacier riding the fake luge and brushing sand off plaster dinosaur bones. Clancy put on a burst of speed to keep from blurting what she knew.

They crossed the plank bridges over the creek that braided through a broad wash. Cottonwoods towered. The air hung sweet with the scent of their buds. Water tumbled over rock, rushed loud through thick willow. A breeze blew in their faces. Layne hollered, "Hey, bear," every four yards.

"They know we're coming." Clancy was tired and hungry, and Layne was pissing her off.

"Given the conditions and why we're here, I think it best."

Clancy could've slapped him. Rosie was already distraught. She didn't need to entertain images of a bear tearing into Ezra's flesh. She didn't need Clancy asking personal questions, either, but Clancy needed to know. The ultrasound in Ezra's camper belonged to someone, and it wasn't Penelope. Try as she might, she couldn't recall the name she'd seen in the corner. "Are you pregnant?"

"God no." Rosie laughed. "I guess this could all be worse,"

CHAPTER 22

OFF ROUTE

◇

Patrick scampered down the switchbacks below Pitamakan Pass toward Old Man Lake. His quads appreciated the break from all the up. Rising Wolf loomed over the Dry Fork and its valley. According to what Mack had told Patrick and Turner, Liz and her dog should be somewhere between here and the Two Medicine Campground. Seven miles of rocky terrain, almost all downhill and ringed by Glacier's red, purple, and green mountains, home to mega- and microfauna in spades. Patrick slowed as he approached the first snowfield. Ice gleamed across the sun-drenched trail. If you slipped, you'd slide a hundred yards, build a healthy head of speed, and meet with rock. He unfastened his pack, dropped it to the ground, and slipped his ice axe free. Behind him, Turner eased his way down the trail. The weight of the pack pulled at the older man's shoulders. They would cross the snowfield twice more as they wound their way down the switchbacks to Old Man Lake. Wind rushed waves across the deep blue water. Patrick studied the snowfield and noted where the trail reappeared. A line of indentations across the iced-over snow told Patrick people had crossed it this season, but there were no fresh boot prints, no dog tracks. He returned his ice axe to the outside of his pack, swung the load onto his back, and turned and started toward the pass. He met Turner, who appeared less winded. Patrick hated to break the news. "Liz took a different route." Patrick pointed to Pitamakan above them. "We have to go back." The man's shoulders drooped. He drew his lips together, closed his eyes. Patrick stepped around him. Turner would be a while.

When Patrick crested the lip of the pass, the wind whipped with such fury that it felt like being underwater. It was as though the air moved too fast to draw oxygen. His pack straps slapped his face. He looked down at whitecaps on Lake of the Seven Winds. He didn't believe Liz was still there. She would have wanted out of the valley, away from its repercussions for her study.

He reached the snowfield across the trail to Cut Bank Pass. Fresh tracks dented the icy crust. The paw prints of a medium-sized canine traversed the snow above the indentations left by boots. Liz had headed into the Nyack, the wildest stretch of the park. Deadfall riddled the area. Thick timber blocked the sun. No bridges spanned its runoff-swollen streams. If Liz stuck to the trails, they had a chance, but if she decided to bushwhack, they'd never find her. Turner was going to hate it.

Clancy blew past the trail junction. If she followed Mack's instructions, she would've taken the right-hand fork that led to Atlantic

Creek Campground and up to Triple Divide Pass, but Clancy refused to participate in Mack's diversion. To have any hope of finding Ezra, they needed to start where everyone else was headed, where'd she'd last seen him: their spike camp.

"Clancy!" Layne shouted. "What are you doing? It's back here."

Layne's voice was no less grating when he was indignant. "This way, my friend," Clancy called.

"We have our orders."

Clancy stopped and looked back. Layne stood at the fork in the trail, his lovely face all distressed. Something about that trail junction bothered her, just as it had yesterday when she'd headed toward the campground with Mack. "Tell me what you think we'll find up there, Layne."

"This is the route Mack assigned. He is the incident commander, my boss and working to find your friend. Surely you have enough respect for him to do as he asked."

"Mack's a great guy, but I am not galivanting up a trail because he wants to prevent us from encountering anything distressing." Rosie caught up and Clancy continued, "Follow your orders." She looked at Rosie. "You in?" The woman nodded and pressed past Layne. "Go ahead," Clancy yelled. "Call it in. Do whatever you need to do, but we're going to look for Ezra where we might actually find him."

Minutes later Clancy could hear Layne muttering behind them. What was it about that trail junction? She needed to register something regarding that spot. It was on the tip of her brain, but she could not pin it down.

Clancy heard a thump, another definitive thump. A grouse flapped up fast beside the trail. Rosie screamed. Fear stung through

Clancy. The grouse's drumming subsided like a basketball giving up its bounce.

"Damn those birds." Rosie inhaled deeply. "They get me every time."

"It's how I hope to die. Grouse-induced heart attack." Clancy hiked as fast as she could. They tore past brush and flowers, grasses, sedges, and huckleberry bushes. The trail sliced through thick lodgepole. Usually Clancy found the shaded closeness of the trees comforting, but today it felt eerie. Shadows dropped deep as though obscuring some threat. Branches hung heavy with strands of lichen. Ezra had made all of them eat witch's hair one hitch. He boiled it, and before he allowed anyone their serving of falafel, he made them each take a bite of the green mush. "Tons of protein," he said. "No need to ever starve in the woods." The taste was earthy, the texture stringy. Clancy had gagged. But she knew Ezra was capable; he could find his way out here, survive.

The muscles knotted across her shoulders relaxed when she heard the rush of the falls. Finally. Clancy darted across the bridge below the waterfall without a glance at the rushing cascade of white. The handrail she'd peeled ran along the upstream side. Clancy didn't touch it.

"I hate this bridge." Rosie inched her way across. Clancy thought about suggesting she crawl but didn't want to embarrass her. The sound of the rushing water had its usual effect, and Rosie would do better without an audience.

Clancy hollered, "Hitting the brush." She plowed through the vegetation, making her way downstream. Layne would be along any minute. She needed some distance. Eventually she squatted at the edge of an open patch of ground. She relaxed and lifted her gaze, then shook her head hard as though she could dislodge what she saw, make it disappear. Her mind must be playing tricks. She needed to eat. Clancy finished, buttoned up, and stepped closer. She made her eyes focus on the shock of reddish hair flecked with gray, a patch of scalp still attached. Clancy nudged it with the toe of her boot, grabbed a stick and flipped it forward. The blood was dark, dry.

CHAPTER 23

CULPRIT

Through his binoculars Patrick watched Liz Ralston affix a length of barbed wire to a Douglas fir using nails she pounded into the tree and bent across the wire. Tree trunks where bears had scratched their backs, snagging hair in the bark, abounded in the Nyack's thick timber. Snags fell in tangled, impassable knots, and Patrick reasoned that only someone on the run, someone out of backcountry camping options, a sociopath, or someone like him craving solitude or planning to scale one of the Nyack's peaks would venture into this area of the park. His money was on Liz ticking most of the boxes. She probably wasn't climbing, but she must have done something that required self-exile. Muffy bounded up and down the trail, her nose to the ground. The dog seemed as thrilled to be here as he was. So far Patrick had seen the tracks of wolverine, grizzly, and black bear. He'd spotted a pair of mountain lion kittens clutching a tree trunk and, until Liz, no other humans. It was his kind of place.

Patrick dropped to a crouch as Muffy ran toward him, barking wildly. "Hey girl," he said in an easy, low voice that worked with dogs, little kids, and sometimes women. He drew his palms firmly across her head and up her ears. The dog's tail wagged, and she flipped onto her back so Patrick could rub her belly.

Turner approached quietly. Patrick handed him the binoculars. "Bingo." Turner smiled. "We got her. I've informed the Com Center of our change in heading."

"What's the plan?"

Turner explained that he'd lucked into a spot of radio coverage and communicated their new route. The Com Center would relay to Mack, let him know where to meet them and what time. "What should I tell them?"

Patrick said they'd hike out the Coal Creek drainage. "It's a trail, sort of." It wasn't well maintained but better than a bushwhack. "We'll ford the Middle Fork. Once we do we'll be right next to Highway 2, across from the Stanton Creek Bar." Patrick glanced at his watch. "Optimistically, we should be there, say, 9:30. It'd be nice to have daylight to cross the river."

Turner nodded. "Catch up to her. Make small talk. You know, the usual trail chitchat. I'll come up from behind and make the arrest."

"I don't like gay guys telling me they'll come up from behind." Patrick smiled.

"You're an idiot."

"It's part of your identity, right? Part of who you are."

"What are you talking about?"

"Being gay. Rainbows. Pride. All of that."

"It's who I am, but it's not everything. I'm also a professional law enforcement officer about to arrest my boss's girlfriend."

"But do you get my point? If I ignore your gayness, pretend it isn't there, don't mention it, don't make fun of it, I'm not accepting the real you."

"Well, then, thanks for mocking me, breeder. I feel validated. Be advised: We're headed into a radio dead zone and I am going to be way too busy catching bad gals to save your sorry hetero ass, so watch yourself."

Clancy scanned the ground, the trees, inspected the rocks, studied the creek, and did it all again. She ran upstream, back toward the trail, and spotted boot prints along the creek bank. She knelt to get a better look. A horseshoe arc of small holes curved along the heel. She set her foot next to the clearest track. The boot that made it was several sizes bigger than her own.

Layne shouted her name. Rosie called to her, too. A piece of his head. People survived the loss of a bit of their skulls. The poster advertising bear spray showed a guy with a meaty hunk of flesh hanging off the side of his face. He was standing up. He was fine. That guy had been mauled and was alive and a poster boy for pepper spray. Had Ezra not had time to use his? Clancy's eyes flitted in every direction. Her skin tingled. She turned around and around. There had to be an indication of what had happened, of where Ezra had gone from here. She climbed a boulder.

"What are you doing?" Layne shouted. "Did you locate evidence?"

Rosie was at his heels. Clancy nodded. She turned to point in the direction of the hair, Ezra's hair, still on the ground downstream. Clancy spotted it, a path of crushed vegetation stretched almost as distinct as the social trails they'd tramped through the grass on the way to their spike camp. It led farther into the trees, through huckleberry bushes and alder.

"This way." She tamped the image of a grizzly dragging Ezra's limp body across the brush and leapt from the boulder. Clancy followed the depression across the bushes. Behind her, Layne and Rosie followed. Branches broke, twigs snapped. Clancy's heart slammed against her chest. She lost the trail, couldn't see the path to follow. She eased back, studying the ground. Clancy felt it before she saw it. The ground tremored. A half snort, half bark. A dark mass streaked through the woods and disappeared.

Layne was beside her. "Holy . . ."

"Fire your weapon."

"That's a threatened species."

"Not at it. Just scare it."

Layne fumbled with his holster and lifted the .357 high in the air. He pulled the trigger. The shot reverberated off the trees. A sound akin to what you hear when you press a shell to your ear filled Clancy's head and hung there, rushing. Her ears throbbed. It felt like she was underwater and listening to the world from a great distance. The needles on the trees hung vivid green. Branches trailed witch's hair. A patch of sky shined blue. She closed her eyes, shut out the deep, silent color, and worked her jaw, swallowed hard. Clancy remembered the bear and threw her eyes open. It was gone.

"Stand watch!" Clancy knew she said it too loudly but couldn't hear well enough to gauge her own voice. Layne nodded and headed in the direction the bear had fled. She motioned to Rosie to follow her. Angry scratches crisscrossed the woman's cheek and forehead. "Look for any sign of Ezra—torn clothing, blood, anything."

Rosie nodded. Her eyes were huge, blank.

Clancy scanned the ground littered with deadfall. Brush, huckleberry bushes, and wild roses grew tangled in the downed trees. She saw Layne. He held his gun with both hands, feet shoulder width apart, knees slightly bent the way they'd probably taught him at the academy. Even from here Clancy could see the weapon shake. He turned slowly, his eyes narrow, his body tense. He stood atop a wide mound of loose dirt. It was dark, freshly dug. Clancy's heart sank, weighed by a slow, sad ache.

CHAPTER 24

AFTERMATH

Mack raced across the log bridge, staring at the back of Roberts's head. They'd heard a shot. *Why would Layne be firing?* He jumped from the cribbing, lifted his radio from his chest harness, and called. No answer. He tried again.

"We're in the forest," Layne responded. "I discharged my weapon, sir. A bear woofed at us." His voice shook. "I saw the hump. A grizzly."

"Where in the forest, Layne?" Mack ran up the trail behind Roberts.

"We're not supposed to use names on the radio. Only call numbers."

"I need to know where you are."

"About a quarter mile or so south and a bit west of the falls." His voice sounded steadier. "Atlantic Creek Falls."

They were off trail between Atlantic Creek and the spike camp, less than a mile from both.

"Clancy found something, sir."

Roberts heard Layne and bounded into the trees. Branches sprang back and slapped Mack's arms as he followed. They climbed over downed lodgepole, plowed through thickets of mountain ash and alder, huckleberry, and wild roses. The crushed vegetation gave off a sharp, verdant smell. Mack felt the hot rush of adrenaline. He could see Roberts ahead of him, hear Nate behind as they barreled through the brush and over deadfall. Branches snapped. Cussing. The vegetation seemed to swallow light. Ancient snags littered the forest floor. They fought to stay upright.

"It's him, sir." Layne paused several beats in his transmission, his mic still keyed. "We found Ezra Riverton."

"Does he require medical attention?"

"Negative, sir." His voice cracked. "Repeat. Negative."

Mack stopped. Roberts turned to him, and Mack shook his head slowly, one time. Nate looked his way. Mack walked up to him and placed his hand on the younger man's shoulder. "Go back. Turn them around, all of them. It's over." Nate nodded. Mack continued, "Retrieve the body bag. Grady's got it with him on the horse. Grab the wheeled litter, too. It's with the guys coming after the searchers but before Grady. Take your time."

"What should I tell them?"

"They probably heard unless they were in a dead spot. Thank them for their time and tell them we have the personnel we need. Once they clock out with Vera, they're free to go." He clapped Nate's shoulder. "Tell them whatever it takes to get them out of here. You'll do fine."

"Should we double-check? That guy's new. What if he's wrong?" Nate's bottom lip quivered.

"He's not wrong about this, Nate. Clancy's there. If Ezra had a chance, she'd be all over that radio asking for anything and everything." He paused. "I'm sorry about your friend."

Nate shook his head sharply.

"Go on, Nate." Roberts stepped closer. "Do as Mack says."

"What about you guys? Where are you going?"

Roberts said, "Remember this spot. Meet us back here." He handed over his radio. "You know how to use this thing?"

Nate made for the trail without answering, and Roberts and Mack continued through the blowdown. Mack spotted bright yellow shirts through the trees, low in the distance. They picked their way toward them in silence.

Once he hit the trail, Nate sprinted. Mack had said to take his time, but he had to move, had to run. He couldn't quite wrap his mind around it. Ezra was dead. Dead. People like them, people who skied and snowboarded out of bounds, chain sawed stoned, occasionally drove drunk, and ingested more than their share of substances, did not die hiking along a trail in the summer, even during a torrential downpour. A bear? Maybe. It seemed surreal. Guys like them most often lived to laugh about the crazy shit they'd done. At least Ezra had grabbed life with both hands—wives, girlfriends, weed, whiskey, snowboarding, and climbing—occasionally messy but never boring. Nate bounded across the bridge he'd help build. He and Ezra had worked together for four seasons. They'd gotten along, given each other shit. Ezra was funny and wild and now he was dead, and nothing would ever be the same.

In all the years Nate had worked for the park, first on the west side and then with Roberts and Ezra on the east side, no trail dog had ever died. Not for lack of risky behavior. It just hadn't happened. Even the woman who fell off the Highline Trail carrying a jackhammer and slammed into the Sun Road had lived. She stuck the landing, feet first and together, like an Olympic gymnast dismounting the parallel bars. She busted bones in her feet and ankles, but by God she lived to tell the tale, rehabbed like a madwoman, and returned to trails the following spring. Ezra's death would come as a shock. The news was going to shatter a lot of folks.

It came to him like the sun through the trees. Skip, the guy who'd had him by the balls for years, who'd made him search Ezra's camper, would finally have to leave him alone. No way would Skip risk his smarmy scheme being exposed. Nate knew too much, and it gave him the upper hand. He could send the guy away for good. Skip was jinxed, always had been. His money couldn't buy him free of it. He had shitty luck. With Ezra dead, Nate was free. Skip's whole cursed enterprise would screech to a halt. It seemed unbelievably fortunate and a damn shame all at the same time.

Nate heard the squawking radios and the chatter of the law enforcement rangers leading the pack. They acted all superior, wielded their narrow swath of power with a vengeance. He wasn't going to tell them jack about Ezra. They could figure out what happened for themselves or wonder. For once it was going to be Nate, a dirty trail dog, telling the guns it was time to go home.

"Howdy," Patrick called, his voice sunny. Liz jumped. Her eyes narrowed. She pursed her lips. He'd never met the woman before, only heard tell of her. She was not what he'd expected, didn't look like a ruthless scientist. She was sturdy with wavy dark hair and bright green eyes. She wore fancy outdoor clothing, the most expensive brands. *Cake eater.* "Didn't mean to startle you. Beautiful day for it."

"Why are you here?"

"Excuse me?"

Liz rubbed Muffy's head. Her jaw jutted, giving her round face an annoyed edge. The dog sat tall at her side. "What are you doing here?"

"Hiking."

"You're that guy from East. You climb. So why are you here?"

Patrick gestured toward Stimson, one of Glacier's six peaks over ten thousand feet. "You ever been up there?" He heard a sharp whistle behind him. Muffy took off. "We could race."

"Hello, Liz." Turner appeared from around the curve, a hunk of jerky in his hand. The dog gobbled and Turner reached inside his pocket for more, keeping Muffy close. "I need to know your whereabouts last night and the night before that."

"I don't have to talk to you."

"We've got a man missing and a woman dead. You know them both. Ezra Riverton and Penelope Keller."

Liz's jaw went slack. She ran her tongue across her teeth and looked straight at Turner. "Penelope's dead?"

"Where were you, Liz?"

She pulled off her work gloves and stuffed them into her pack. "How did she die? Suicide?"

"Why would you think that, Liz? Because you killed her husband?"

"I know my rights." Liz pulled on her pack, clipped the hip belt, tightened the shoulder straps, fastened the chest strap. "I'm not saying a word until I speak to my attorney."

"No time. We need to know what you did, and we need to know now."

"Last I saw her, Penelope was very much alive, flirting with my new packer."

"Turner found her this morning in Ezra's camper," Patrick tried. "Any idea where we should look for Ezra?"

Liz stared into space. "Ezra's gone?"

"I am not a patient man, Liz. Tell me where you were the last two nights." Turner gripped Muffy's collar.

"I camped at Katoya last night. I'm not telling you anything more until I've spoken with my lawyer."

"I'll write the ticket for camping without a permit and one for your dog. Where were you the previous night? The night Ezra was last seen in the trail crew spike camp?"

"You won't write me tickets for anything. Not if you like your job." Liz's hunched back and darting eyes gave her the look of a cornered animal.

"Don't make me shoot your dog." Turner drew his weapon.

Liz took several steps toward him. "You wouldn't."

Patrick looked at him in horror. "Jeez, Turner. Relax."

"Care to try me?"

Liz shook her head. "I didn't kill anyone."

"Glad to hear it. Now tell us what you did do."

"Like I said, I want to speak to my attorney."

"And people in hell want ice water." Turner tugged the dog's collar and rubbed its head with the butt of the gun. His voice came even and calm. "We are trying to save a man's life."

"None of this will be admissible."

"You're not on trial, Liz. Just tell us what you did so we can find the guy." He pressed the barrel behind Muffy's ear.

Dazed, Clancy went numb. Her hearing still wasn't right. She looked up, away from what she did not want to see. The lodgepole boughs curved skyward, lifted toward the sun. They appeared outstretched as though offering friendship or aid.

"Mauling. It's a straight-up grizzly mauling." The firearm trembled in Layne's hand.

"Put the gun away." Clancy's voice came even, calm.

"You know why bears bury their prey?" He paced, three steps toward the creek, three steps back, peering into the trees. "Birds..."

"Not now, Layne." Clancy cut him off. Rosie sat on the ground staring at Ezra's fingers caked with dirt, knuckles scraped raw.

Clancy said, "I'm telling you, put the gun away, Layne."

"What if the bear comes back?"

"They're here." Rosie pointed. Mack and Roberts moved slowly, making their way through the deadfall with care.

"We've got this," Mack called. "Take the rest of the day off."

"Rest of the week for you, Clancy," Roberts hollered. "See you at the shop on Monday."

"I'd like to help." Layne started toward them.

Clancy waited until they broke through the trees. "There's a piece . . . a part of his head and some hair, back by the creek."

Mack shrugged out of his pack, unzipped the top pouch, and

tossed her a roll of orange flagging. "Mark it for us." Mack nodded at Layne. "Good work."

Clancy reached down and took Rosie's hand, pulled her to her feet. It was going to be a long hike out.

Mack opened the main compartment of his pack and tugged a body bag from inside.

"I thought you sent Nate after that," Roberts said.

"Guy needed a project. He's too young for this. We'll make up something about needing two in bear country."

"Two? Who else were you expecting to find?"

Mack tossed Roberts a pair of blue medical gloves. "Girl Scouts aren't the only ones who like to be prepared." The men crouched on either side of the mound and got to work.

PART III

NOTHING TO THE FACTS

Tuesday, June 22, 2004

CHAPTER 25

WITHHELD

◈

Clancy stirred her margarita, leaned against the porch rail, and stared out at the mountains. The shadow of Dancing Lady crept over Lone Woman, the obelisk at its base. Puffy clouds billowed above the peaks while a wall of deep blue built to the south. Each salty sip of the drink quelled her urge to jump into her truck and drive Looking Glass fast with Merle Haggard cranked just to feel the heady thrill of narrowly missing a curve, of almost plunging over the side into the depths, and the glory of surviving, the wash of relief at still being alive, not suffering the sorts of ills as the people in the songs.

Grady hadn't shown. She should not have come herself. Ezra was dead, and eating a platter of Mexican food drenched in melted cheese and salty sauce seemed gauche.

"Clancy!" Marty wore a string tie, a pressed pearl-button shirt, and his cowboy hat. His open face ran with a confluence of lines born of wind and sun and age. Exactly which age was a mystery, somewhere between fifty-five and eighty. He was short, not much over five six, but Clancy knew him to be as strong as the guys on her crew. She'd seen him heft the metal kitchen boxes they'd mantied like Christmas presents. He hoisted the loads that weighed a solid seventy-five pounds against the mules, steadied them on a raised thigh while he balanced on one foot, and deftly twisted the ropes into knots that held fast. A packer's variation of tree pose. He'd push at the box once he had it on the mule, test its sway, and announce, "It'll ride."

"Looks like you could use another." He nodded at her drink.

Clancy handed him her empty glass. "I've never seen you in your town clothes."

"Taking my wife out to supper. She's still primping, sent me to get our name down for a table."

The hostess popped onto the porch and called a party of five. A bench cleared. Marty tossed his head in its direction, and Clancy sat. He entered the restaurant. Clancy watched clouds scud across the sky and tried not to think, just be. Marty reappeared, carrying two margaritas on the rocks. He plopped down beside her and brought his ankle to rest on a knee. "I heard about your friend. I'm sorry." He took a sip. "Awful. You were the one to find him."

Marty's words barely registered. Clancy stared at his boot. The pattern on the heel arced, a rainbow of pinprick indentations. "Where'd you get those?" She set her drink on the armrest.

"The boots?" he asked. "These are Whites. Top of the line. They've been hand-making them for over a century. You can find them at the ranch supply place or that Western store in downtown Kalispell."

"Did you get off your horse on the far side of the creek when you came to get us yesterday?"

Marty raised an eyebrow, "The mules got skittish right in there. Something had them nervous. I was lucky to stay in the saddle. You couldn't have driven a knitting needle up my ass with a sledgehammer."

Clancy laughed. Marty didn't. She asked, "Do you know anyone else who wears boots like that?"

Marty shrugged and cocked an eyebrow. She realized she might as well have asked if he knew someone who drank beer. "Smokejumpers, wildland firefighters, power linemen. A bunch of us wear Whites. Why are you so curious about work boots?"

"When I found . . ." Clancy clamped her teeth, swallowed the emotion that ached her throat, threatened to surface. "A sign of Ezra, there were boot prints nearby, close to the creek. The heel had that arch, like yours."

Marty leaned to study his sole, righted himself, and took a long swallow of his drink. "You get to be happy, Clancy."

She had no idea what that had to do with anything. "I forgot to tell Mack. I can't believe I didn't tell him. Someone was there recently, sometime after the rainstorm, someone wearing boots like that." Clancy jumped to her feet. "I need to call him."

Marty stretched out his leg and reached into his hip pocket. "Use mine."

"You have a phone?" Clancy would not have taken Marty for a cell phone user.

"Birthday gift from my wife. Not that it works worth a damn around here."

She grabbed the device, flipped it open, and bounded off the porch. She would call the Com Center. They'd know how to reach Mack.

"Forgive me." Grady ran toward her, removed his hat. He looked different, exposed. Sweat matted his dark hair to his scalp. The top of his forehead was lighter than the rest of his face. "Liz never showed. I've kept you waiting. I'm sorry."

Mack took the curves leading to East Glacier as fast as he could. He drove past Red Blanket Ridge and the trees that had held the dead and eased off the accelerator just enough to stay on his side of the road. He was headed for trail crew housing. Mack hoped that with Ezra's body recovered, Nate and Roberts would feel at liberty to tell him everything they'd been refusing to say. Earlier that afternoon, Roberts had done whatever he asked. Grim project. They'd worked well together, bagged the remains, loaded them on the wheeled litter, hiked them out.

Usually at the end of a search, even those that ended in a recovery and lacked the elation of saving the lost, Mack experienced a pleasant weariness. If nothing else, he'd alleviated the pain of not knowing for the victim's loved ones. He would have a beer, watch the fading sun rim the clouds in color and the blue bright summer twilight seep into the sky, then retreat to his bed and sink into a solid sleep. But this situation felt different. On the surface it appeared straightforward. Ezra had headed out in the storm to visit Penelope and never made it. A bear had gotten him.

But given the bait spilled on the tent and in the campground, Liz's study and the sabotage, Mack didn't believe it was that simple.

Bears killed people, but rarely, and usually only as a means of protecting either cubs or a food source. Mack hadn't found evidence of either. Glacier's bear management policy dictated that he kill the bear. He vowed to postpone that unpleasantness. If he could prove something else had happened and Ezra had already been dead when the bear buried him, no animal would have to die.

As he crested the top of Looking Glass Pass, he hit a stretch of gravel that bounced the truck toward the edge. He overcorrected, veered into the opposite lane for a moment. Mack thought about Liz. What were they going to do if she was pregnant? Barring any new information, all the evidence pointed to her. Using her bear bait as a weapon, she'd become her own worst enemy. He wished he'd been able to speak to her on Turner's radio, but when he and Patrick had dropped into the Nyack, they'd entered what was largely a radio dead zone. Ever since Mack learned that she'd gone over Cut Bank Pass instead of down to Old Man Lake, he had wondered if Liz knew the area lacked communication and headed there intentionally.

Pockets of reception existed in the Nyack. Maybe Turner would find one and the Com Center would relay an update. The sky to the south was an angry blue. Mack hoped they could beat the weather.

Layne had been waiting for Mack at the trailhead. The kid was a wreck. Finding a body wasn't easy on anybody, and Layne felt chagrined about standing on the mound that held the remains. The young man needed to feel useful, and Mack needed to interview trail crew. So he sent Layne to collect Turner, Patrick, and Liz as they came off the trail.

One thing he knew for certain: Roberts and Nate had information they'd thus far refused to share. Mack was going to find out what that was and then deal with his girlfriend. He accelerated out of a curve and sped down the straightaway.

CHAPTER 26

EQUALIZED

◆

Patrick studied the darkening sky and picked up the pace. They still had miles to go, several creek crossings, and the bonus of fording the raging Middle Fork at the end of their journey. Turner was ailing and having trouble keeping up. Except for Muffy, they were all exhausted. With luck, the rain would hold off until they were safely on the other side of the river and headed to town in a Park Service truck.

Liz had told Turner as he held his gun to Muffy's head, "With Penelope's help, that dirtbag Ezra was destroying my study."

Patrick pulled Turner aside and convinced him that they should get moving or they'd be spending the night back here. They made good time until they had to climb over or around the deadfall knotted across the trail.

"It's the great equalizer, isn't it?"

Liz was only a few feet behind him. She sounded wistful. Patrick figured she'd realized that her study, the culmination of her career, was over. "I'm not following," he told her.

"Take you and me, for instance," Liz continued. "It doesn't matter that I'm a doctoral candidate on the cusp of revolutionizing wildlife research, not here. This place doesn't care. Out here, I'm no different than you."

"But in the front country you're better than I am?"

"We occupy different echelons of the social hierarchy." She laughed. "You have to admit, if we both were to call Senator Donaldson's office, only one of us would get a personal response." Her voice was jocular. "Let's just say I have more resources at my disposal." She patted the logo on her jacket. "And better gear."

Patrick almost admired her unapologetic sense of superiority. He walked for a stretch, his ire building. "My pack's not loaded with a concoction of rotting cow blood. I haven't been messing with the king of the food chain. That might make a difference at some point." He liked to think the place would exact revenge.

He glanced at her and caught an eye roll so intense it forced her whole head back. "Judge me all you want. I have science on my side. Science and the power of the United States government. I am advancing wildlife research. So go ahead, sneer. Act morally superior, but guess what? We live in the real world, the world where knowing the number of bears is critical to managing them. Science rules the day and always will. Simply loving an animal, as sweet as that might be, is not enough to ensure its continued existence." She stopped moving. Her voice rose. "If you want grizzlies to survive, you should be helping me. Every last one of you monkey-wrenchers should help."

The trail led to a fast-running creek, and Patrick plunged into the icy water, not bothering to try to pick his way across atop rocks or logs. His feet throbbed with cold. His legs didn't obey his brain. He concentrated on one step and then another until finally he barreled out on the other side. He set his teeth against the pain and turned to see Liz waiting for Turner and Muffy. The dog strained against the lead Turner had fabricated out of parachute cord. He kept Muffy close, insurance against Liz making a break for it.

Liz grabbed a hefty stick, and for a moment Patrick wondered if she would brain Turner. "Let her go. She'll swim it if we make it a game of fetch."

"You bolt and I'll kill her. Clear?"

"Hurry up," Patrick hollered across the stream. "We've got weather moving in. If we don't move along, we'll have to ford the river in the dark and the rain."

Turner untied the lead. Liz showed Muffy the stick and then hurled it across the stream. The dog dashed through the water. Liz and Turner followed more slowly and with a great deal less enthusiasm. Muffy fetched and dropped the prize at Patrick's feet. He tossed it a ways for her. Turner splashed onto the bank and uttered a fantastic string of curses. He unfastened his pack and dropped it to the ground. "Blisters," he said. Liz plopped down a few feet away from him. She kept her pack fastened tightly to her body. She'd hardly taken it off. It looked heavy and could not have been comfortable after the miles they'd covered. "What do you have in there?" Patrick asked.

"We going to be here a while?" she asked, ignoring his question and tossing the stick Muffy brought her.

"What are you hiding?" Patrick asked.

"I always come prepared."

"As much as I hate to take the time, I've got to doctor my feet."

Turner had his moleskin, medical tape, and collapsible scissors laid out with surgical precision atop a rock. He peeled off his socks. His feet were a grotesque white and mottled with tiny indentations. The knuckles of his toes were red and raw. Quarter-sized blisters bulged from his heels.

"What will happen to Muffy?" Liz rubbed the dog's head.

"I'll take her wherever you ask." Turner offered, cutting a circle slightly larger than his blister from the center of a patch of moleskin.

"Mack's never liked her." Muffy flopped onto her back and Liz rubbed her wet belly. "I can't think of anyone." She looked up at Patrick. "You're good with her. Will you take her? Just till they let me go?"

Patrick shook his head. "Too much wildlife where I live. A dog like Muffy would harass the bears, chase the elk, kill the fox kits."

"How about you?" Liz looked hopefully at Turner, and Patrick saw how charming she could be.

"Park housing." Turner pressed the moleskin to his heel. "No pets."

Patrick pulled the skeleton hand from his pack, dug out a pair of wool hiking socks, and tossed them to Turner. "Those are my lucky socks. I need them back. Clean. No gay germs."

"I'll use the special detergent." Turner narrowed his eyes. "What is that?"

Patrick held the plastic skeletal hand and shrugged. "I wanted to make Rosie laugh."

"The plan is to incarcerate me and leave my dog by the side of the road?" Liz demanded.

Turner almost smiled at Patrick. "That is just plain wrong. You are twisted. And you need serious help wooing women." Turner pivoted and shot Liz a withering look. "We have to get out of here first." He finished padding his heels and pulled on Patrick's socks. They were a mite too big but loads better than what he'd removed. "If it comes to it, I'll see that Muffy gets to Martha."

"Who is Martha?"

"I would've thought you knew her, both of you being animal people and all. She's a vet with a practice between Browning and Cut Bank."

Liz said, "Vets euthanize homeless animals."

Turner laced his boots. "Martha works with a whole army of dog people. A Karelian like Muffy, they'll find her a good home." He whistled and the dog promptly came and sat. He fed her jerky and refastened her lead. Thunder rumbled low and distant. A shelf of gray cloud edged their way.

CHAPTER 27

HOG FARMED

Through the kitchen window, Josie Meeks watched light ease from the sky as she scrubbed a pan. Mrs. Thomas, the ranch owner who had faked cancer when she'd discovered her husband cheating, walked slowly up her trail and disappeared into the aspen. That was what had brought the trouble. If Josie allowed herself the luxury of blame, she could have laid it squarely at the feet of Fred Thomas. His inability to honor his marriage vows led him to attempt to assuage his guilt when he thought Maureen had taken ill. He'd hired Ezra Riverton to build a private trail, a place that his wife with her fragile immune system could hike while avoiding Glacier's crowds and their germs. Mr. Thomas had cheated for years, bringing women with him to the ranch, the place she and Grady and their parents worked. They'd interpreted Mrs. Thomas's inaction as tacit approval. Turned out, she'd simply been busy raising their three kids and had trusted Fred. They were still married, for now, but Mrs. Thomas called the shots. She'd given Josie's parents a raise.

She didn't blame Mrs. Thomas, not even for pretending to have cancer. Josie knew shame and the lengths to which one would go to escape it. She glanced at the book on the counter. Her dad had gotten it for her. It showed development week by week, compared her baby's growth to various fruits. Beyond the window, pink gathered along the edges of the clouds and a house sparrow sang as though the very spinning of the earth, the rising and setting of the sun depended upon its song.

The phone rang. It was Grady calling from outside the diner in East Glacier. He told her he'd been part of a search that had found Ezra's body. "Bear got him." As she hung up, Josie welled with relief.

It had been that day, the day that happens every April where the plains stretch up to meet the mountains, when the sun holds real warmth and radiates powerfully enough to raise color on bare skin. Josie had mucked stalls in a T-shirt, and her arms felt cold and tender inside the sleeves of her hoodie. Her face felt hot, sun-kissed. She'd come to the bar for a carry-out pizza and stayed. A band played honky-tonk. The beer tasted good. She didn't figure she needed to tell anyone she wasn't old enough to legally drink it.

As Josie drained her glass, another full one appeared. The trail builder said he wintered in Whitefish. "A town with more money than sense," Josie said. That was what her dad called it. Josie had loved the place the time her family had visited. Even in February,

Christmas boughs and bows and bells hung from lampposts and swung high across the road. Snow collected along their edges, just piled there soft and silent. There was no wind. As her family drove through downtown, they saw people wearing furs and big Western hats, and that was when her father said it. "This town's got more money than sense."

In the bar that April night, the trail builder laughed like she'd said something funny, and Josie guessed maybe she had. Her mind felt loose. She wanted to dance. The band played a two-step, the sort she and her dad danced to across the kitchen when he'd had a couple but before he'd had too many. As though he could read her mind, Ezra took her hand and led her onto the floor. He danced crazy without touching her. She glided and twirled, and it was fun. The band played fast and they moved with the music and the beer flowed and everything Ezra told her, his mouth so close to her ear that his breath tickled, struck Josie as hilarious. They yelled over the music about bears and the park and Whitefish in the winter, the rough bunch of ranch hands Ezra roomed with, and the trail Mr. Thomas had hired him to build for Mrs. Thomas because she had the cancer and no immune system.

Josie told him about Richard Hugo and the poems her mom read to them as they drove to distant Montana towns for rodeos and stock shows and sometimes, just because. She told him, "The day is a woman who loves you." She said, "We owe nothing to the facts and everything to the truth."

The lights that signaled closing hurt Josie's eyes. Panic lifted in her belly. Her dad and brother were off moving cows, but her mom would be worried.

The night felt damp and cold, colder than it would have had the day not been warm. Josie shivered as she found her truck. Ezra lifted the keys from her hand and drove them to the bunkhouse. Stars scattered thick, like fresh gravel. She started across the patchy snow and wind-worn ice toward home. She slipped. Slammed down hard. Ezra took her hand and led her inside, into his room.

Josie awoke to a dry mouth, throbbing head, and spotty memories of smoking, or trying to, from a tube of red glass that reminded her of a hummingbird feeder. She remembered kissing, the roughness of Ezra's beard and thickness of his tongue, the warmth of his skin on hers, his man smell. He pushed and pushed, pressed his heaviness inside. It hurt, but she didn't want to say. She remembered pain, a sharpness that felt like it could split her in two. Finally, he emitted a low animal sound and finished. She bled. And then nothing. She didn't remember anything more.

She gathered her clothes, heard guys talking. An excited voice. "You won, man! Money's all yours."

"Shut up, you asshole. She's still here."

Josie realized with a dry shriveling in her center that she'd been hog farmed. She'd heard the term in the barn, the hired hands slapping at each other and laughing. She'd made Grady explain it. All the guys threw in money. Whoever slept with the ugliest girl won.

Josie had brown eyes, thick hair, and her mother's cheekbones. She would have been completely forgettable, a noncontender, if not for the puckered scar that ran above her lip to her nose. She pulled her sweatshirt hood forward, looked down, and stepped into the hall. She dashed, pushed her feet into her boots, and flung the door wide. Ezra hollered something. She bolted. Sunlight screamed from the sky, careened off the crusted mounds of dirty snow.

Josie chewed on her hoodie string as she stepped into the new house. They still called it that even though it'd been five summers since her dad had threatened to quit and Mr. Thomas had sent their new home on two flatbeds. Her mom pressed a cool hand to Josie's forehead. "Get yourself a shower." Josie would've preferred her mom to yell, chastise her, give her shame something to defend against, but she did not.

Josie got sick that day. She got sick again several weeks later, just when she'd started to feel better. The shame and regret had burned away with hard work, school, sunshine, and the blooming of buttercups. Heat rose to her face whenever she so much as glimpsed Ezra beyond the barn, tools over his shoulder, headed for the aspen. They had not spoken. She hoped they never would. Ezra finished the trail and left, and she told herself she never had to see him again, and she almost believed it.

When she threw up, Josie knew she didn't have the flu, but that was what she told her mom so she could stay home and fret. She couldn't see her way out of the situation. There were places—probably in Missoula, maybe in Whitefish. But Josie knew that even if she could muster the energy and make the arrangements, she couldn't go through with it. She sank into despair. Nothing relieved it—not the massive spring storm that dumped three feet of heavy, wet snow, not the crescendo of chorus frogs lifting off the pond once it melted, not the trill of a northern flicker that continued long after you thought it had to end.

Clouds pressed low over the mountains. The wind whipped catkins from the aspen. Her mom waved and called out the car window for them to be good. It was Memorial Day weekend, and her parents were headed to Great Falls for fencing supplies. Josie clamped her teeth and waved back. Grady saddled up and rode out to check cows.

Josie scanned each stall, made sure no animals were present, and drove the old truck inside. She slid the barn doors closed and found the hose her mom used to water her barrels of pansies. The barn smelled of hay and manure, dust and dirt and animals. Dull light eased through the windows. She climbed in on the passenger side to make things easier later and listened to the wind. She did not feel sad. Calm enveloped her. She breathed deeply. She thought about the trip her family had taken to Whitefish one winter, how the snow had collected on the Christmas boughs, piled on the roofs of houses as they sat warm and well lit, amid the stillness.

Grady returned. He'd forgotten his chew. He noticed the barn doors closed, the truck gone. "Why?" he asked as he drove her to Browning and the hospital. Josie told him everything, starting with her plan to get pizza and take it home to eat on the stoop and watch for birds. Instead, she'd met up with the ranch hands and the trail builder and they'd convinced her to stay and have a beer. She told him what she'd heard them say the next morning and watched anger draw Grady's back straight. She told him, though she didn't believe it, that the trail builder probably wasn't a horrible person, he'd just gotten caught up with the wrong bunch, the hands from Havre, the guys their dad ran off as soon as they'd finished the spring work.

Grady wasn't having it. "Decent people don't play games like that."

"I'm pregnant." She blurted it before she could change her mind. She watched the shame and knowledge of what this news would do to their parents set his jaw. The land rose and dipped, lifted green in places while stubborn bits of snow clung to the shadows. He reached over and set his palm on her leg, gave it a squeeze. His touch, the warmth of his hand, caused something inside her to lift.

Grady told the doctor about the baby, and the doctor ordered an ultrasound. Josie mustered the courage to ask the technician, who was big and older and Blackfeet and the only other person in the room, if he could see the baby's lip, if he could tell if it was going to be like hers.

"Not like yours," he told her with a lift of his chin. "Perfect in its own way."

Josie knew it was the sort of line that would cause her dad to sneer, say something like "Laying it on a bit thick, aren't you?" But the technician knew why she was there, knew she'd been hurting, and she was grateful for his kindness. She lay back and stared at the screen, listened to the hummingbird-fast *whoosh* of her baby's heart.

And now, on this summer evening weeks later, Josie felt free—free from the fear of running into Ezra, the dread that he might try to take her baby or be part of its life. She'd wanted him gone from this earth, had prayed for as much. She grabbed a blanket and burst out the door. Josie, who had spent her whole life trying not to be seen because her lip made people uncomfortable and she did not want their pity, spread her quilt across the ground. Planks of light stretched from behind the mountains. Even though Mrs. Thomas, the hands, and her parents might see, she lay on her back and raised the hem of her shirt, pressed the waist of her pants low. She wanted her plum-sized baby to know the beauty of this day giving way to night and the glimmer of the first star.

CHAPTER 28

WHAT PASSES FOR LOVE

F lotsam littered the floorboard of Grady's truck, insurance cards and junk mail, a thick metal ring, possibly from a bridle, a broken Barenaked Ladies CD—nothing out of the ordinary, but Clancy found it all riveting. She collected the tidbits of information the way she did small treasures like heart-shaped pebbles, snail shells and bits of wasp nests. Grady was a fan of the Ladies, was a State Farm customer, and got his mail at a post office box in Babb. His last name was Meeks, and he wasn't tidy. Her margarita buzz had mostly subsided, but when Grady offered to drive her home and help retrieve her truck in the morning, she accepted and felt drunk all over again.

They'd had drinks with Marty. Grady slugged an overpriced lemonade while they talked about the search, where they'd found Ezra, bears, Liz, her study, mules, the packing schedule, and a job opening in the barn that Marty said would suit Grady. "Get you out from under the thumb of that rich guy." The alcohol lulled Clancy into a sense that the world could wait. She handed Marty his phone without bothering to use it. The hostess at the Mexican place told them it'd be at least an hour until they got a table, so Clancy and Grady walked over to the diner while Marty stayed on the porch and waited for his wife to join him. After they ordered, Grady stepped out to use the pay phone and check in with his family. He wasn't gone long.

Clancy watched him consume a loaded double bison burger, fries, breaded mushrooms, and two slices of pie, one apple and one berrylicious. He mocked her chef salad as "hardly enough to make a turd." It felt good to laugh.

When they got to his truck, he told her he'd be right back and dashed into the Mexican place with a thermos. Clancy was giddy. The combination of alcohol and attraction and the prospect of watching the sunset together at Two Med had her awash in happiness. Guilt wormed its way between her and her joy, but she tamped it down with the thought that Ezra, more than most, would discourage any sort of maudlin vigil or moratorium on pleasure.

The truck door flew open, and Grady held the thermos aloft in triumph. "Margaritas."

"You don't drink." Clancy laughed.

Grady grinned wide. "You do." He loosened the lid and poured it full.

Clancy sipped. They'd added the salt straight to the mix. It was the perfect combination of savory and sweet tinged with the flavor of coffee and she was tempted to down the whole thing. "Are you trying to get me drunk?"

"Nobody'd hold it against you. Not after the day you had."

The sun angled warm yellow light through the pickup window. Grady buckled in and they were off. As they passed the East Glacier Ranger Station, Clancy spotted Mack's truck parked in front of Park

Service housing. "Turn," she hollered, pointing right. "I need to talk to Mack." Grady swung the truck around the corner.

"Back there." A large gravel lot surrounded the trails shed. Clancy drained her drink and screwed the cup back on the thermos.

"You sure you want to talk to law enforcement?"

"Drinking's not a crime. I need to tell Mack about the boot prints near Atlantic Creek." The vehicle stopped and she hopped out. "You coming?"

He tossed the keys onto the dash. "What's Mack doing here?"

The evening held the scent of pine. The temperature was dropping with the sun. Clancy wished she'd thought to grab her fleece from her truck. She followed the sound of voices, Grady moseying behind. The guys were drinking beer and hanging out with Mack on the porch of the trails shop.

"Clancy!" Her name went up like a cheer. They were lit. "Grab a beer." Roberts stood and edged his chair forward as an offering. "Get one for your friend there, too."

Grady shook his head. "I'm driving."

"One beer. Nothing bad ever came of one beer."

"Leave him alone, Roberts," Mack said with a smile.

Roberts stepped forward and offered his hand. "Nice to see you again."

Grady shook hands all around and addressed Mack. "I waited for Liz. Gave her a good hour. Think we should worry?"

Mack slapped his forehead and said he was sorry he'd forgotten to tell him. Patrick and Turner were hiking her out of the Nyack. "Seems she switched up her itinerary. I sent Layne to meet them."

"They're going to ford the Middle Fork?" Clancy asked. The river would be raging with snowmelt.

Mack nodded. "That's what the Com Center relayed from Turner."

"Better them than me." Roberts popped the tops on two cans of Schmidt. He handed one icy can to her and the other to Grady. "You entertaining our Clancy this evening? She looks tipsy. Hurt her, you'll answer to us."

The color on Grady's face deepened. Roberts took it as encouragement. "Look, son, we spend more time with her than anybody. Don't take it personal. It's our duty to vet her suitors."

Clancy spat a mouthful of aspirated beer. "Only so you can mock me."

He threw his arm across her shoulders. "Doesn't mean we don't love you."

Clancy didn't mind. The affection felt nice. Roberts, probably like a lot of people, was easier to be around when he was good and buzzed. "Can I talk to you?" she asked Mack and tossed her head toward the trees. She smiled at Grady and told him she'd leave him to the wolves, but not for long.

Darkness gathered low in the pines. They stopped at the edge of the trees. "How are you holding up?" Mack asked.

Clancy shrugged. "I'm going to miss him. It's not real yet. Grady's a nice distraction." The beer was cold in her hand.

"You've had a bad run."

She swallowed hard, wasn't prepared for the flood of sadness. "When I found that," she stopped to collect herself, "bit of Ezra near the stream, I saw a bunch of boot prints." She took a sip of beer. "I ran into Marty on the Mexican Palace porch."

"Marty?" Mack asked, confused. "Marty the packer eats Mexican food?"

"How many Martys do you know?" She laughed, and the laughter smoothed the edges of her sadness. "His boot heel had the same pinpricked arch as the tracks along the creek bank." She looked up at the sky. A satellite glimmered, and out of habit she made a wish. She wished for time to reverse. She wanted to go on the climb with Sean, reach out and grasp his hand as he jumped the gap on top of Going to the Sun, boot-ski down the mountain, and drive him home, where they'd grill burgers and drink a couple of their dad's beers. She wanted to stay with Ezra to finish the dishes in the rain and wind and get him to play cribbage in her tent until the storm passed. She wished for no one she loved to die.

"You think Marty had something to do with Ezra's death?" Mack asked, perplexed.

Clancy shook her head. That was ridiculous. "I asked him if he dismounted there. He said he didn't. But he said something spooked the pack string near that spot." She repeated his line about the knitting needle, and Mack laughed like she knew he would. "He also said that lots of people wear those boots. Whites is the brand—wildland firefighters, power linemen, people who work outdoors." She went on to say how the pounding rain would have washed out prints, so the ones she saw indicated someone traipsing around after it had passed.

Mack tipped his head toward the porch. "Why didn't you tell me this in front of the others?"

Clancy felt like a rat. "Nate and someone else," she began, "someone really angry, trashed Ezra's camper last night. I went to see if Ezra was there, to look for some indication of where he might have gone. I hid in the bathroom while they ransacked the place. They've all worked fires, Ezra, Roberts, Nate. Any one of them could have boots like that." She felt weary.

"Any idea about what they were looking for at Ezra's camper or who the other guy might be?"

She told him they'd discussed a shipment. Something valuable. The angry guy, whoever he was, sounded desperate to find it. Mack told her that Patrick, the climber, had said an urban-looking fellow had sat next to him in the diner, offered to pay him if he showed him to Ezra's place.

"Nate's the one who knows. You have got to get him to tell you while he's loosened up but before he's too far gone." Clancy told him how the guys stopped making sense after they'd been at it a few hours. "The coherency window is closing." They made their way back toward the porch. "I know the bear fed on Ezra, but what if something or someone had already killed him?"

Mack nodded. "I had the same thought."

A red-winged blackbird called. The trill of chorus frogs filled the air. Clouds darkened the sky.

"You sufficiently hazed?" Clancy called to Grady. He flashed her one of his half grins. Her insides went weak. As they made for the truck, Roberts hollered, "Admin leave until Monday. Don't go showing up till then. You got five days to rest. Come Monday, work as usual."

Nate yelled, "Hey, cowboy, you forgot your beer."

Clancy raised her can and called back, "This. This is what passes for love around here."

Grady ushered her to the truck. He opened the door and held out a hand, which Clancy took as she climbed into the cab. Whoops and whistles rose from the porch.

CHAPTER 29

CONDITIONS

◆

Patrick's heart pounded steadily. Bear sign everywhere he looked—scat, tracks, claw scratches deep in tree bark, massive digs amid patches of glacier lilies. The clouds gathered and built creating a premature darkness. He felt tired and nervous and moved faster.

"For the love of God, will you slow down?"

Patrick almost laughed. He was trying to make up time because Liz had refilled her water bladder, which had added fifteen minutes to their journey and over five pounds to her load. She'd been so careful not to remove much when she rummaged for her filter that Patrick wondered again what all she had inside her huge pack. Was she guarding bear bait or something more sinister—a gun, cocaine, embarrassing photos of Mack to use as blackmail? If it were him hauling that huge load, he'd be cranky, too. Patrick called over his shoulder, "Only one way out and it's going to be a lot easier if we beat the storm."

"A laudable goal, but I have work to do." She shrugged out of her pack and dropped it between her feet. She extracted a length of barbed wire with the poky bits covered in duct tape from beneath the outer stuff compartment. She crouched and began the tedious task of removing the tape.

Patrick strode back, resenting every extra step. "I don't want to cross the Middle Fork in the dark."

"Who knows how long it'll take for this situation to blow over and when I might make it back here. They've probably found the bastard at this point and have nothing on me." Liz tugged tape from the barbs.

"What did you do?"

She stood and lifted the wire as high as she could on a tree that bore fresh claw scratches. She swiftly pounded nails and used her collapsible hammer to bend them over the wire as she held her pack fast between her knees. "I found Ezra's headlamp at a destroyed hair-snag station." Liz stuffed the hammer in the main compartment. "You'd think my boyfriend would be in my corner. I needed his help." She hoisted the pack and swung it onto her back. "When I got to his place, I found Muffy tethered and muzzled, defenseless. She could've been killed." Liz fastened her buckles, pulled the straps taut. "You watch, I'll triumph. It's what I do."

Patrick led Liz down the trail, a tunnel through the thick trees. He reined in his pace. Where was Turner?

"I spotted you hiking with that girl in pigtails," Liz said.

"You were watching us?" Patrick's skin crawled at the thought of Liz lurking in the woods spying on them.

"Awfully young for you, isn't she?"

Patrick reminded himself that he was being paid to hike. It felt like he was earning every penny.

"What do you want to bet that dirty hippie orchestrated this whole disappearance act to get back at me? He'll ruin my work any way he can." She was right behind Patrick. "But then, I'm not the only person he wronged."

Muffy barked. Patrick stopped and moments later Turner appeared. He looked stronger. He told them he'd hit a patch of reception and gotten an update. "They found Ezra's body near Atlantic Creek."

Patrick's thoughts flew to Rosie. She would be heartbroken. It would be hours before he could see her.

"It appears he was mauled," Turner said.

Liz started to speak but stopped. Her face drained of color. She pressed past Patrick and took off down the trail without a word.

"She's involved. Mark my words," Turner said. "That woman's guilty of something."

Patrick almost felt sorry for her. In the fading light, Liz faced a radically different future. A bear had killed Ezra in the valley she'd strewn with bait. Sabotage was the least of her problems. Thunder rumbled low, still distant. Flashes of lightning strobed across a bank of gray cloud. Patrick turned and followed Liz.

Mack jotted notes, his back stiff against the chill of evening. He hoped Nate and Roberts had information that would clear Liz, or at least provide another suspect. Nate said, "My other condition is that my buddy, we'll call him 'Ray,' never gets mentioned."

As soon as Clancy and Grady had left, Nate had pushed up his glasses, flipped his *Virginity Rocks* ball cap around backward, and started talking. Mack leaned against a post with his legs stretched out in front of him. He cursed the pinch of his Kevlar vest. Nate took another drink of his pale ale. "How many conditions is that?" He looked at Roberts. "Did I get them all?"

His boss gave him a nod. They both held beer bottles beaded with condensation. Nate slouched atop a massive cooler that contained enough alcohol to float a johnboat. And he had about as many conditions as there were beers in the cooler, starting with complete immunity for himself. Nothing he revealed could be shared with Ezra's parents, Clancy, Rosie, or the press. Once he told Mack what he had to say, he would prefer to never speak of it again. He would never, under any circumstances, testify at a trial resulting from what he said. Whatever law enforcement folks—park rangers, tribal cops, sheriff's deputies, highway patrol, FBI—Mack decided to involve, he could not reveal the source of his information. Given all that, Nate swore that what he was about to tell Mack was the truth.

Mack dutifully jotted it all down. He had no idea if he could make good on all he'd promised, but he would worry about that later. "Ray's last name?"

The evening cooled into the brief, magical stretch when the light angles just right and everything comes alive. Robins sang. Squirrels chittered. A fox slipped through the shadows. "Don't bother. You won't find him." Nate began with "Back in high school," and Roberts popped into the shop and returned unfolding a camp chair. Mack nodded his thanks and settled into the seat.

Nate told about the night he'd celebrated making the Olympic ski team and how he'd been drunk and stoned and wrecked a friend's sports car. He would've lost his spot on the team, everything he'd trained for, his shot at the big time and sponsorships, had it not been for Ray, the owner of the wrecked vehicle, who happened to be more sober and stepped up, saying he'd been the one driving. "Ray's folks owned a custom jewelry shop in Whitefish. They had money, hired a good lawyer to defend him." He said Ray's sentence was to perform community service for the rest of the school year. Ray organized magazines in the town library every Saturday, and that was the end of it. Legally, anyway. But Ray had him by the balls. He never let Nate forget. Favor after favor after favor. "When Ray came up with this latest venture and needed my help, I told him no. I wasn't getting involved. No way was I committing a felony, no matter how well it paid. I didn't want any part of it." Nate took a long draw on his beer. "Ray wouldn't leave me alone till I found someone who would do what he needed."

Questions churned in Mack's mind, but he knew better than to interrupt. He took notes and kept silent. "Ray's idea, and it's a pretty good one, turned stolen jewelry into cash." He told Mack how Ray traveled the country as a high-end closet installer and pinched the right pieces—tennis bracelets, necklaces adorned with precious stones, pricey earrings—nothing worn every day, nothing quickly missed like wedding rings. Nate stood and fished a bottle from the ice. Roberts grabbed one, too. Mack's mind reeled, trying to make sense of what a jewelry thief had to do with anything.

"Ray mailed shipments to Ezra. Ezra paid locals, all Natives, twenty bucks for their name, Social Security number, and phone number. He used that info to set up an email address and an eBay seller account."

"Ezra had internet access at his camper?" Mack asked.

"He used library computers in Columbia Falls and Whitefish. We get four days off between hitches." Nate said that when pieces sold, Ezra mailed them to the buyers from East Glacier. The beauty of the arrangement lay in the jurisdictional quagmire. The FBI wasn't going to prosecute a Native kid for a piece of stolen jewelry, and that was in the unlikely event that it ever came to their attention. "Ray reasoned that the FBI has homicides, disappearances, drug rings to investigate. They're too buried in real crime to care about jewelry."

Nate tipped the neck of his bottle toward Mack. "Ezra had the reservation connections and needed cash to buy his house from Penelope." It had been a great arrangement for all until Ezra missed a deadline. He failed to forward Ray his share of the most recent profits and hadn't acknowledged receipt of the latest treasure trove. Ray being Ray decided to rectify the situation. "Only Ezra was in the woods, and Ray's not a hiker. Too much dirt."

Nate stood and bounded off the porch to hit the brush. Mack felt vindicated. He'd known there had to be more to Ezra's death. Ray must have been the man Clancy had heard ransacking Ezra's camper and the guy who'd tried to pay Patrick to show him where Ezra lived. The waning sun further narrowed the distance between shadow and darkness. Birds fell silent. The breeze picked up, rustling the trees.

They grabbed fresh beers and settled back in their seats. "Why don't you want me to say anything to Clancy or Rosie?" Mack asked Nate.

Nate removed his glasses and rubbed his eyes. He looked straight at Mack. "They loved Ezra. They'll want to love him even more now that he's dead. This scheme, his involvement, would only taint their memories of the guy. There's no point."

"You and Ray tossed Ezra's camper last evening?"

Nate looked surprised. After a moment, he sighed. "You ever do anything you wish you hadn't?"

Mack smiled, gave a single nod. The kid had no idea. "The money Ezra borrowed," he looked at Roberts, "what was that about?"

"My guess is a mortgage payment." Roberts raised his bottle. "Whatever he used it for, I'll never see it again."

"Anything more you gentlemen need to add?" Mack watched the rain clouds gathering to the south.

"We found the shipment in Ezra's camper. Ray took it." Nate replaced his glasses and pointed at the sky. "Lightning."

"Do you think Ray had a hand in Ezra's death?" Mack might as well ask the real question. At this point he had a story he couldn't corroborate about illegal activity outside his jurisdiction from a witness who refused to testify to any of it and who had just told him the incriminating evidence was gone.

"Doubtful," Nate said matter-of-factly. "He's too squeamish, doesn't like to get his hands dirty, literally or figuratively. The chances of him venturing into grizzly bear territory by himself during a thunderstorm—pretty much nil. If you met him, you'd understand. He's soft." Nate drank his beer. "I suppose he could've hired someone, but he seemed surprised and frustrated when Ezra disappeared. If he'd had anything to do with it, he would have known Ezra was gone and why."

"Who would he hire?"

They looked at each other and laughed. "One of us," Roberts said.

"Did he?" Mack asked. "Did one of you kill Ezra?" The first drops peppered the ground. The smell of rain-raised dust wafted off the lot. Liz had told him the word for that, *petrichor*.

"We both probably felt like it at some point, like how when you're growing up you sometimes want to kill your brother. But no. Neither of us had anything to do with Ezra's death. We went to our tents, waited out the storm." Roberts's bottle clamored into the garbage. "I give you my word on that."

"Do you know anyone who wanted to hurt him?"

"That bear?" Nate shrugged. "Penelope."

"And Liz," Roberts offered.

Nate nodded. "Ezra waged war on her study. He didn't keep it a secret. He recruited folks to do the same."

"He was sabotaging?"

"Wrenching that study is an east-side pastime akin to golfing at the lodge, playing poker at Hook's Hideaway, and drinking beers at Kipp's," Roberts said. "Lots of folks had a hand in it, but Ezra paid the price."

"You two? Were you involved in the sabotage?"

Roberts's mouth twitched, almost smiled. "No visual, no foul."

"What's your theory on Penelope?"

Roberts motioned to Nate to hop off the cooler and grabbed another. "She fed Ezra hair-snag station locations. She was young. It's sad. She must have been torn up about Ezra disappearing, probably just got too wasted."

"Anything else I should know?" Mack asked.

The two men shook their heads. Rain pocked the gravel. Nate's bottle rattled into the garbage. He gave Mack a nod and dashed toward their housing. Roberts shook Mack's hand and palmed him a baggie. "Don't go wasting that on Liz."

Mack made for his truck. He didn't mind the rain. As he opened the door, light poured from the cab. He opened his hand. Several blue pills crowded the plastic corner. *Viagra. He could sleep with anyone.* He stowed them in the top of his pack next to the pregnancy test. Mack turned the key and flipped on the wipers. Hadn't Liz had a pair of Whites boots in her closet in West Glacier? Hah! He could always ask Roberts.

CHAPTER 30

THE CROSSING

Flames licked the paper, transformed it to gray ash that smoked and disappeared forever. To chase the chill, Clancy set lengths of pine atop the kindling in the stove. Grady poured her more margarita and raised his mug of cold coffee. "To better days."

"Better days."

"Where do you get your wood?"

Clancy tossed her head toward the window. "The shed." They laughed. She told him that when the campground maintenance folks cleared deadfall or dropped a snag, they bucked it up for her cabin and the evening interpretive programs. The margarita delighted her. It took all her willpower to not drain the glass.

Grady scoffed. "The government knows how to work it. No one can cut wood in the park unless it's them and it serves their purpose. They keep the rest of us in check, and the park's theirs to exploit. Never mind that in the 1895 Agreement the Blackfeet retained usufruct rights."

Clancy bristled. Was Grady one of those antigovernment, separatist types? "I'll grant you that a lot of Park Service people have a proprietary sense about the place, but I don't think burning deadfall from the campground is terribly exploitative."

"I'd get a ticket if I did it." Lightning struck against the darkness. "Just like I'd be arrested if I got caught hunting in the park."

Clancy asked him about usufruct rights and Grady explained that the 1895 Agreement had sold the eastern portion of the reservation to the US government for $1.5 million. The Blackfeet retained the right to hunt, fish, and gather timber for as long as the land was public. "The people were starving. They signed under duress." He told her how in May 1910, the federal government created Glacier Park—its eastern portion comprising the same land the Blackfeet had sold in 1895. The federal government maintained that the land was now no longer public; hence the Blackfeet no longer had the right to hunt, fish, and gather wood. In the early 1970s Woody Kipp, a tribal member and American Indian Movement activist, drove through the entrance gate at St. Mary so law enforcement would arrest him. In the ensuing court battles, tribal members won back the right to access the area but nothing else. "More than once my dad and I have been tracking an elk until it crosses the boundary, heads into the park, and becomes just one more thing in the long list of what the government took."

"How do you know all this?"

"Relatives. My grandpa and my mom went to college. I read. It's not a secret."

Clancy felt bad. Her cabin, the campground it sat in, had all been taken from people struggling to survive.

"Don't look so distressed." Grady smiled his lopsided grin. "It's been this way a while. It's not changing anytime soon." He thrust his chin in the direction of the porch. "Let's go watch the storm."

She grabbed her down jacket, hat, and gloves.

Grady raised an eyebrow. "You cold?"

"Aren't you?" He wore a long-sleeved shirt, blue silk kerchief, jeans, and cowboy boots. As they stepped onto the porch, thunder slammed. Clancy jumped.

He laughed. "It's gotta be almost sixty degrees out here." She pulled on her gloves, and Grady's arms surrounded her. His front pressed warm against her back, the reverse of yesterday on the horse. She leaned into his solid strength. Thunder slammed so close it rattled her teeth. Grady went inside and refilled her glass. When he returned, Clancy kissed him. His lips were soft. He cradled her neck in his palm, traced her jawline with his thumb. His hands were rough. The first fat drops of rain plinked against the metal roof as the storm tore through the treetops and drove rain under the porch.

After several minutes, she yelled over the wind, "Inside!" Dripping, they retreated to the warmth and the firelight. They kicked off their boots, dropped their coats, shucked their pants, and scrambled to the top bunk. Clancy relished the feel of the flannel sheets against her legs, the weight of the down comforter, Grady's warmth. The only light, save for the flashes of lightning, flickered through the cracked damper of the woodstove. Rain hammered the metal roof. He kissed her neck and she squirmed with delight. His hand reached beneath her fleece, found her shirt and then her camisole. He gently eased his lips away from hers and touched her forehead with his. "It's like peeling an onion."

"Layers, the key to survival." Clancy laughed. They lay still and listened to the storm. "This is nice," she said. "But."

His hand retreated. "I worried there'd be a 'but.'"

"I'm enjoying this. You. I just don't want anything more. Not now. Not tonight. Not when I'm drunk."

He rolled onto his back. "Would you like me to go?" he asked gently.

Clancy thought a moment. "Not particularly. Not if you can stay and kiss me and . . ."

"Not press for more?" he offered and pulled her close. He kissed the top of her head. She inched closer, found his lips with hers. Rain pounded. Firelight danced shadows around the room.

Patrick shivered as he shifted his stocking cap, fleece jacket, long underwear, and rain pants to the top of his pack, where he hoped the river wouldn't reach. If it did, he'd have bigger problems than wet layers. Rain dripped off his nose and onto all he hoped to keep dry. He almost laughed. The heavens had opened in a full-on deluge for the last quarter of a mile. They were all soaked. Poor Muffy, wet dog was not her best look, or smell.

Darkness fell with the rain. Their headlamps shined feeble circles of light against the roiling Middle Fork of the Flathead—the last obstacle in their return to the land of hot food, hotter showers, and soft beds, where he hoped Rosie waited. He'd have a buddy collect her, bring her to his place so she wouldn't be alone with her grief. He would give her the bed, take the couch.

The river swelled with snowmelt and rain and ran darker than the darkness of the night. Rain pocked its surface. The current lifted and swirled. Turner kept trying to get through on his radio, which Patrick found silly. Even if he got in touch with the Com Center, what could they do, send a boat with a motor? And how long would that take? A ten-minute crossing outweighed the bleak prospect of a cold, sleepless night with the same ford looming in the morning. There was one way to the other side, and that was through it. Just like the family in *We're Going on a Bear Hunt*—how many times had his mom read him that book? They had to go through it. The river wasn't getting any lower. They might as well get it over with. Turner slammed his radio to the ground in frustration.

"They teach you that at FLETC?" Patrick asked.

"When we get back, I'm sending the radio guys on that hike we just did. Damn things don't work. You would think, what with modern technology, I could contact someone twenty miles away."

Patrick agreed, but frustration wouldn't get them across the water. "River's wide here and fairly level. It's likely as good as it gets. I'm tallest. I'll be in the middle. Liz, you toss the stick for Muffy and we'll link arms." Liz had been silent as a monk ever since they'd gotten the news about Ezra. Patrick figured she was at the end of her rope, exhausted and anxious. She showed Muffy a stick and flung it into the blackness. Muffy splashed in after it. They linked arms and stepped into the icy water.

It took Patrick's breath. The river pulled at his feet like something alive and looking to do him in. He glanced down. "Unbuckle your hip belts! Haven't you watched your own safety video?" As a group they took tentative, awkward steps. The water rose, pushed at Patrick's thighs. It soaked Liz above her waist. He pulled her closer with his elbow and pretty much dragged her. Buoyed by the water, she weighed almost nothing. A wave lifted and swamped Patrick's ribs. God, it was cold. His legs numbed completely. He urged them on, forward toward Rosie and warmth and dry clothes. It was like walking on tree trunks. Patrick clamped his teeth. Turner muttered curses. Wind lashed the rain against their faces. Light from their headlamps rolled and dipped across the swells. Patrick focused on one step, then the next. Liz pressed forward beside him.

In an instant she was down. Under. She flailed and splashed. Her head popped up only to disappear again beneath the undulating surface. Her arm slipped free of Patrick's. Her hand clasped his wrist. Her fingers dug deep. An eddy tugged at her. Her grip tightened. He pulled his arm free of Turner's and hoisted her so her head broke the surface. He powered through the deep water, trudged into the shallows tugging Liz behind him. He splashed and slipped and willed his way ashore. As he dragged her onto the rocks, Liz sputtered and coughed, turned her face away, and was sick. Turner lumbered out of the water behind them. Patrick watched the river rush past, dark and indifferent.

Mack braked and swung the truck into the parking lot of the local steakhouse. As he dashed for the door, the deluge soaked him to the skin. He stepped inside. The place was packed, lit low, and warm.

"Mack. Never thought I'd see you here." The woman beside him pushed paper in the park warehouse. She'd once made him write a letter of justification for a roll of duct tape. "Especially not in uniform." She sounded friendly, but Mack knew better. The park attracted all kinds. She leaned in close. Mack could smell the wine on her breath. "And," her eyes shined, "especially not tonight. It must be horrible to discover your girlfriend's a murderer."

"Excuse me?" Mack desperately wanted to get away from her.

"What other explanation is there? Two young lovers dead. One wrecked Liz's study, the other was Liz's employee." She drained her wineglass. "Liz has always been intense. But then," she tittered, "you'd know more about that than I do." The woman pointed an acrylic nail at Mack. "You should date someone nice. Sandy in the Com Center likes you."

Mack's ire rose. He opened his mouth to tell her to stop talking. Someone called, "Sharon! Your round." He looked across the room. A pack of Park Service folks gathered at the tables against the wall. It looked to be a post-SAR night out. Mack felt a knot of dread build in his chest. Whatever it was Liz had done, neither of their lives were going to be easy, not for a while.

"What can I get you?" the woman behind the bar asked.

Did everyone believe Liz was a murderer? He thought about the cat inside the physicist's box with the radioactive material. As long as he didn't look, the cat could be alive or dead, and until Liz peed on that test, they were pregnant and not. The possibility that the woman who would give birth to his child could have taken someone's life rattled him. What if their baby was born in prison?

Mack made himself focus, asked what they had hot and ready. She told him chili and baked potatoes loaded with butter, sour cream, cheddar cheese, and bacon bits.

Mack ordered both, to go.

As he signed the credit card slip, his radio squawked. "601, 721."

Mack stepped out the door and into the rain. "601. Go ahead."

"501 reported from the Stanton Creek Bar. He and his party request transport. They're north of the highway."

"Copy that. On my way." What the hell had happened to Layne? Mack had sent him to meet them hours ago. He ran to his truck. Supper would have to wait.

CHAPTER 31

SKIN TO SKIN

◆

"You earned yourself a set of extra-tall dry clothes," Patrick told Liz. Her eyes opened. He grabbed his stocking cap, hand knit by Rosie and complete with a dorky pom-pom, and tugged it onto Liz's head. She started to shake. Patrick knelt on the rocks and began removing her boots. His fingers, stubborn with cold, struggled with the laces. Liz's whole body trembled. Her teeth chattered.

"I got through. They're on their way." Turner was at his side. He settled his palm across Liz's forehead. "She needs skin-to-skin."

Patrick cursed the sopping-wet shoestring. "I nominate you."

"My boss's girlfriend. Wouldn't be appropriate." He heaved a sodden sleeping bag from a low compartment of his pack and tossed it on the ground. He dug in his pack and retrieved an emergency blanket. He lifted Liz's wrist and pressed his fingers against it. "Thready."

"You carried a sleeping bag all day?"

Turner nodded, wide-eyed with exhaustion. "Mack said to come prepared to spend the night."

Patrick shook his head. Maybe they should have bivyed in the trees, mostly out of the rain, on the other side of the river. In the morning they would've been able to see and had fresh legs. But here they were. Second-guessing was pointless.

The rain eased. Heavy clouds pressed low. Patrick got Liz's boots off and started to peel her out of her fancy trousers. "Grab her under the shoulders." Together, they wrestled her from her clothes. She said nothing, offered no cooperation. Turner laid out the sleeping bag and the silver blanket. Liz was not slight. She trembled. They placed her inside. Patrick shed his wet clothes, wrung out his boxers, and pulled them back on. Beneath an ancient cottonwood, he lay down and pressed his chest against her. Liz's back burned with cold. Her feet had been reduced to frozen clumps. Turner piled jackets and spare clothes on top of them. Patrick settled his arm across her, feeling no affection, only the small, fierce hope that his warmth would absorb her coldness, seep beneath her skin, flow into her. He didn't like Liz and hated her study. Penelope and Ezra were gone. So much was beyond his control—park rules, weather, Rosie's affections—but this, warming the person next to him, a person suffering and cold, this he could do.

As Mack drove, rain lashed the windshield. Even with the wipers going full bore, Mack could hardly see. He had the heater going full blast and still felt cold. He knew his discomfort had to be mild compared to what Liz, Turner, and Patrick were experiencing. They had to be wet and exhausted, possibly hypothermic. He toyed with the idea of radioing a West Glacier ranger who might be able to get to them faster, but he was already on his way. And he needed to talk to Liz. Their conversation had waited long enough. The rain eased, and just as he increased his speed, Mack spotted Layne's truck. He grabbed the radio and called him.

"Go ahead," the young man answered, sounding relieved.

"Wrong spot." Mack flipped his lights. Blue and red pierced the night. "Follow me."

"Copy."

Layne's headlights reflected in Mack's rearview mirror, blinding him. He turned off the flashers and tamped down his annoyance. The poor kid. He'd been waiting where the river ran on the south side of the road. Mack realized he should not have sent him. The guy didn't know the Coal Creek drainage from his own thumb.

Clancy listened to Grady's soft snores, enjoyed his warmth, the feel of his body curled next to hers. The storm had passed. Only the occasional drip plopped against the metal roof. She'd been drifting off when she heard the *scritch-scratch* of a mouse and the slap of a trap. Experience had taught her not to hop up and deal. She got squeamish when it came to suffering. Suffering. Clancy hoped Ezra hadn't. She hoped something, though it was hard to imagine what, had killed him before the bear had found him. He loved grizzles. It seemed a cruel irony if one had gotten him in the end.

Where was Ezra's bear spray? He carried it, always, on the hip belt of his pack. They all did. The Park Service issued them a canister along with a hard hat, earplugs, and work gloves. Had the bear buried it along with him and his pack?

The crew would never be the same. Critical Incident Stress Debriefing was all the rage in the Park Service. Clancy would have a front-row seat as some poor soul from the head shed attempted to get Roberts and Nate to talk about their feelings. Her coworkers were not pillars of emotional stability. All the pot in the world wouldn't allow them to sufficiently numb, but that didn't mean they wouldn't try. If it could happen to Ezra, it could happen to any of them. Maybe that was what complicated grief—fear.

Clancy would track down Nate and ask what he'd been up to in Ezra's camper. She doubted he'd own up and tell her, but whatever he did say might shed some light. They kept things from her. She figured it was because she didn't smoke with them, but it was more than that—the sorts of things Nate hinted at—background and social class. They came from and inhabited different worlds. Clancy worked trails because she wanted to, and if that ever changed, she had options like returning to college. The same wasn't true for the rest of them.

Whatever Ezra had been mixed up in, well, he wasn't anymore. Clancy was going to miss him, his quirky Ezra-ness, hiking together mile after mile, the way he made her laugh, his chocolate. She didn't know what had happened to him, but she believed that if hadn't been for the DNA study, Ezra would still be alive. Liz and her staff traipsing through the backcountry with bottles of bovine blood and rotten fish, Penelope camped in the same valley while the lure manipulated the bears' movements and behavior. None of it would have occurred if not for Liz and her project. Who did those biologists think they were, messing with the grizzlies, wolverines, and lynx? They'd killed one wolverine implanting a tracking device and caused another to abort—and for what? To document that a wolverine's territory could encompass a hundred miles and that the bad-ass creatures required snow, the deeper the better. Even before the study, biologists had known that. Why'd they have to count everything? Why couldn't they just allow wildlife to be? Preserve some mystery? Clancy felt like she was witnessing the death of wonder. Not every question had to have a verified answer on a spreadsheet. Hard dark pressed the windows. Clancy listened for the next drip to hit the roof.

Patrick coaxed a small fire to life beside Liz. He blew gently on the embers, raised flames to lick the twigs and pine cones stacked with care. She wore Turner's dirty socks, Patrick's spare long underwear, polypro shirt, and the pom-pom hat Rosie had knitted. Patrick had tied the laces of Liz's boots for her and wrapped Turner's emergency blanket around her shoulders. He had spread her clothes across a downed cottonwood, smooth and white with age, hoping they'd dry. He called Muffy, ordered the dog to stop terrorizing the creatures of the riverbank and warm her owner. The dog had been barking incessantly, sending something tearing through the brush.

Patrick talked to Liz about his woodstove and wool blanket, popcorn and hamburgers grilled to perfection and topped with bacon. She was eating the emergency food he always carried, a protein bar and potato chips. "Energize and exercise, the antidote to hypothermia." He needed to get her moving. He wondered about hyponatremia—severely low sodium levels caused by overconsumption of water and indicated by vomiting, fatigue, cramps, and confusion. Maybe Liz suffered from it, too. He had not seen her eat all day, but she'd sucked on the valve of her water bladder constantly.

The fire needed wood, as dry as possible. "Be right back," he told Liz. She kept her vacant gaze trained on the low flicker of flame.

Patrick spotted a downed tree and traipsed through a thicket. He popped branches from the lee side. If they didn't yield to his hands, he slammed them free with his boot. A light drizzle fell, helped nothing. A gust freed moisture from the leaves of the cottonwoods and flung it in his face. He told himself the weather would relent and soon they'd see stars. He had half an armful of wood when he spied the motherlode in the form of a down, long-dead pine and countless needle-ridden wrist-thick branches. His spirits lifted at the thought of a raging bonfire. Turner would probably write him a ticket. Patrick shined his headlamp against the darkness and made for the tree. Turner had scrambled up the hill to flag down whichever Park Service employee had drawn the short straw and would come to collect them. Patrick had thought about rifling through Liz's pack under the guise of locating her spare clothes. But his desire to get a fire going and get home trumped his curiosity about what she'd been protecting inside her pack all day.

Patrick heard a splash. Barking. He turned. The fire glowed. The emergency blanket sat in a heap. Liz was gone. More splashing. Patrick dropped his load of wood and ran for the river. He muscled through brush, scrambled across the rain-slick rocks. As he reached the water, the beam of his headlamp caught the bob of Muffy's head. It rushed downstream and out of sight. "Liz!" Patrick called as he ran down the shoreline. He would have sworn she was incapable of walking to the water, let alone swimming.

Turner scrambled down the bank. Mud slid ahead of his boots. "What happened?"

"Light!" Patrick demanded. "I need more light." Turner ripped off his headlamp and handed it over. "I think she went in after Muffy." Patrick drew both beams slowly across the river. Rain fell inside the bands of light. The water ran swift. The surface bobbed and dipped.

A call, high and sharp, pierced the night. It was primal and alive. Both men froze. Fear iced down Patrick's back. The screech came again, originated from behind them. Behind and above. Patrick swallowed. Every cell in his being wanted to run. He made himself breathe. Moving slowly, they turned toward the sound. Patrick shined the feeble lights against the darkness. He swept the area, back and forth, back and forth until he saw it. He trained both beams on the middle branches of a cottonwood. Two eyes, bright and round like massive marbles, flashed black. The mountain lion looked straight at them. It crouched close to the tree trunk. Even coiled and tense, the cat appeared impossibly huge. It drew its top lip back, screeched again. Patrick saw its teeth.

"Shit," Turner whispered.

Patrick lowered the beams. "Easy. We back away, easy. Do not meet her eye. Stay close. We need to look like one big mother of a beast that she does not want to mess with." The two men inched backward. Patrick glanced up. Her eyes flashed.

The gunshot made Patrick jump. The world went silent. Turner had his arm extended and his .357 aimed at the top of the tree. The mountain lion leapt, stretched long, longer than Patrick was tall, and disappeared into the darkness.

Vapor rose from the blacktop. Mack had trouble seeing. He almost flew past the wide spot in the road where Turner, Patrick, and Liz and all her answers waited beside the Middle Fork of the Flathead. He slammed the brake, swung the truck into the turnout, and jerked to a stop. Layne sailed in behind him.

Mack stepped from the vehicle. No one was there. He thought they'd be by the road, waiting, desperate for the heat of the truck, anxious to get home. He motioned to Layne. and they scrambled down the muddy hillside. Turner and Patrick dashed along the riverbank, yelling, "Liz! Muffy!"

"Where is she?" Mack hollered.

Turner turned their way and shook his head slowly. Mack broke into a run, met Turner on the rocky shore. The man looked like hell. His lips were dry, his eyes bloodshot. His sodden fleece clung to his Kevlar vest. "We think Muffy went in the river and Liz tried to save her."

Patrick paced the riverbank. Weak headlamp light danced across the water.

"Liz was spent, Mack. If Patrick hadn't hoisted her out of the river, she would have drowned. He carried her to shore, did skin to skin, got her into dry clothes. She didn't have any strength left. And that was before she went in after Muffy." He looked at the river rolling past. "I don't think she could have made it."

"You're saying she's dead?"

"I'll call it in. Get help headed this way." He hobbled a few steps and stopped. "There's a mountain lion around. Might be how Muffy ended up in the water. Be careful."

Mack took a long breath and blew it out slowly. He walked to the river. Layne stayed at his side.

"You've had a rough day, sir."

"She did something, Mack," Turner called. "You should have seen her when I told her Ezra was dead. Guilty as hell."

Turner and Patrick declined Mack's offer of the truck cab. They scoured the riverbank, searched and called. Clouds spread across the night sky. Occasional gusts whisked water from the cottonwood leaves. Twice Mack thought he heard brush rustling. But each time he found nothing and chalked it up to the breeze, a critter, or wishful thinking. Mack shined his Maglite in a careful 360. When it passed over her clothes draped across a smooth cottonwood snag, Liz's name caught in his throat. He knew those clothes. She wore them hiking, camping. He'd helped her out of them more than once.

He called to Patrick, "What was she wearing?" Patrick and Mack strode toward one another. When they met, he told Mack about Turner's socks, his own spare base layer several sizes too big, and the pom-pom hat.

Mack and Layne headed downstream, drawing their lights across the swells and riffles of the river. Mack called for Muffy, hoping that if Liz had lost consciousness, the dog might be at her side. If Layne had been there to collect them, none of this would have happened. Liz would be inside a Park Service truck. Why had he sent Layne? Why hadn't he gone himself? Nothing Nate and Roberts had told him made a damn bit of difference. If only Mack had come here instead. They searched, calling and shining their lights. Occasional pinpricks of stars appeared through gaps in the long stretch of cloud.

Mack's beam glanced off something purple caught along a thicket of willow. He lifted it from the cold water and saw it was the hat that Liz had kept stuffed in her pocket that morning in his office, the morning she'd surprised him and locked the door and told him she might be pregnant. But Patrick said she'd been wearing a different hat before she went in after Muffy.

Mack wrung the slick fabric free of water. A single, persistent thought made him shudder. As he ran upriver, back to Patrick and Turner, his heart slammed in his chest. He reached them and drew a long breath. Dread built in his gut. "Did either of you see Liz go in the water?"

"Negative," Turner said.

"I heard a splash," Patrick said. "But I didn't see her, no."

Mack showed them the hat. "It's Liz's favorite. She sometimes keeps it jammed in her back pocket." The men shook their heads. They had no explanation to offer. Emergency lights pierced the darkness. Help had arrived. Mack felt empty. He believed Liz was gone. The river rushed past. Clouds pressed low. Fog collected, closed in, hung just above the water.

CHAPTER 32

MORNING

◆

The next morning, the air was damp and cool. The campground lay shrouded in cloud. Clancy brushed her teeth in the tiny bathroom behind her cabin. The roar of a diesel engine shattered the quiet. Clancy listened as the truck rumbled into the distance. Grady had been sleeping when Clancy had climbed from the bed, slipped into her clogs, and made for the bathroom. Outside, mist hung low, gathered in the trees, and lent the campground an air of enchantment.

Now, as the sound of the truck faded to silence, she pushed back against her disappointment, told herself she still needed to get a fire going in the woodstove, warm the cabin. It just wouldn't be the same without him there. The haze that had seemed so glorious a few minutes before pressed dank as Clancy made her way to her front door. She knew what she needed—a long hike. She just couldn't bring herself to pack a lunch, fill water bottles, not yet. She climbed back into bed. Even though they hadn't had sex, he'd left. Just like all the others.

Clancy had been drinking beer at Kipp's one spring evening when a Native guy struck up a conversation. After a while, his buddy told him, "Move on. She's one of the dry herd." She insisted the guy flirting with her explain. He told Clancy "the dry herd" referred to the droves of young women who came to the reservation to wait tables and clean rooms in the big lodges back in the day. He said a lot of the women rode the train from Minneapolis and were Midwestern Catholics who wouldn't put out. Some of them stayed, married into the tribe. Most of them returned to their homes on the plains, their virtue, so the story went, intact.

"So since the 1920s the Blackfeet have been characterizing seasonal female workers as sexless bovines?" Clancy's question pretty much ended that conversation. Grady was Indian, but he seemed different from the guys at Kipp's. Or maybe not. Sadness pressed down like the blanket of moisture.

Forty minutes later there was a knock, and her door creaked open. Clancy bolted upright and smacked her head on a beam.

"That had to hurt." Shopping bags hung from both of Grady's hands. "Your fridge." He shook his head. "Sour cream is not a meal." Light poured through the door. "It's like that line from *Say Anything*: 'There's no food in your food.'"

"I thought you'd left." Clancy's head hurt. Neither the tequila nor slamming it into a log had been helpful.

"We need breakfast." He set the bags on the floor.

"Why didn't you tell me you'd be back?"

"I wrote a note. You were in the bathroom." He lifted a piece of paper from the counter. Clancy wished she'd noticed it earlier. "You could have talked to me."

"You would have wanted me hollering at you through the bathroom door in the middle of the campground?" He shook his head, perplexed.

"You could have waited, communicated."

"Are we fighting?" he asked. "Would you like me to leave?"

Clancy rubbed her eyes. "Leaving is what got me upset." She didn't know. Maybe it would be better if they called it, just jumped ahead to the inevitable. Instead of waiting for her answer, Grady filled the counter with potatoes, a carton of eggs, a package of bacon, a green pepper, onion, tomato, and a massive bottle of orange juice.

"You cook?" she asked from the bunk.

"I'm a fan of food. Unlike some people."

She climbed down from the bed and told him she'd make coffee.

"Cream." He tossed her a pint from a bag on the floor.

The sun cleared the eastern hills, beamed in earnest. The smell of fresh rain and damp pines hung in the air. Campers emerged from their tents and RVs. Rain did that, encouraged sleep and easing into the day. Clancy and Grady sat at the picnic table enjoying their omelets and sipping coffee.

She told Grady that once they retrieved her truck, she was going to hike Dawson Pitamakan, going up Pitamakan first because her crew had constructed stone steps up Dawson and Roberts had insisted they use monster rocks. Scaling the beasts made her suck air every time. "Ezra and I spent a lot of time together in this valley. The walk will do me good." A nuthatch called.

"Care for company?" Grady swiped a smear of hot sauce with his toast.

"You hike?"

"How hard can it be? I walk around outside quite a bit."

"Eighteen miles in cowboy boots?"

"My boots are comfortable enough to walk in. Just don't tell Ms. Ralston." Grady sighed. "I should probably figure out my work situation."

"Liz should be in jail."

"She may have bailed out by now."

Clancy told him the scary backcountry permit writer sometimes let people use the phone in the ranger station. "You'll have to charm her, and don't tell her you work for Liz." She said the Blackfeet permit writer couldn't stand Liz, and she had cause. A couple years ago, Liz had conducted bear training for Two Med's trail crew, fee collectors, and backcountry permit writers. Two of the women were Blackfeet, one a paraplegic. Liz kept getting the two confused, calling them the wrong names. She botched their last names, too. The permit writer eventually told Liz, "Jamie's the one in the wheelchair. And it's Bear Medicine, not Bear Grass." What made it worse was the fact that both women wore nametags. Liz just couldn't be bothered to read them.

"I wonder how she took the news about Penelope." Grady stacked their plates and silverware.

"Knowing Liz, her only concern will be about the impact on her study."

Mack woke up tired. For a long, disorientating moment he could not fathom where he was. The window above his head framed tall pines.

He breathed in the distinct Two Medicine smell and recalled that he'd crashed on Turner's couch. Years ago, a naturalist had told him Two Medicine's fragrance owed itself to the age of the trees. The valley hadn't burned in over a hundred years. Mack hoped it could hold off twenty or so more. He did not want to be district ranger during that catastrophe.

Turner was already gone. Mack helped himself to a shower, dressed in yesterday's clothes, and headed for the ranger station to see about coffee.

Clancy and Grady stood at the counter. "I'll bet Mack knows," she said as he came through the door. "Grady's trying to get ahold of Liz."

"My guess is Grady's got a day or two off." Mack motioned them outside and told them about the river, about the dog and the mountain lion and Liz's fatigue. He said he hoped the swift-water rescue team that had started at first light would have news soon.

Mack was just beginning to acknowledge the tinge of relief he was experiencing along with his sense that she was gone. He tamped down thoughts that suggested she'd engineered her escape, pinned his hopes on the rescue team finding definitive answers. He breathed deep the smell of the trees.

Clancy stopped short. Grizzly tracks pressed into the mud of the trail and veered onto the rocks. She crouched and placed her palm at the bottom of the footpad. Her fingers splayed inches shy of the top of the track. Grady cussed softly and did a 360 scan of their surroundings—the massive back side of Rising Wolf, the Dry Fork

Valley leading to Old Man, Mount Morgan, Pitamakan Pass, Red Mountain, Spot. The air carried the scent of wild animal, musky and rank. The sun beat down on the red rock of the creek bed. Bear grass and brush covered the hillside.

"I'd feel better if I could see the bear, at least hear it," Grady said. "And I can't help but wonder what Ruth's doing now." He grinned.

Clancy laughed. "She's probably out to pasture and bored, wishing someone would have had the decency to ride her into the backcountry today so she could catch the scent of bear and know she's alive."

They started moving. Grady said, "Tell me about your brother."

Clancy wasn't sure if he was hoping for a diversion from the bear or genuinely interested, but she was happy to oblige. She told him about Sean, who loved *Star Wars* and refused to eat anything green with the exception of pickles, who could stick out his tongue and curl it up to touch the tip of his nose. Sean, the son of a park ranger and a botanist, who would rather play a video game than hike, ski, mountain bike, or raft. Sean, who'd just bought his first car and hated heights and was allergic to dogs and horses, who had a big head and thick hair and had just started shaving every day. Sean, who dreamed of seeing a space shuttle launch and attending a *Star Wars* celebration in Indianapolis. He loved planetariums and rockets and planned to major in computer science at Montana State. He taught himself programming, learned Java, and could do math in his head.

She told Grady how Sean had climbed Going-to-the-Sun Mountain by himself, leapt the gap, signed the register. She said he must have tried to find a way to avoid jumping the same expanse on his way down, which sent him into the class 5 cliffs where he fell, and how Ezra downclimbed, finally located his body, and recovered it.

"Hell of a thing for you to go through. I don't think I'd survive if I lost my sister." Grady spoke about Josie, said she was five years younger and still his best friend in the world. They'd grown up on a ranch without other kids around—had only each other except in the summers, when the owners' kids would visit and Grady and Josie would get them to pee on the electric fence and try to ride calves and eat the horse feed. He talked about his home, the creek that ran through it, the barns and pastures, meadows and mountains. He told Clancy about the dumb things the cows did and the wildlife that passed through.

She told Grady about growing up as a Park Service brat. How her family had lived in all sorts of amazing places—Acadia, the Tetons, Grand Canyon—but none of them, not one, compared to Glacier. She said how after Sean died, she'd needed out from under the hurt and taken to drinking. "I feel like I owe you an explanation about last night." Clancy said that whenever she hooked up, in the morning she felt ashamed and never wanted to see the guy again. "I didn't want that. Not this time. Not with you."

"You don't owe me anything," Grady said. "That's not right, those guys taking advantage."

Clancy shrugged. "It was me using them."

Grady told her how things had been for him growing up: "Normal—too much alcohol and anger, not enough money." He told her his mom didn't drink anymore, but his dad did. "Enough for both of them." He said there'd been plenty of good times, too. Lots of work, animals, below-zero cold, deadly chill factors, and weather like the June storm a couple years before. It dumped four feet of snow, killed calves, and drew the bears down out of the mountains to feast on them. Clancy remembered it. She'd seen birds dead on top of the mounds of snow as though they'd frozen and fallen from the sky. They'd endured the four-day power outage not more than ten miles away from each other, Clancy in St. Mary and Grady outside Babb.

They hiked in companionable silence for a while, enjoying the view, scaling the switchbacks above Old Man to Pitamakan Pass. The trail crossed stretches of snow rotting in the sun. They got to the top and Clancy stopped to pull on layers. Grady pointed down at Lake of the Seven Winds and the valley beyond. "Liz came up here from down there?"

She nodded. The wind whipped steady. Clancy had to holler to be heard. "She dropped down into the Nyack. I'll show you."

Clancy leaned into the wind, following the trail worn into the talus. They came to a snowfield. She pointed at the dog tracks.

"Muffy." Grady said the dog's name like a cuss word.

The trail led to the backside of Mount Morgan. Once they turned south and got squarely behind the mountain, the wind eased. The valley below was a dense mass of timber dotted with lakes and rimmed by snow-covered peaks. "Liz dropped down there."

Staring down at the thick trees, he said, "Good place to feel alone."

Mountains lifted like peaks of meringue across a pie as far as they could see. Ezra was gone, and Clancy blamed Liz. It felt good to have someone to condemn. "Did she really believe she could outrun them? Did she think Mack would just look the other way?"

"Liz had evidence Ezra was sabotaging her study," Grady said. "She probably just meant to warn him, send a message. When she took off, she didn't even know he was missing."

"You're defending Liz? Someone poured bear bait on his tent. She's the prime suspect."

"Everyone makes mistakes. Sounds like Liz paid for hers." He studied the valley. "I would not jump in the Middle Fork after that dog."

"Liz lured a grizzly to our camp." Anger heated her face. "That's not a mere error in judgement. Ezra's dead."

"Are we fighting again?" He asked with such earnestness that it made Clancy laugh, and she started walking.

"Almost halfway," She called over her shoulder.

Grady cussed.

A log lay across the trail. It was one Clancy had bucked over a week ago, back before they'd gone on their Atlantic Creek hitch. Ezra had missed clearing it. It was a good eight inches in diameter and a couple feet long. She kicked at it. "Ezra's messing with me."

Grady hoisted the round and, giving it a toss, swatted it like he was serving up a tennis ball.

"Remind me not to arm wrestle you." She told him she had trouble with the chain saw, mostly getting it started but also pinching the bar, and how patient Ezra had been.

"You work trail crew and you can't run a saw?"

"I can. I'm just not good at it. It scares me."

"That's like a packer allergic to horses."

"Exactly like that." The ache of missing made her surly. Clancy would've liked to have told Ezra, *And then he compared my fear of a machine capable of removing my leg to a flipping allergy.* Roberts and Nate wouldn't muster the kind of righteous indignation she craved. Ezra. There was no one like him. Never would be again. She took the spur trail that led to No Name.

A wall of rock lifted above the lake. Circles radiated from where fish met the surface. The air was blessedly still. A biting fly chomped her ankle. Clancy stomped to send it away and pulled a Nalgene from the side pocket of her pack. She stomped the other foot, lifting flies into the air. Thinking of the mules, she wished she had a tail to swish. She remembered Marty had told her his string had spooked crossing the creek. "Did you notice anything at the Atlantic Creek ford that morning you gave me a ride?"

Grady studied the shore. "Why?" He plucked a stone and skipped it. It skimmed across the water, touching seven times before it sank, disappeared forever.

"Marty told me he had some trouble there. I wondered if your girls were bothered, too." Clancy plopped on a boulder and pulled peanut-butter-and-jelly sandwiches from her pack.

"They're mules." Grady shrugged. "They get skittish. Especially in bear country."

"You scared of bears?" she asked, handing him his lunch.

"I prefer to think of it as being respectful of their power."

Clancy pulled off her boots, shed her socks, and dipped her toes in the cold water. She told Grady she was looking forward to a beer. He'd taken off his shoes and socks too and rolled up his jeans. His feet and ankles were shades lighter than his face and forearms. He waded into the lake. "If there's a ranch hand my dad wants rid of, he comes up with some excuse about why the guy can't ride. Set him afoot and the dude's gone by supper." He smiled. "Now I know why."

Clancy didn't feel hungry and put her sandwich away. She tossed rocks, listening for the satisfying *plunk*, watching for the flash and spark of sun against the splash. "What do you think happened to Ezra?"

"'We owe nothing to the facts and everything to the truth.'"

Clancy dropped a handful of rocks and turned to him. "Where did you hear that?"

"The truth thing? That's a line from my mom's favorite poet. He drove around Montana in some gas-guzzling boat of a vehicle and wrote poems about the little towns he visited, their churches and bars, the people. My mom kept his collection in the jockey box and read out loud to us as we drove to Great Falls or out east to gather cows or wherever." Grady said his mom had attended the University of Montana. "Hugo's a legend."

"Ezra started saying that line about the truth this summer. He said it a lot. That and a line about the day feeling like a person who loves you."

"That's one of Hugo's, too." A marmot whistled and Grady jumped. Clancy laughed but stopped when he reached under his T-shirt and she glimpsed the handgun tucked at the small of his back. He'd hiked with it the whole day.

"That makes me nervous."

"My gun?"

"Statistics say you'll use it to shoot me."

"Statistics don't know me." Droplets sprang in the air and glinted in the sun as he waded to shore. The rock wall and trees pressed close. A wave of exhaustion washed over her. She didn't have it in her to argue about guns or anything else. Clancy needed to be back on the trail and moving, back to where her eyes could relax into the distance. She didn't want to think or set the pace. She wanted only to sink into the numb rhythm of walking and just be.

CHAPTER 33

DEBRIEF

◆

Four days later and against Mack's better judgment, he stepped inside the Hudson Bay District Office in St. Mary wearing his backpack and civilian clothes—hiking shorts, polypropylene shirt, nonissue boots. He'd taken comp time so he could get a jump on his days off. Mack didn't mind working weekends. It was important for the people with spouses and families to have their Saturdays and Sundays free. Vera chose to work Sundays for the pay differential. He'd take her help whenever he could get it. He'd slept in and then spent over an hour finding and organizing the backpacking gear he hadn't used for months. Two nights camping in Glacier's backcountry, the cure for any ill.

He had spent the last several days ignoring his usual duties to meet with grieving parents. Penelope's folks were flying her body back to Des Moines today. Ezra's parents wanted to spread his ashes in the park. They were waiting for the coroner to release his remains and for park headquarters to issue the permit. Mack offered to organize a memorial, but they wanted no part of a gathering, their sorrow private and all-consuming.

He'd escorted Liz's folks to the river. He had wanted to say something, to tell them he'd known her well, but he was no longer certain that was true. Telling them she'd been part of his life, that they had been a couple, seemed to unduly complicate what was already difficult. Her folks had to be in their late seventies and required assistance across the rocks. Mack stepped away to give them time alone at the water's edge. They knelt and laid a bouquet, then helped one another as they struggled to stand, as though the weight of their grief proved too much and could only be borne together.

Now, Mack shook free of his pack. Vera wolf-whistled. "Careful, or you'll blend in so well you'll have to follow the rules."

Mack smiled. "What would I do without you?"

"That you?" Turner popped through the office door. He would serve as acting district ranger while Mack was in the backcountry. "Five items. I've got five, maybe six. Can you stand it?"

Mack followed him into the office. Turner looked to have found his element. He had file folders in neat stacks and a checklist in front of him. Mack sat. He liked the view from this side of the desk, nothing but blue sky and trees.

"Easy one first. I think we should hire that Patrick fellow," Turner said. "A backcountry technician job. He knows the park." When they'd dropped Patrick off that dark night, Rosie had been waiting on his porch. Turner held out his hand, and when Patrick shook it, Turner said, "Give her time. She'll come around."

"Sounds great." Mack smiled. Turner was in for an education. "Find the money in the budget. Check in all the random funds like rescue cache equipment and office supplies, that ilk. Once you've got a respectable amount theoretically amassed, write up the PD."

"PD?"

"Position description. Run that by Vera and then Barb in personnel. They'll both be crabby about it, but they'll make it better. Then it needs to go to Truman Dyer for approval. Talk to him before you send it or you don't have a prayer. Let him know how helpful Patrick was during the incident. Like all of us, Truman has a fondness for certain people. Clancy's friends are among them. Then they'll want to advertise it publicly. Check with Barb and see if you can get special dispensation for an emergency hire or some such nonsense so you can get the guy you want instead of some hard-drinking, unemployable New Jersey military veteran. Again, they'll grouse about hiring regulations and all the rules they're legally bound to follow. Remain courteous, but don't give up. They do this sort of thing all the time when they hire one-half of a couple and need to find a job for the spouse."

Turner finished jotting notes. "Done by the time you get back." They both laughed. "The report on that scat you bagged came back. Perfectly normal. No human DNA."

"Nastiest-smelling scat I ever encountered." Mack reached forward and flipped the photo of Liz and himself on the summit of Otokomi against the desk. He didn't want to look at it and doubted Turner did, either. "Maybe it all smells that bad and I just don't usually come across it quite so fresh."

"Report came back on Penelope." Turner tapped a folder. "Just like I figured. Pulmonary aspiration leading to asphyxiation. She choked on her own vomit. Died like a rock star."

Mack closed his eyes lightly. Penelope's parents were wrecked. This news wouldn't help. Maybe they didn't need to know. He would wait, see if they asked.

"Now for the more complicated stuff." Turner lifted a sheaf of papers from a file and offered them to Mack. "Autopsy report on Ezra. The doc called before she faxed it. She said what with the condition of the body, the work was 'less than straightforward.'"

Mack itched to get outside. "I don't want to read the thing, Turner. Just tell me."

"It complicates matters. Considerably."

"Dear God, have you been hanging out with Layne? How did he die?"

"He drowned."

Mack was silent. Complicated and then some. If Ezra drowned, who or what fished him out? A bear could have caught his scent but probably not immediately. It might have been drawn to the area because of the bait and happened upon him. Who else might have been there? Liz? Penelope? Whoever left the boot tracks Clancy had described? Mack wished he could have seen those prints. Maybe he would've been able to tell something—gender, approximate height and weight.

Clancy had been right. The bear had fed on Ezra, but it hadn't killed him. "We've got more work to do there. Someone or something pulled him from the water. Real question is, how did he go in? With the rain, he certainly could've slipped off that excuse for a bridge, but if that were the case, he probably would've been able to climb back out."

"It gets better," Turner said. "He suffered a severe blow to the head, possibly from a fall. His face was bruised antemortem and his body both ante- and postmortem. Doc said the bruising looked compatible with both being dashed against rocks by the current and being dragged by the bear." Turner paused and let that sink in. "Most fascinating of all," Turner paused again and opened the file, pointing to a highlighted section, "his ribs were cracked. 'Damage consistent with someone performing CPR.'"

"Could that have been done by the bear?"

"I had the same question." Turner tapped the file. "Doc said possibly. No way to know with a hundred percent certainty, but her money's on someone trying to resuscitate him."

"Whoever sent him in didn't want him to die." Penelope sprang to mind.

"Maybe he just fell."

"Maybe," Mack allowed. They were not going to figure this one out in the office, not that morning and possibly not ever. "At least the bear didn't kill him. We don't have to shoot it."

"Cup's half full."

Turner was organized and methodical. Mack had the fleeting thought that they should switch jobs. He could spend more time outside at Two Med and Turner could shuffle the paperwork, compile the policy binders.

"Don't know if I should bother you with this next one before your days off, but I found it curious. The Walton ranger reported that she found the lock jimmied on the Park Creek patrol cabin. Said the perp raided the food cache, but nothing else seemed amiss."

"Any sign of a dog?"

"Exactly what I asked once again. Not that she noticed. But then, she wasn't looking. And no one's expecting dog prints back there. You'd just write them off as another coyote."

"I've been wondering," Mack hated to bring it up but wanted Turner's take, "what happened to Liz's pack?"

Turner's eyes grew big. "Her pack. I have no idea. It was so dark. With the weather, who knows? It could have been there."

"When I went back, her clothes were still on the cottonwood, but no pack. Maybe something dragged it away? Or maybe one of the swift-water rescue folks took it to headquarters?" Mack chose not to share that Vera had seen Liz withdraw cash from an ATM. He saw no reason to saddle Turner with the questions it raised. Liz could have orchestrated her disappearance, planned it all along. Mack hadn't decided how he wanted to handle that possibility. Turner knowing about the money would limit his options. Mack told himself he would have time to mull it over in the backcountry.

Turner drew his lips into a line. The missing pack complicated the Liz situation as surely as Ezra having drowned and someone having performed CPR muddled Ezra's death.

"Another thing's been bugging me. Liz's hat, the one I found washed up against the willow." Mack had bagged it and marked it as evidence. "Patrick said she was wearing his hat, one with pompoms."

"The river's hydraulics are nasty." Turner cocked an eyebrow. "Maybe she lost it during the ford, when she went under?"

"Maybe." Another puzzle they weren't likely to solve this morning. "Where would you go?" Mack asked. "Up to Atlantic Falls to look for evidence of someone murdering Ezra or Park Creek to look for signs of Liz and Muffy?"

"The Atlantic Falls hike is prettier, but we know Ezra's dead."

"Agreed." Mack stood. "You're doing a good job."

"You have your radio?" Turner asked.

He nodded. Weariness settled in his bones. "But no one else needs to know that, and I may choose not to turn it on."

CHAPTER 34

CLOSER

◆

That same Sunday morning Clancy watched Grady hoist a bundle resembling a massive brown Ho Ho and secure it behind his saddle. "What are you packing?" Clancy asked. He probably had his gun along for the ride, too. They'd borrowed horses from the Park Service barn in St. Mary. Marty had made sure Clancy got a good-natured old mare.

"Bedroll." He smiled and winked, and Clancy felt herself blush. They rode the five easy miles to Red Eagle Lake. The sun was warm. The glacier lilies and pasqueflowers had given way to lupine, camas, and larkspur. They fished. Clancy stayed on the rocky shore because the frigid water made her feet throb. Grady rolled his jeans, braved the depths, and outfished her two to one. She tossed her fish back. He extracted a camp stove and collapsible-handled pan from his saddlebags and fried his catch in butter. Clancy picked the meat free from the iridescent skin and tried to ignore the accusatory eyeball. "You don't have to eat it." Grady laughed. "Food isn't supposed to be a punishment."

They'd spent their days hiking and fishing, playing chess and cribbage, canoeing and now riding. They'd enjoyed epic make-out sessions and slept entwined but chastely in her top bunk. Clancy dreaded going back to work. She wasn't ready. This was her last day of freedom. Nate and Roberts were great in many ways. Few people had made her laugh as much. But given their penchant for self-medicating, their grief was bound to come out sideways. Ezra's absence would echo through the crew's routine, and the real missing would begin.

After lunch Grady hauled the bedroll up a rise far back from the trail and away from the horses. He kicked away cones and, between two Douglas firs, unfurled what amounted to a portable mattress. It felt ridiculously comfortable as it molded against her body, cushioning the ground. The sun beat down from the center of the sky. Grady lay beside her. No alcohol addled her brain. No substance numbed her body. He kissed her neck, her cheek, her mouth. He eased her out of her shirt and camisole, and his callused hands grazed her skin. As he knelt above her, he brought his palm to cup her cheek. His warm brown eyes bored into hers. She felt revered. Her whole body tingled in the way of a limb that has been still and under pressure too long and stings with the thrill of awakening. Any shred of resolve she might have mustered melted beneath the warmth of the sun and the press of his skin on hers.

Afterward he took her hand, and they walked the ridge. To the east the land lifted and dipped a vibrant green. Yellow patches of arnica and balsam root spread across the hills. Copses of trees, pine and fir, bunched greener than the ground, and the leaves of aspen flashed greener still. The world stretched before them, on and on beneath the bright sun, until it met with sky.

The same Sunday, twenty miles south as the crow flies and along the same mountain range, Patrick eyed the broad shelf of Calf Robe. A cornice of snow extended from the mountain like a frozen white wave. Rosie set an easy pace through the cow parsnip that crowded the trail. She wore her hair in a haphazard ponytail. She'd taken a week off work. Patrick insisted they climb a peak a day. The park worked its magic. Patrick found sky pilots and Jones columbine to show her. He pointed out mountains poking the clouds that swept their tops and shadowed their contours, told her their names. They hiked past gnarled whitebark pines, spied ptarmigan, pika, mountain goats, and bighorn sheep. At the summits they beheld the expanse of peak after peak shining with snow and running with waterfalls, and for a time, the strain that weighed her eyes eased. The climbs left Rosie spent and able to sink into the sound sleep of physical exhaustion. She spoke of little beyond Ezra and the fun they'd had, the plans they'd made. She told Patrick about finding his remains, told him the same tales again and again, the telling a balm against the hurt. Patrick listened. Each evening, when they returned to his place, he cooked her meals of wild game and fresh vegetables, gave her his bed and slept on the couch.

Today's goal was Calf Robe. Rosie stopped. She pointed. A western tanager, bright yellow and sporting a reddish-orange head, perched on a branch. Rosie smiled. Patrick wanted nothing more from the world than this—the sight of Rosie finding a flicker of joy, a bit of beauty to pull her through.

The dusty shade of the barn felt cool, a respite from the heat and sun. Clancy paused to let her eyes adjust. Marty stepped out of a stall and held the reins while Clancy dismounted. He said, "You look more comfortable on your own two feet."

"I didn't fall off, so that's something." She loved the smell—dust and hay and animals. Marty asked after the fishing. "We didn't get skunked. Wish I liked to eat them." She followed his gaze toward the sunlight pouring through the open barn doors. "Grady saw your boss in the pasture," Clancy explained. "Went to talk to him about the job you mentioned the other night."

Marty reached under the horse and uncinched the saddle. "You and Grady look to be spending a lot of time together. Where'd the two of you meet?"

Clancy froze. That was it. That was what had been bothering her about the trail junction in the Cut Bank Valley, the one that led up toward Atlantic Creek Campground and Triple Divide Pass or else kept going straight toward Atlantic Falls and their spike camp. Her voice shook. "Do I need to do anything? Bring her water, feed?"

Marty told her he'd take care of the horse. "You ever figure out who left those boot prints near the falls?"

"Getting closer," Clancy called as she dashed for the rectangle of light. "Closer all the time."

CHAPTER 35

LONELY LAKES

◆

Mack finished his spaghetti, rinsed his cook pot, and hung his food bag in a tree a good two hundred yards from his tent. In the end he'd decided against both the Cut Bank Valley and the Park Creek drainage and instead hiked in and set up camp at Lonely Lakes, of all places—and he did feel lonely but on top of that was something akin to rage. The two small lakes reflected puffy cumulus clouds. Angled sun caught and brightened their bellies. The rocky cirque spread like an invitation. With his tent pitched, pad and sleeping bag laid out, water purified, and supper eaten, he had little to distract him from the feelings he'd kept tamped down for days.

Years ago Mack had passed the long winter driving to Whitefish to learn to downhill ski. His instructor explained to him about the fall line. Once you passed the point where the mountain sloped and gravity took hold, you were headed down. If Liz were still around and had been pregnant, he would have dropped over the fall line, plunged into a life tethered to her for the rest of his days, bound by their child. The thought made his jaw clench.

Ezra had hocked stolen jewelry. Jewelry the owners might never miss. He and Nate's buddy had a slick system of turning it into cash—none of which had occurred inside Mack's jurisdiction. He'd alerted the tribal police and the sheriffs in both Glacier and Flathead Counties. It seemed all of them, given their lack of interest, must have bigger law enforcement fish to fry. Stolen tennis bracelets couldn't compete with meth and child abuse, drunk driving and missing women. Lord only knew where the jewelry crimes had originally been committed. You didn't see many tennis bracelets in Glacier County. Mack couldn't remember seeing so much as a tennis court.

The park had culled a few more. Penelope was dead. And, just as he'd predicted, the search had found Ezra within a mile of where he'd last been seen. The young man drowned, and either someone tried CPR or the bear damaged his ribs. If somebody pulled him from the creek and tried to resuscitate him, were they responsible for sending him into the water? If so, Mack believed they'd talk. Sooner or later, people unburdened themselves. He just had to bide his time, listen, pay attention. The mystery would unravel eventually. Whatever had happened, the young man was dead and Mack blamed Liz. He believed she'd poured bait on Ezra's tent, which must have drawn the bear that fed on him to the area. Even though Mack suspected she might still be alive, he doubted Liz would ever answer for her actions.

The day after she went missing, when the swift-water rescue crew came up empty and Mack returned to the river to find her clothes but not her pack, he recalled what Vera had seen. Liz withdrew cash from an ATM the same night she hiked out of the Cut Bank Valley and grabbed Muffy. That was also the night she left the "I love you" on his machine with the message canceling the meeting with east side law enforcement to address the sabotage.

Even if Liz had withdrawn the maximum amount allowed, it wouldn't get her far. Maybe to a job in a lab or at a wild animal sanctuary somewhere in the vast expanse of the West. Someplace in Utah or Nevada where she could claim a fire, flood, or some other catastrophe had destroyed her driver's license and Social Security card. Her pack had disappeared along with her. Had she thrown a stick into the water for Muffy as a diversion, sacrificing her dog so she could escape into the night? What kind of person killed her pet to save herself? He would never know if she was pregnant. The box would remain unopened, contain both possibilities forever.

Here was the truth—he hated Liz's study and all that she'd put him through. Along with his anger, he felt relieved that she was gone. It was like he'd been given a gift. And this was true, too—he hated himself for putting up with her for so long, for being with a woman who used him, a person who at her core was so self-absorbed, so riddled with insecurity and ambition that she was not kind. It was fear that had kept him with her, fear that he was incapable of a real relationship, that no one else would want him. Liz was a penance he'd served for his long-ago sin. He told himself he had done his time. Come fall, when the park and life slowed down, he vowed that he would address his shame, find a way to work through it. And there was always recreational Viagra.

The wind kicked up, whined through the sweet pine, and lifted waves across the water. Mack watched clouds rimmed in light drift across the sky.

CHAPTER 36

NOT SORRY

Clancy tilted the passenger seat forward and rifled through the detritus in the back of the cab of Grady's truck. The same odds and ends she'd found the night he'd bought the margaritas—mail, music, random tack. Her hands shook. The day he'd found her sprawled on the trail, the morning Ezra had gone missing, Grady had come up past their spike camp. But he'd been going to meet Liz and Penelope. Penelope had camped at Atlantic Creek. They were working farther up the Triple Divide trail. Grady had gone past the junction he should have taken. Way past. No one in their right mind would lead a pack string extra miles. Not without a compelling reason. She made herself breathe, climbed inside and sifted through the stuff on the seat—rope, jumper cables, a socket set. The creak of the driver's-side door made her jump.

"Looking for these?" Grady held up a pair of worn leather boots. He tilted the bottoms toward her. The canted heel bore the arced pattern she'd seen on Marty's and in the mud beside the creek where she'd found Ezra. She closed her eyes lightly, wished she could go back, back to earlier that afternoon, stop time on the ridge with the view. Grady tossed the boots behind the seat and climbed in. "I can talk and drive at the same time." His voice was flat, his jaw set.

A breeze blew through the truck. Rangers and maintenance workers crisscrossed the parking lot. She thought of his gun, how he carried it everywhere, and that Ezra was dead. "I'd rather we discuss this here."

Grady shook his head once. "Can't risk it." He wouldn't look at her. She stepped onto the pavement, pushed the backrest into place. The wind gusted, rushed the tops of the trees. A paper cup bounced across the parking lot. She told herself she could walk away, beg a ride home. But if she did, she would never know the truth. She climbed into the truck, fastened her seatbelt, and pulled the door closed.

Grady drove slowly through the Park Service compound. As he turned onto the highway, he said, "I realize you'll have to tell Mack or your dad, but if you could give me some time. After I take you home, drop you off, I'm going to need a few hours."

"Hours?"

"I need to get across the line."

"What line?"

Grady tossed his head. "Canada."

Outside her window spread the St. Mary Valley with its crazy blue lake surrounded by mountains. It was the view they printed on postcards, made into puzzles, slapped on ornaments. Beyond the first tier of peaks, she could see the shelf of Going-to-the-Sun. She liked to imagine Sean up there, awash in endorphins, drinking in the view, resting and triumphant before he started down and back home.

"I'm not going to jail. Not for this," Grady said.

"What did you do?" Heavy timber lined the road. The truck rumbled up the mountain.

"He's dead. And I'm not real sorry." Grady kept his eyes on the road. "It might be different for people like you—tell what happened and everyone says, 'Thanks and have a nice day.' But that's not how it works for folks like me."

"Like you how?"

"I'm Indian, Clancy. Indian enough. I don't have money. Not that kind. I'd get some shit public defender and end up in prison." He took the curves below Divide fast, braked hard as he swerved to miss the cattle half on the road as they grazed the borrow pits.

Clancy took a long breath. "I won't tell a soul. You have my word. But I need to know what happened." She waited and then added, "You owe me that." The road had no shoulder. Paintbrush poked red against the smear of green. Clancy didn't figure they needed to rehash her inability to keep a secret. She asked why he came up the trail past the spike camp. Told him that they both knew Liz and Penelope were working up the Triple Divide trail. "You should have veered right at the junction. Instead, you led the pack string past the falls." The truth of it weighed her chest.

"Would you believe me if I told you I smelled smoke?"

Horses grazed in a meadow. An old corral with posts weathered to gray sank toward the earth. Marshes pooled across the valley floor, reflected blue sky and puffy clouds. White Calf loomed in the distance. "Would you be telling the truth?"

Grady watched the road like it held answers, like it could lead them someplace worth going. "Liz had me bring the stock up the

Medicine Grizzly trail. She'd flagged a route down from the Triple Divide trail to lure saboteurs to her motion-sensor camera."

Anger bit at Clancy's throat. "That doesn't explain anything. You brought the stock below Atlantic Falls, past our spike camp. Why?" Her mind raced. She remembered the evening they'd sat on her picnic table, the sliver of moon, his arm drawing her close, his smell, the warmth of him. "You're the one who told me a guy can have more than one pair of boots."

The highway ran straight. Grady sped up and said he might as well start at the beginning. The ranch owner, Mr. Thomas, the man his family worked for, had hired Ezra to build a private trail for his sick wife. Turned out she wasn't even sick, only pretended to be. "He'd been catting around for years, would bring women to the ranch. We all assumed his wife knew. She didn't. And when she found out, she was so devastated, she lost a bunch of weight. She told my mom that someone at her church asked if it was cancer. She didn't deny it. Mr. Thomas heard the rumor and hired Ezra to build her a trail." Grady eased the truck through gentle curves. "By the time she fessed up, it was too late."

He said that one spring night Ezra and the ranch hands he roomed with played a game. They called it hog farming. Everyone threw a twenty in the center of the kitchen table, and whoever slept with the ugliest girl won the pot. Grady told Clancy about his sister. "Josie was born with an unfused palate." He said a surgeon tried to fix it, but he'd never done the procedure before. "Left her with a wicked scar." That April evening Josie went to the local bar to get pizza. Ezra and the hands were there, too. "At the end of the night, Ezra drove her to their trailer." Grady glanced at Clancy. His face was blank. "He won." Grady said that Josie was pregnant. For weeks and weeks, she'd kept the baby a secret and sunk to a dark place. She'd tried to kill herself. Grady had found her.

Clancy felt sick and cracked her window. The air helped. Grady said he had hiked in the night of the storm. He planned to convince Ezra to do the right thing—send Josie money and promise to stay away from her and the baby. The weather rolled in, and he was about to turn back when he saw someone coming toward him. Ezra had just crossed the bridge below the falls. Grady confronted him. Ezra got angry. He looked stoned. He said that Josie had seemed lonely that night. He asked Grady, "Where were you?"

"I punched him. Hard." The road curved and dipped and Grady kept his gaze trained on the asphalt. "He got up, turned, and started back across the bridge. But I wasn't finished." Grady said he jumped up after him. Ezra looked over his shoulder, lost his balance, and fell. "His head hit a rock." Aspen pressed close, surrounded the road in a tunnel of green. "By the time I fished him out, he was gone."

Clancy remembered the back of Grady's hand, the bruise she'd noticed that night at her picnic table. The road curved sharp, like a bent knuckle. Grady braked, took the bend fast, and sped downhill. Aspen leaves flashed in the breeze. "I tried. I did. To bring him back."

Clancy bit down so hard her jaw hurt. Small hills stretched to the east. Mountains lifted to the west. Sun blanched the sky. "You did CPR?"

Grady nodded. Clancy imagined that night, the darkness and rain, Grady pushing Ezra's chest, trying to jump-start his heart, his mouth—the same mouth that had kissed hers—on Ezra's, driving air into his lungs. She thought how desperate he must have been, frantic to breathe life back into Ezra. "You pulled him out, tried to resuscitate him. Then what?"

Grady said the storm eased. "I was scared. I never meant for him to die." He told her how he ran the entire way to his truck. He didn't want to go home, where his mom would climb out of bed to ask him how his day had gone and drag the truth from him. He drove to St. Mary. He was due at the barn before dawn. He built a fire next to the river, got warm and dry, unfurled his bedroll, and watched the clouds break and stars appear until he had to go to work.

"How's your sister?"

"She's starting to show. Keeps asking if she looks pregnant or fat." Grady's voice was flat, matter-of-fact. "She's got us."

"I am so sorry." What could she say? "What Ezra did, that wasn't the person I knew." As she said it, Clancy realized it wasn't completely true. She could imagine him trying to fit in, playing that vile game. He was just so much more—the guy she worked with every day was funny and kind. He'd managed to downclimb to her brother, recover his body. He'd never once grown impatient with her grief, her need to talk about Sean and his death. He was her friend. Clancy's entire body felt heavy. She was disappointed in Ezra, frustrated with Grady, and angry with herself. She should have realized sooner. It was all there—the trail Grady was on when he insisted on giving her a ride to her crew, the boot prints that mirrored Marty's—a fellow packer—the lines of poetry Ezra had spouted and Grady knew, too.

Grady steered the truck past the dirt road that led up the Cut Bank Valley. The hillsides stretched browner than they'd been the week before. The prairie smoke waned, faded. He glanced her way. "None of it was your doing. You don't have to be sorry."

But Clancy felt culpable, guilt by association. All the times she'd listened to the guys on her crew, the way they spoke about the women they bedded, "Parkwide" and "the Bicycle," and she hadn't called them on it, hadn't stood up to them and told them it was wrong. Not really. Sure, she'd tease them occasionally, but Clancy hadn't been brave enough to say how shitty it was to treat a human being as though she existed for their entertainment, their use. Clancy thought again about that night at her picnic table with the thin moon overhead and how she'd tried to justify Ezra's messy love life to Grady. She cringed at how it must have sounded, Grady knowing what Ezra had done to his sister. "I still feel bad." The road ran up a long hill. "The night I told you about the people in Ezra's camper, you knew they had nothing to do with his disappearance."

Clancy realized she would never ask Nate what he'd been up to that evening, tossing drawers and emptying cupboards. It made no difference. He could have his secret. She would have hers. This one, she would have to find a way to keep.

Grady's jaw tightened. His hard eyes met hers. "I didn't know I could trust you." He told her those people, whatever had gone on in Ezra's camper, none of it was his concern. "I planned to happen by in the morning, discover Ezra's body, report it." He reached over, his hand seeking hers, wanting assurance.

She tucked her palm beneath her thigh. He'd lied, deceived her, played a role in Ezra's death and kept it all to himself. It'd been Grady all along, not Liz, not Penelope. Clancy still couldn't get her mind around the truth. "Why didn't you? Why didn't you tell us like you planned?" Clancy knew Grady must have been frightened, desperate for things to be other than they were.

He drove the tight curves. "When I got to the stream bank, the spot where he'd been the night before, Ezra was gone. I thought maybe he hadn't died. Maybe he'd been hypothermic when I pulled him out and somehow survived. I smelled smoke, and then I spotted it. It came from the area where Liz told me Ezra and your crew camped. I was looking for help, someone to tell." He swallowed. "That's when I found you."

Clancy glimpsed an aspen trunk bound by several colorful lengths of fabric. She'd been told Sun Dancers prepared for months, tied their prayers to trees with certain colors of cloth in a prescribed order, and when they fasted and danced, they did so for all of us, for everyone, the whole world.

"You lied to me." She stared at him.

His face weighed with strain. "Couldn't see a way around it."

"The night you came to my cabin, that first night, why?"

His hands tightened around the wheel. He told her that after he gave Penelope a ride to the trailhead, he drove the mules to the barn. He knew he'd left boot prints along the stream but had no idea where Ezra was. He took care of the animals, changed into his spare boots, and stashed his Whites in a dusty corner of a stall. "I was trying to figure out what to do next. I thought you might know something that would help. Marty told me you stayed in the cabin in the Two Med campground." He glanced her way. "I'm not proud of why I went to see you that night, but believe me, all of it since, everything between us, is real." He accelerated into a straight stretch of road. "I wouldn't pretend about that."

They blew through the junction at Kiowa and started up Looking Glass. Clancy watched for the swirl of rock, an example of the collision of tectonic plates. Newer, harder rock pushed up and under an older, softer layer, swirled it. The world upended.

"No wonder you knew the ultrasound wasn't Penelope's."

Grady said his mom had mailed the scan to Ezra with a letter. They'd never heard back.

"What Ezra did to your sister, that's rape. Why didn't you go to the police?"

"Clancy!" He said her name with such vitriol it made her jump. Just a few hours ago, he had been so tender. What they'd done, it had felt right. Knowing what she now did changed everything.

"Josie was so ashamed she wanted to die. She wasn't about to go blabbing it to anyone—not to me or our mom, let alone a cop." They crested the pass. Snow-dappled mountains lifted above the valley and into the distance like a choir on risers. "What Ezra did was low, ignorant. But being an asshole isn't illegal. She was underage and drunk. She went with him into his bed. The worst night of Josie's life hashed over in a courtroom and on the front page of the paper, everyone knowing. No way."

Clancy wished he wasn't right, that the truth was different. She wanted the world to be more just. A fresh wave of defeat washed over her. Ezra had behaved despicably. She wished he was alive so she could give him the hell he deserved. At the same time, she refused to reduce Ezra—the person who'd found Sean and sat with her in Sun Rift Gorge as the sorrow sank in, acknowledged her pain day after day, hike after hike, the guy she teased, who made her laugh and shared his chocolate—to the worst thing he had ever done. Ezra was more than that one drunken night, too.

Clancy tried to focus on the view. Aspen grew thick on both sides of the road. A single organism, hundreds of years old, it survived by sending runners up through the soil, dispatching fresh shoots to try their luck aboveground out in the world. She wondered what life would be like for Josie's baby. "Why didn't you just let Mack run with the idea that the ultrasound was Penelope's?"

Grady shook his head once. "She's got a family, too. Wouldn't have been right, them thinking that when it wasn't true."

She thought about all Grady had told her. "How did you know where to find Ezra the night of the storm?"

"Liz told me your crew was camped in that valley. She showed me on the map."

Ezra and Penelope were dead. Liz was missing, probably drowned. And for what? It all seemed a complete waste. Flat-bottomed clouds puffed white. A hawk rode a thermal. The mountains looked red, distant against the washed-out summer sky. "Why? Why would Liz show you where Ezra was camped?"

Grady explained that Liz had worked with the ranch owner, Mr. Thomas, the man with the sick wife who wasn't sick, to solicit donations of cash and supplies for her study. When Liz needed a packer, the man recommended Grady. He suspected Mr. Thomas must have told Liz about Josie's predicament. He knew Josie was pregnant and that Grady and his parents despised Ezra. "He's not dumb. He probably figured it out." Liz already suspected Ezra of study sabotage and welcomed Grady and his grudge to the team. "She told me we shared an enemy and that made us friends."

"Liz couldn't have known what would happen."

"Liz manipulates people. Ask Mack."

Clancy knew that if it hadn't been for Liz's DNA study, Ezra and Penelope would still be alive. "Why did you go in to find Ezra that night? Why not wait? Confront him in the light of day."

"Have you ever been so upset it took over? I had to find him, let him know the damage he'd caused. Once I knew where he was, I couldn't sleep. I didn't eat. I couldn't let it go."

Grady turned onto the Two Med Road and drove more slowly. He eased the truck around curves and cows, past pullouts and crosses, over the cattle guard at the boundary. He rolled to a stop at the entrance station, gave the attendant a nod, and said, "Tribal member." The truck's engine protested the giant hill and the hairpin curve. They coasted toward the lake. He turned at the ranger station. Dread built in Clancy's belly. "I can walk from here."

Grady guided the truck slowly past the picnic area. "I'll see you home." Wind shuddered the water, snapped tents, bowed the tops of the trees. He drove through the campground. Neither of them spoke. He pulled up to her cabin, stopped the truck but didn't kill the engine.

She climbed out. "I wish it were different."

"I know you do." He nodded but didn't look at her.

She closed the door and stepped aside. He backed down the drive. Clancy watched his truck rumble away until it disappeared, leaving nothing but a black ribbon of empty road.

CHAPTER 37

THE GIFT

The next morning Clancy flung a shovel full of dirt, pine needles, cones, and twigs. At the last possible moment, just before the detritus rained down, she spied a calypso orchid. Rare and delicate, these beauties grew in deep shade. She thought of them as clandestine. Clancy tossed her shovel aside and dropped to her knees. She worked quickly and with care. She loved everything about the calypso orchid, its pinkish-violet spires that poked like rays of sun, its perfect hood, the leopard-spotted tongue that cradled a round bit of yellow the way a jewel box presents its jewel. She sifted handful after handful of dirt and debris until she located it, the stem broken, severed from its roots.

Clancy yanked open her pack and removed the book she'd found on the windshield of her truck that morning. A plastic THANK YOU bag had protected it from the moisture beading the glass. She had overslept and was late. She tossed it onto the truck seat as she climbed inside. She drove slowly through the campground and flipped open the inside cover, hoping for an inscription. There was none.

At the trails shop she pushed the book inside her pack. It rode there as she hiked, tucked low and away like a secret she intended to keep. After work, she planned to buy herself a bag of powdered donuts, brew a mug of tea, and read at her picnic table, where she could glance up at the side of Rising Wolf and maybe glimpse a grizzly, mountain goats, or bighorns.

Roberts's voice made her jump. "Stop milking it." Some paper pusher in the head shed had put him in charge of the crew's Critical Incident Stress Debriefing, which had consisted of Roberts and Nate smoking a bowl before they left the shop. Clancy pressed the orchid carefully between the pages of *Making Certain It Goes On: The Collected Poems of Richard Hugo*.

She returned the poetry to her pack. Maybe tomorrow, after she studied the poems and imagined Grady driving some Montana highway, looking forward to the next town and recalling the lines describing its bars and people, she could let him go. But today she wanted to try to understand, to read words that he had read, to feel close to him, if only for a little while.

"You've had a rough week," Roberts barked. "We all have. But drains don't clean themselves."

She wished every day dawned like a man who loved her, but some mornings stung with having been left behind. Roberts hadn't changed and probably wouldn't. It was what passed for love around here. And for now, it would need to be enough. Clancy shouldered her pack, grabbed her shovel, and started up the trail.

ACKNOWLEDGMENTS

In the mid-aughts biologists conducted a bear DNA study in the Northern Continental Divide Ecosystem. Their efforts spanned five years and millions of acres with the goal of accurately assessing the number of grizzlies living in the vast, wild area that includes Glacier National Park and the Bob Marshall Wilderness. The number scientists published, 765, was twice that of previous population estimates. The controversy surrounding grizzly bears, their protected status under the Endangered Species Act, and plans to eventually hunt them, persists. *Baited* is a work of fiction and does not depict real people.

This novel would not exist without the help and support of many. I thank Carol Savage for her wisdom, humor, and reading multiple drafts. I am grateful to Debra Magpie Earling for her guidance and for writing with unflinching beauty. I thank Dan Carney for his expertise and kindness. Any mistakes are mine. I am grateful to Greg Michalson for his diligence, direction, and kind heart. I am also grateful to Michael Kenneth Smith and his sponsorship of the fellowship at Porches Writing Retreat in Virginia. My thanks to Trudy Hale for her warmth and hospitality. I am grateful to Scott McMillion at *Montana Quarterly* for publishing short stories. For reading and commenting on the manuscript, I thank Kara Basko, Terre Ryan, Romy Loran, and Barbara Andreas.

For support and inspiration, I thank the people of East Glacier, especially Karlene Morgan, Beth Hagan, Pat Hagan, Joann Flick, Amy Conrey Andreas, Ursula Mattson, Colleen Erickson, Laurie Litner, Berta Rink, Roz Schildt, and Michelle Peterson. I sincerely appreciate the friends who cared for my children, especially Emma O'Connor Haynes, Nicole Whitney, Lisa VanDeHay, and Weiko Emerson. I thank my Park Café co-workers, especially Kathryn Hiestand, Neal Miller, and David Dittloff. Pie for Strength. I am grateful to my Park Service coworkers for all the stories. For abiding friendship, my thanks to Jennifer Bertsch and Emily Swanson.

I am especially grateful to my family: my parents Christine O'Brien and the late Lawrence O'Brien; my siblings Jackie O'Brien, Kevin O'Brien, and the late Tom O'Brien; as well as Edna Kuchta, Steve Shirk, Jolene Pravecek, Jeff Pravecek, Matt Lyson, Dr. Isabella Nair, Quinn O'Brien, Brittany O'Brien, Sinjin Nair, Dr. Venu Nair, Judy Howser, Jeanine Teroy, Robyn Campbell, Lonnie Kersey, and Pat Kersey. I am beyond grateful to my children. I thank my husband Mark, my rock, my light, my love.